NOT in a generation has there appeared so unusual a master of detection as Rabbi David Small of Barnard's Crossing, Massachusetts. His complex religious training enables him to see the third side of any question, and he operates on a special brand of internal radar as unpredictable to others as to himself.

In this newest adventure, trouble comes once again to Barnard's Crossing. A mysterious death. And wherever there is mystery—and trouble—you will find Rabbi Small, who from his special "third side" conjures up some astonishing answers to a very entertaining puzzle.

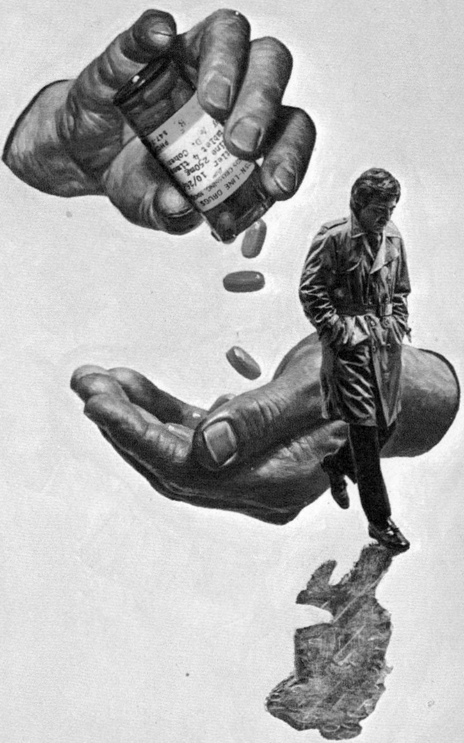

Wednesday the Rabbi Got Wet

A Novel by **HARRY KEMELMAN**

A FAWCETT CREST BOOK

Fawcett Publications, Inc., Greenwich, Connecticut

WEDNESDAY THE RABBI GOT WET

THIS BOOK CONTAINS THE COMPLETE TEXT OF
THE ORIGINAL HARDCOVER EDITION.

A Fawcett Crest Book reprinted by arrangement with
William Morrow & Company, Inc.

ISBN: 0-449-23291-3

Alternate Selection of the Literary Guild, November 1976
Alternate Selection of the Jewish Book Club, January 1977
Full selection of the Mystery Guild, February 1977

Printed in the United States of America

10   9   8   7   6   5   4   3   2   1

Wednesday the Rabbi Got Wet

1

"I suppose *you're* happy about the outcome of the election."

Rabbi David Small turned and saw that it was Joshua Tizzik, a thin little man with a long nose and a mouth twisted in a perpetual sneer, who had fallen in step with him.

The evening service had just ended, and Rabbi Small was strolling back to his car in the parking lot, savoring the balmy air of the October Indian summer. The rabbi was thin and pale and walked with a scholarly stoop although still under forty. He fixed nearsighted eyes on Tizzik and said, "If you mean that the election of Chester Kaplan and his friends signifies a renewed interest in the temple's religious function as opposed to its social function, then of course I am. If, on the other hand, you're suggesting that I had anything to do with it, then you're mistaken. I never meddle in temple politics."

"Oh, I'm not saying you campaigned for him, but don't try to tell me you're not happy he won."

"All right," the rabbi said good-humoredly, "I won't." He had found over the years that it was pointless to argue with the perpetually dissatisfied Mr. Tizzik.

"And don't kid yourself about any religious revival,

9

Rabbi. Organization and ordinary politics did it. For over a year now, Chet Kaplan has been holding these At Homes every Wednesday evening—"

"I've never been to one."

"No?" Tizzik was frankly incredulous. "Well, take a small town like Barnard's Crossing. What can you do of an evening? There's the Friday night service at the temple, and you know half the people come just because it's a place to pass the time. Saturday nights, maybe you go out to dinner or a movie. And that's pretty much it. So when Kaplan started these At Homes, it was something to do, a place where you could meet people. You'd have a cup of coffee or a glass of beer and a couple of doughnuts—"

"But what do you do there, Mr. Tizzik?"

"Talk—mostly about the temple because it's a common interest. We discuss religion. Everybody is an expert on that. Sometimes, Kaplan will have somebody come to give a little lecture. He's got a friend from New Hampshire, Rabbi Mezzik—" He laughed. "I told him once we ought to start a vaudeville team, Mezzik and Tizzik. Well, this Rabbi Mezzik, he goes in for meditation. He talks on Judaism and other religions like Christianity and Buddhism and how they relate to our religion."

"And then Chester Kaplan tops it off with a political speech?"

"Oh no, nothing crude like that. But he has this group that are into this meditation business with him, the guys that were on his slate for board of directors. They're like an inner circle. Sometimes, I understand, they go upcountry to a camp they rent for a couple of days, and have all kinds of discussions. And pray, for all I know, because this Rabbi Mezzik, he's involved in it. But then the rest, those who came because it was something to do, well most felt where their host was running for president, they ought to give him their vote. Then just before the election, the inner-circle guys, they phoned everybody who had ever attended a meeting. They got the names from a guest book Chet has you sign."

Rabbi Small nodded. "Yes, I can see where that might be effective. But let me suggest another possibility. As in all small towns, there's only one synagogue here in Barnard's Crossing because the Jewish community isn't big enough to support more than one. So it was established as a Conservative temple in order that the Orthodox on one side and the Reform Jews on the other can both feel not too uncomfortable. It's a compromise. My guess is that the Conservatives have a clear majority, but there are shades of opinion among them running from almost Orthodox to almost Reform. Most years it has been two men from the middle, two Conservatives, who were running against each other. This year, the other candidate, Mr. Golding, was definitely of the Reform wing. So the Orthodox and the near-Orthodox and most of the straight Conservatives voted for Mr. Kaplan. It was probably as simple as that."

When they reached the rabbi's car, a sudden thought occurred to him. "Whom did you vote for, Mr. Tizzik?"

Tizzik smiled deprecatingly. "Look, Rabbi, I drank his beer and I ate his doughnuts. So what could I do? I voted for Kaplan. At least, I know that when I come to say Kaddish like tonight, Chet Kaplan will be there, and if necessary he can lead the prayers."

2

Since it was Akiva Rokeach's first conference with the rebbe, Baruch, the *gabbe,* felt he should instruct him on how he was to behave. "You understand, Akiva, that with the rebbe one doesn't argue," he said severely. "Reb Mendel is a *zaddik,* that is to say a holy man, like a saint." Baruch was a small, stout man, balding, with grizzled hair pushed back from a high forehead where a prominent blue vein pulsated noticeably when he was angry. He held the last half-inch of an unfiltered cigarette between nicotine-stained thumb and forefinger, took a final puff, and then regretfully dropped it in an ashtray where it continued to smolder. He was a nervous, irritable man, but as the *gabbe,* or secretary and general factotum to the rebbe, he was important. Only through him could one get in to see the rebbe. "Even when the rebbe seems to make a mistake," he continued, "as when you think he has misquoted during his discourse on the Law, you do not point it out or contradict him. Instead, you should ponder the reason why Reb Mendel deliberately misquoted." He paused to light another cigarette. "Most of all, when he renders a verdict, you accept it without protest."

"I understand," said Akiva Rokeach humbly.

The vein in the *gabbe*'s forehead throbbed at the interruption. "For he has the Insight, you understand, and it is not to be expected that his thought will be like yours."

This time Akiva merely inclined his head in acquiescence. Although he had been associated with the group for more than half a year, it would be the first time he would be seeing Reb Mendel in his study alone, and he did not want to jeopardize the opportunity by irritating the *gabbe*.

Baruch looked at the young man standing before him in frank disapproval—of his long hair, of his unruly blond beard, of his patched blue jeans stuffed into heavy boots. "You have a *kvitl?*" he demanded sourly, and when Akiva did not seem to understand, he translated impatiently, "A request, a written request. You don't expect the rebbe to wait while you explain, do you?"

"Oh, oh yes. I have it here."

"And a *pidyon?*"

Akiva drew out a five-dollar bill from his wallet and presented it, a token in advance of his gratitude to the rebbe for the privilege of talking with him in private. Baruch glanced at it and made a notation in his book.

"Wait here and I will see if the rebbe can see you now." He knocked on the door of the study, waited a moment and then entered, closing the door carefully behind him. He returned shortly and motioned the young man to enter.

Akiva had never been so close to Reb Mendel before. At the *farbrengen,* the festive gatherings, as the newest member of the group, he had to remain on the fringe. And when the *zaddik* expounded Torah and philosophy after the third meal on the Sabbath, he had been at the extreme foot of the communal table, separated from him by almost the length of the hall.

Now Reb Mendel sat tall in his thronelike chair behind a large carved walnut desk. He was thirty? forty? forty-five? It was hard to tell. The large spade beard was beginning to gray, but the hand that occasionally stroked it was that of a young man.

"Ah, our young Viking," Reb Mendel murmured, and nodded to a chair beside the desk.

"I beg your pardon, Rebbe, I didn't hear—"

Reb Mendel smiled. "Nothing. A little private joke. You wish to live here for a week?"

"I have a week's vacation," said Akiva. "I thought I could best spend it here in prayer and meditation."

With only a flick of his eyes, the rebbe glanced at the card Baruch had placed on his desk. "You have been with us only seven months," he said. "You do not have the training or the background yet which would make it worthwhile. You have had no previous religious education, not even the little that most Jewish boys get in preparing for their Bar Mitzvah."

Akiva inclined his head. "My parents are not religious. My father is an agnostic and I was brought up in agnosticism. I was not sent to the religious school like the other boys in the neighborhood and we did not belong to the temple."

"Your parents live here in Philadelphia?"

"No, I come from Massachusetts, from a small town north of Boston called Barnard's Crossing."

"And when did you last see them?"

Akiva colored. "Well, I haven't seen them for some time, but I talk with them on the phone every now and then, especially with my mother."

"With your father you quarreled." It was not a question; it was stated flatly as though he knew. "Tell me about it."

"My father has a drugstore, and when I graduated from pharmacy college and passed my licensing exam, I went to work for him. We never really got along."

"But that was not why you left—and never returned."

Akiva nodded readily, even eagerly, to show he had

14

no intention of keeping anything back. "There was this place I used to go to, it was a kind of nightclub. They had a back room where there was gambling—"

"And girls?"

"Yes, they had girls, too. Well, I was a little short on my bill there one night, and I gave them an IOU for fifty dollars. Then somebody, not the proprietor—he claimed he bought it from the proprietor—came to see me at the store, only it had been hiked to a hundred and fifty."

"You asked your father for the money?"

"Well, no. He wouldn't have understood. He's very like square. He would have gone to the police."

"So you took the money out of the cash register?" the rebbe suggested.

Akiva nodded without embarrassment. That was what was so wonderful about the group. One could be completely honest with them. "It was no sweat. You see, I opened in the morning and I closed at night, so I totaled. Mostly I'd take the figures at night, but if I was in a hurry I'd leave them for the morning. But one morning I overslept, and my father opened. Of course I was planning to replace the money in a couple of weeks."

"But your father caught on before you had a chance to."

"That's right. There was an awful row and I split."

"Where'd you go?"

"I just wandered around the country. I was in California for a while. And then I worked my way back to Philly."

"Why here?"

"Because I'd gone to the College of Pharmacy here, so I knew the city."

"And what did you do while you wandered around the country? And how long has it been since you left home?"

"About three years. Most of the time I worked. I'd

take a job in a drugstore—pharmacy jobs weren't hard to get—and I'd work for a while and then I'd move on to another place."

"Because you were not at ease with yourself," said Reb Mendel flatly.

"No, I—" He remembered that one must not contradict the rebbe. "Yes. But I also wanted to try out different lifestyles. I was into yoga for a while, and Zen." He took courage. "I understand you, too . . ."

Reb Mendel smiled, a broad sunny smile that showed even white teeth, and for a moment he seemed very young, no older than Akiva. "While doing my doctorate in anthropology, I lived among the American Indians for a while, studying their religion. Later, I spent some time in India, studying Eastern thought and Transcendental Meditation. But ultimately one must find the equivalents in one's own culture. One must go home. I did. And so must you, Akiva."

"But if I stay here, if only for the rest of the week—"

Reb Mendel shook his head. "You do not know enough to profit from it. I am informed that in the time you have been with us, you have learned to read your prayers in Hebrew . . . haltingly. But of course you don't understand what you're reading. When we talk here, we talk in English to be sure, but also in Yiddish and occasionally Hebrew, neither of which you understand. You would be wasting your time. You have a few days left of your vacation, so I tell you to use them to go home."

The young man made no effort to conceal his disappointment, and Reb Mendel's expression softened. "Don't you see," he said kindly, "the quarrel with your father impedes your spiritual progress. So long as you have something in your past which disturbs and interferes with your concentration, you will never know the tranquillity that is necessary for the ecstasy we strive for."

"It wasn't only that," Akiva pleaded. "We never really

16

got along. He had old-fashioned ideas—even about running the store. Lots of stuff he wouldn't carry because he'd say it wasn't in keeping with the dignity of a pharmacy. Even the way you filled prescriptions, it had to be just so. Like where every pharmacy in town used plastic tubes for putting up pills, he still used glass bottles because he said the tubes weren't air-tight, although there are only a few pills like nitroglycerin that deteriorate in the air."

"And this was a hardship?"

"No, but it's old-fashioned. The bottles cost more and instead of just sliding the label in like you do with tubes, you got to paste them on. I'm just giving that as an example. Like we used to stay open later than the other stores in town because he felt it was the responsibility of a pharmacy to the community. Sometimes, doctors would call up in the middle of the night and I might have to go to the store to compound the medicine and maybe even deliver it."

"And over this you quarreled? It was a good deed, a mitzvah. You were helping a sick person."

"We didn't fight over that. I'm just trying to give you an idea of how he felt about the store." He smiled wanly. "That's how I happened to oversleep that morning. If it was a mitzvah, I sure didn't get any reward for it."

"One doesn't perform a mitzvah in the hope of reward. If one does, then it is no longer a mitzvah but a business transaction that you are trying to make with The Almighty. And one does not always recognize the reward when it comes." He thoughtfully stroked his beard.

"Yeah, I suppose," Akiva agreed moodily, staring down at his hands. Then he looked up and tried once again. "He didn't pay me what he'd have to pay a regular pharmacist, and I worked longer hours. That was because I was his son. He'd say, 'The store is yours. In a few years I'll step aside and you'll take over the way I did from my father.' Like it was a family tradition," he added bitterly,

17

"like a bank or a railroad or some big corporation. But it was only a small neighborhood drugstore. And if it was mine, how come he raised such a stink when I took some of what was mine?"

"This family tradition, you have no feeling for?"

The young man shook his head. "To me it's just a job. If I go home, he'll start in about carrying on the tradition and I'll just fight with him again."

Reb Mendel nodded his head slowly as he considered. Finally, he spoke, in tones that would brook no further argument. "This disagreement with your father, it bothers you. It is not something you can forget. And for that reason it is a psychological and spiritual infection that must be cured or it will spread and bring about your spiritual decay. Go home, Akiva. Go home."

3

As Rabbi Small entered the basement chapel of the temple where the weekday services were held, he automatically made a head count, and then on the chance that one or more of the men might have stepped out for a cigarette, he asked hopefully, "Do we have ten? Are we a minyan?"

"No, Rabbi. You're the ninth, but Chet Kaplan should be along any minute."

It occurred to the rabbi that the religious renaissance Kaplan claimed for the congregation had so far not made it easier to gather a minyan. There was no problem evenings, but evidently the religious fervor was not yet strong enough to induce them to get up half an hour earlier to make the morning service.

As soon as he entered the temple, the rabbi had put on the black silk skullcap he kept in his pocket. Now he took off his jacket and unbuttoned and rolled up his left shirtsleeve. He took one of the narrow silk prayer shawls from the pile on the bench in the rear of the room, touched the two ends of its embroidered collar to his lips, and perfunctorily muttering the blessing, he draped it around his shoulders. From the small blue velvet bag he had brought with him he drew out his phylacteries, the little black boxes with their leather straps which contained strips of parchment inscribed with quotations from the Bible proclaiming that they were to serve as "reminders on your hand and on your forehead . . . that with a mighty hand the Lord freed you from Egypt." He began to put them on, first the hand box, strapped above the muscle of the left arm and hence next to the heart; then the head box, placed above the forehead next to the hairline, his lips moving as he recited to himself the appropriate blessings.

The others had similarly prepared themselves and were sitting in the middle of the room talking, mostly about Hurricane Betsy, which weather forecasters had been tracking for the last several days and which still might strike the Boston area. Irving Hovik, something of an amateur meteorologist, was explaining with wide gestures that ". . . she can still turn in. She gains strength over the water and loses it over the land. So if she turns in and hits us head on, it can be bad, but if she hits south of here and then moves up the coast, she'll lose a lot of her power, see? It depends on how much spin she's got."

Over to the side, at the end of the aisle and away from the rest, the rabbi noticed a tall young man whom he had not previously seen at the services. His blond hair was long and he had a heavy beard. He wore a blue denim jacket and blue jeans stuffed into leather boots. Instead of a narrow silk prayer shawl such as the others wore, he had a long woollen one that came down to his knees.

Just as the rabbi was about to welcome him, the young man grasped the edge of his woollen prayer shawl in either hand and, raising his arms, he crossed his hands in front of his face, thereby enclosing himself in a cylinder of cloth. It reminded the rabbi of his grandfather, who had been an Orthodox rabbi; just so, he used to momentarily shut out the world to organize his mind for prayer and communion with God. As he watched, the cylinder of white began to gyrate slowly from side to side in a kind of ecstasy. It crossed his mind—with a touch of regret? of annoyance?—that over the years his own recital of the blessings accompanying the putting on of the phylacteries and the prayer shawl had become more or less perfunctory.

Chester Kaplan, a short man of fifty with a round head and smiley face, came hurrying in. He shed his jacket on one of the back benches and rolled up his left shirt-sleeve. "We got ten?" he asked.

"Yeah, now. You're the tenth. Let's get cracking."

"Jeez, Chet, you know some of us poor slobs got jobs to go to."

"I know, I know. I had trouble getting my car started." He began to put on his phylacteries.

The young man lowered his prayer shawl and draped it once again about his shoulders. The rabbi came over and said, "I am Rabbi Small."

The young man nodded and smiled. "Yes, I know."

20

He took the proffered hand and said, "I'm Akiva Rokeach."

"Are you new in town, Mr. Rokeach?"

"I'm visiting for a few days."

"Well, we're happy to have you." He looked about and smiled. "Without you, I guess we would not have had a minyan this morning." Then he offered the traditional courtesy to the stranger. "Would you care to lead the prayers?"

Rokeach blushed. "No, I better not."

Courtesy also forbade pressing anyone who refused, so the rabbi called out, "You want to lead, Chester?"

"Okay," and Chester Kaplan took his place at the reading desk in front of the Ark. Throughout the service that followed, although the greater portion was murmured in undertones, the rabbi was able to hear his neighbor reciting the prayers, and he quickly understood that the reason the young man had refused his offer to lead was that his Hebrew was uncertain.

Since it was Wednesday and hence not one of the days on which the Scroll was read, the service was soon over. As the men removed their phylacteries and rolled up the straps, they resumed the conversations the service had interrupted.

Chester Kaplan came bustling up to the rabbi. Confidently tucking his hand under the rabbi's elbow, he whispered in his ear, "Got something I want to ask you."

The rabbi let himself be led to the door and then to the parking lot beyond, although he expected no important request or significant revelation. By temperament Chester Kaplan was given to intrigue and its outward manifestations: the confidential whisper, the knowing nod and wink, the little grimace invoking silence at the approach of a third person. Now at the rabbi's car and safely out of earshot of eavesdroppers, he asked, "Have you

21

thought any more about that business we discussed at the last board meeting, Rabbi?"

"You mean about the retreat? Well, I haven't changed my mind about it."

Kaplan pursed his lips in momentary annoyance. Then he smiled, a bright friendly smile, his eyes crinkling with good humor. "You made the point that the temple couldn't afford it," he said. "All right, you've convinced me." He looked at the rabbi, his eyes wide with candor. "I thought originally, if we put on a big drive, we could raise the money. But after inquiring around a little, I decided you were right and that it would be a tough proposition to promote." He smiled and gave a little nod of the head to indicate that he was man enough to admit when he was wrong.

"Well—"

Kaplan clutched the rabbi's arm. "But what if the money was no problem? What if I were to tell you that there is a chance of getting the property without it costing the temple or the membership one red cent?"

The rabbi smiled. "The difficulty in raising the money was just one of my objections. I'd still be against it."

"But why, Rabbi? Why?" His tone registered puzzled hurt.

"Because it smacks of Christianity rather than Judaism," said the rabbi promptly. "It suggests convents and monasteries, an ivory-tower attitude. *Retreat*—the word itself suggests retiring from life and the world. That's not Judaic. *We* participate."

"But prayer and meditation, Rabbi, they're part and parcel of our religious tradition."

"Sure, and that's what the temple is for. If you want to pray and meditate, why can't you do it at the temple or in your own home for that matter? Why do you have to run off to the country?"

"We don't have to, but—"

"Is it because some other temples and synagogues have gone in for it? Or is it because you'd like to have something positive, something material, that you can point to as an accomplishment of your administration?"

"Naturally, I'd like to make a major contribution to the development of the temple," Kaplan said stiffly.

"Well, you already have."

"I have?"

"Certainly. You're the first president we've had since Jacob Wasserman who is an observant Jew. That's a major contribution in itself."

Kaplan nodded thoughtfully. "Don't think it's a fluke, Rabbi. There's a new spirit around. I was elected *because* I am an observant, religious Jew. I might point out that a number of my friends, people who think as I do, were also elected to the board of directors. Why? Because there's a yearning for religion. And not just going through the motions. There's a religious renaissance, and I can feel it. And it's why I was elected."

"Well . . ." The rabbi smiled deprecatingly. He did not think it politic to mention Tizzik's explanation, or even his own.

"The young fellow who was sitting next to you, the guy with the beard, did you notice how he *davened*? With what fervor and intensity? It's a sign of the times. Who was he, by the way?"

"I don't know. A stranger visiting in the neighborhood. His name is Rokeach, Akiva Rokeach."

"There he is now." Kaplan nodded toward the far end of the parking lot where Rokeach was climbing into a low-slung sports car. They watched as he raced his motor and then set the car in motion to make a wide sweep toward them. He braked the car momentarily to wave to the rabbi. "I guess you don't remember me, Rabbi," he called out.

"Should I? Do I know you?" the rabbi asked. But evidently the young man did not hear over the throb of the engine, because he laughed and sped away.

"He must know you," said Kaplan.

"No one I remember, unless he was a student at one of the colleges where I've talked to Hillel groups. Maybe he asked a question." He looked at the president curiously. "You think the way he *davened,* rocking back and forth, is an indication of religious fervor?"

"What would you call it?"

The rabbi shrugged. "A style, a mannerism picked up from those who taught him to *daven,* and that must have been fairly recently judging from his halting Hebrew."

"That's just the point, Rabbi. That's exactly what I mean. He's new at it. He must have got interested in religion just recently. And it means a great deal to him because he's just visiting, you said, and yet he makes a point of coming to the minyan. He's not exceptional, believe me. At these Wednesday evening get-togethers I've been having at my house, you hear so many similar stories that—"

"Is that what you do Wednesday nights? Get together and swap testimonials?"

"We discuss all kinds of things," said Kaplan stiffly. "Any kind of input is welcome. Why don't you come some Wednesday night and find out for yourself?"

"I might at that. Tonight—"

"Tonight there won't be much that would interest you," Kaplan interposed quickly, and then added, "Of course, you're welcome, but—"

"I was about to say that I couldn't make it tonight. I have one of my sick calls. Old Jacob Kestler—I promised to come and sit with him for a while."

"How about next Wednesday? Mark it in your calendar. Or any Wednesday you're free."

"All right, I will."

4

At precisely seven o'clock Wednesday morning, as on every other day of the year, Marcus Aptaker, the proprietor of Town-Line Drugs, came down to breakfast. He was a methodical, systematic man and the things he had to do regularly he did automatically. Freshly shaved, rimless eyeglasses gleaming, his thin brownish-blond hair was plastered down as though painted on. He was neatly dressed in his blue suit—the blue for Mondays, Wednesdays and Fridays; the gray for Tuesdays, Thursdays and Saturdays. On Sundays, because the store was open only half a day and it was therefore a half holiday, he dressed in slacks and a sweater. To be sure, when he got to the store, he would hang up his jacket and put on a cotton store jacket, but it was as a doctor might put on a lab coat to make hospital rounds. The important thing was to be properly dressed going to and coming from the store, because as a professional man attention to dress was a responsibility he owed to his position.

He was seated at the dining room table when his wife Rose entered a few minutes later. She was still in her bathrobe, her hair pulled back from a round pleasant face and hanging down her back in a loose braid. She served him his breakfast of freshly squeezed orange juice, eggs,

25

bacon and toast. With a nod at the other place setting on the table he said pleasantly, "I suppose Arnold will be sleeping late today."

"No, he got up early. He's already gone," his wife answered.

"Gone? Gone where? And without breakfast?"

"He said he'd be back for it. He went to the temple for the morning service. He said you were supposed to pray first and then eat."

"Is this some special holiday? I hadn't heard anything about it."

"No, it's just the daily service. They hold it in the morning and in the evening. When my mother died, my father went for a whole year, every morning and every evening."

"Ridiculous," he said and drained his orange juice.

She had brought a cup of coffee for herself and sipped at it while he ate. "What harm does it do?" she asked reasonably. "A boy living alone? Better he should be interested in religion than in some of the things young people are involved in these days."

"Did you talk to him after I went to bed? Did he say anything about his plans?" Marcus asked hesitantly.

"Just that he had to get back to Philadelphia by Monday. He just had the week off."

"I mean his plans in general. Did you talk to him about the store? Did you tell him about Safferstein?"

"I told him we had a buyer for the store and that you said you wouldn't sell unless you knew definitely that your son would not take it over."

"And what did he say?" he asked eagerly.

"He said you should go ahead and sell. You could retire and we could travel or go to Florida or—"

"And then what would I do?" he demanded. "So I travel for a while, for six months, even a year? Then what? I'm sixty-two years old and I'm in good health.

26

What do I do after I've traveled? Sit around and wait to die?"

"But if he's just not interested . . ."

"He's got to be interested," Aptaker insisted, his voice rising. "I put almost forty years into that store, and my father fifteen years before that. It's a family enterprise. Do you just walk away from something you've worked at all your life and your father before you? It's not just a way of making a living. It's something we've built over the years."

"Yes, and you work sixty or seventy hours a week there. Why should a young boy like Arnold be interested when he has a good job where he works forty hours a week and doesn't have the headache and the responsibility?"

"But working for wages! If he has his own business—"

"So in time maybe he'll get his own store. Why should he tie himself up with this one that's been going downhill—"

"It's not going downhill," he shouted and banged on the table with his fist for additional emphasis. "We netted more this year than last year."

"A few hundred more."

"All right, so a few hundred more. But a young man could build it up—"

"It's the location, Marcus." She shook her head sadly. "You can't build up a location. You can fancy up the store, put in a new front, some new fixtures, but if the location is going down, it won't help."

"Locations change. If that high-rise for senior citizens goes through, it will be an A-one location for a drugstore again. If the location is so bad, why does a smart real estate man like Safferstein want to buy it?"

"Like he said, for his brother-in-law. I can imagine what the situation is. His wife has a brother whom he has

27

to help support. So he figures he'll set him up in his own store and get him off his back. But for a young man like Arnold—"

"I tell you he could do well here," Aptaker insisted. "I'd make it easy for him to take over. I'd take back notes and he wouldn't have to worry about paying them on time. And I'd come in a few hours a day to help him, not for regular pay but just for expense money."

"So talk to him. Tell him what you have in mind."

Aptaker's shoulders drooped in despair. "I can't talk to him. It's like we don't talk the same language."

"What do you expect? If you talked to him like you talk to anybody else, like you talk to a customer or to McLane, quietly, reasonably—"

"I can't talk to him like to McLane," he exploded. "He's not just another pharmacist applying for a job. I can't sit down and discuss wages and working hours with him. He's my son. He should feel that the store is his, that I'm just holding it for him until he can get around to taking it over like I took over from my father."

"But how can he understand how you feel unless you tell him?"

"I shouldn't have to tell him. He should feel it himself. If you have to tell him, then right away, it's no good."

Rose Aptaker sighed. "Go to the store already, please. Arnold should be coming home soon, and the way you're feeling now, I don't think it's a good idea you should be here."

"So I have to hide from my own son?"

"You don't have to hide, but sometimes it's a good idea if—I don't know, lately you're so irritable. Go to the store, please, and I'll talk to him again."

28

5

"Say, Miriam, do we know anyone named Rokeach?" the rabbi asked his wife when he got home. "Akiva Rokeach? Do you recall my ever mentioning the name?"

She was small, with the trim figure of a young girl. She had wide blue-eyes and an open frank face that would have appeared naive were it not for the firm determined chin. The mass of blond hair piled on top of her head threatened to come tumbling down about her neck and shoulders as she shook her head in vigorous denial. "A name like that I'd be sure to remember. It sounds like an Israeli name."

"He's certainly not Israeli. His Hebrew is bad and his English has no trace of accent." He told her about the incident at the temple.

"He doesn't have to be a *sabra,*" Miriam pointed out. "He could have emigrated, you know, and come back for a short visit. A lot of them take Israeli names. Or they translate their names into Hebrew. Does Rokeach mean anything in Hebrew?"

"Why yes. It means druggist, an apothecary."

"An apothecary? How about Aptaker? That means apothecary too, doesn't it?"

"In Russian, I believe. I wonder—"

29

"The proprietor of Town-Line Drugs is a Mr. Aptaker. Could it be his son?"

"You know, Miriam, I think you're right. Remember a few years back—"

"Of course. Jonathan got that terrible attack in the middle of the night and you called the doctor—"

"And he called Mr. Aptaker at his home, and his son opened the store and got the medicine and delivered it." He screwed his eyes shut in an effort to recall young Aptaker's appearance. "He had no beard, of course, and his hair was cut short. It could be."

"I didn't see him." Miriam smiled ruefully. "I was with Jonathan. He wouldn't let me out of his sight."

"And I never saw him again either," the rabbi said. "I went there a couple of days later to pay for the medicine, and he was gone. I seem to recall that I spoke to his father, and he was rather stiff and formal with me. I got the feeling that perhaps he resented having been put to the trouble since I didn't normally trade there."

"Well, if it's Aptaker's son, you can thank him properly now that he's back."

"I gather he's not. Just visiting, he said. Maybe he'll be at the evening service and I'll get a chance to talk to him then. I would have this morning—I sensed that he wanted to talk to me, but with his usual officiousness Kaplan came over and dragged me off."

"You don't like him much, do you, David?"

"Who, Kaplan? Oh, I like him well enough." His face twisted into a sour smile. "Though I liked him better before he became president of the congregation." He laughed shortly. "Since his election, we appear to be in competition. The president is supposed to be the executive director of the congregation while the rabbi guides its religious life. Usually we're on opposite sides of the fence. They want to shorten the service or update it by substituting modern poetry for some of the prayers, or they want to get the temple to take sides on national politics."

"But you've always been able to set them right," she interposed.

"True. But then we were in opposition. I represented the religious side, while they represented the secular. But with Kaplan—"

"He's trying to be both the president and the rabbi of the congregation. Is that it?"

He nodded grimly. "Just about. He holds weekly At Homes for religious discussions and lectures. Every few weeks he leads a group up-country to some camp and holds a retreat of prayer and meditation and religious discussion."

"And you object to that? What was it my Aunt Gittel used to say—'Is it a flaw that the bride is pretty?' "

"You can err on the right just as much as on the left," her husband retorted. "And you can be so meticulous in your observance of the regulations that you lose sight of the reason for them in the first place. But where the error is in the direction of excess, criticism becomes almost impossible. It's like those airline people who instead of calling a regular strike tied up the airports by adhering rigidly to the regulations. What could you say to them? Don't follow the regulations? Can I say to Kaplan and his group, don't be so religious? At the last meeting he proposed that the temple buy this property in New Hampshire to establish a permanent retreat. This new idea of retreats, and of the special group, or the commune, or the chavurah—whatever they call it—withdrawing from the world and society to expand their precious souls, it's contrary to traditional Judaism."

"It's attracting the young people, though," Miriam observed. "I was reading—"

"What's the point in trying to attract young people to traditional Judaism by changing it? So if they do get interested—hooked, is the expression I've heard—it's not Judaism. It's something else that has only a superficial resemblance to it. I've read about them, too. There is a group that celebrates Rosh Hashonah by baking a birthday cake with candles for the world, if you please. Another, down in Florida, tried to rent a lion from some outfit that supplies them to the movies to see if they could make him lie down with a lamb. What's the sense of attracting young people, if they turn out to be nuts? Some are in the neo-Chasidic movement. This Akiva may be one of those, judging from the way he was gyrating and rocking back and forth while *davening*. They're terribly concerned about such things as having the mezzuzah affixed to the doorframe exactly right and that it be hand-written by a scribe on real parchment. Otherwise, presumably, it won't work. And all of them are so self-righteous and so condescending to what they call 'establishment Judaism' as though for the last couple of thousand years we've just been going through the motions and haven't really understood what it's all about. It's the same attitude that led to the recent 'improvement' in our colleges."

"Whew! I had no idea you felt so strongly."

He shrugged. "Maybe I got carried away. It was just that it occurred to me that when this Akiva, if it is he, brought that medicine in the middle of the night, he was doing a real mitzvah. It certainly was more of a religious act than his coming this morning to pray."

6

Marcus Aptaker arrived at his store at half past seven, a good hour before he normally opened for business, and within minutes his resentment and annoyance with his son fell away from him. He liked to come in early so he could do his paperwork leisurely, pecking out necessary correspondence on one of the two ancient typewriters in the prescription room, checking statements against bills, making out checks for supplies. Then he would wander about the store, straightening a package on the shelves or turning a bottle so that the label showed; sometimes changing stock from one shelf to another; or even just touching things as a lover might touch his mistress to be sure she was there, to make contact.

For he loved the store. It gave spice and variety to his life. Every customer who came in to buy was a problem to be solved. Should he suggest an alternative to the item he did not stock, or would the customer resent it as officious? Should he show a higher priced item? Should he offer an opinion at all? Then there were major decisions: should he transfer the toothpaste next to the tooth-brush rack so that the one might suggest the other, or should he keep them far apart so that the customer, in naturally going from the toothbrushes to the toothpaste, would have to pass still other items which he might be tempted to buy? These were all problems that presented themselves one after another all through the day. And he solved them, each in turn as they came up. It was challenge and accomplishment.

And also, he loved the things he sold. Although he did not smoke, he delighted in the smell of the tobacco when he slid open the door of the cigar showcase, or the feel of a briar pipe as he passed it across the counter to a customer; the delicate shape of the flagons of perfume and the new line of men's toiletries packaged in masculine solidity; the cameras, the pocket radios, the clocks and watches; the colorful boxes of candies, and the mechanical pencils and ballpoint pens in their special rack; the sunglasses, and the new display of rubber gloves that had come in only last week, the rack cleverly designed so that as one flat box was drawn out, another automatically took its place; the expensive line of French soaps; the tiny scissors and nail clippers, all in gleaming chrome; and best of all, the special patent medicines that a pharmaceutical house had made up for him under his own label.

Also he liked the people who came into the store, but he liked the idea of the counter between them, because while amiable and friendly as became a good retailer, his professional status required that he not be too friendly. That was the beauty of it, that he was not just another tradesman like the grocer or the hardware man. He was a businessman *and* a professional man, a member of the corps of doctors and scientists and researchers who were engaged in the healing and care of the sick and like them with a diploma and a degree and a license to practice with all the duties and responsibilities thereunto pertaining.

At eight-forty, the first customer came in, and Marcus

Aptaker came forward to greet him, his face automatically assuming the retailer's smile of polite inquiry.

7

"Did you eat someplace?" demanded Mrs. Aptaker. Her son, on his return from the temple, had said he didn't want breakfast, that he wasn't hungry.

"No, but—"

"But me no buts. How do you think it makes me feel when my own son won't accept food from me? So you've become pious and my dishes aren't kosher? All right, I'll give you some cereal and milk in—in—the mixing bowl. It's glass, so you can eat anything in it. Isn't that right?"

He did not have the heart to point out that the spoon was not glass and hence, from his point of view, not kosher, but he reflected that the injunction to "Honor thy father and mother" was of equal importance to the dietary laws, so he said, "All right, I guess since it's glass, I can eat from it."

He poured the dry cereal into the bowl and added milk.

"A couple of eggs, Arnold? I can make them so you could eat them from the shell. That would be all right, wouldn't it? And a cup of coffee. If you want, I could give it to you in a glass."

"Sure, Ma, that'll be fine."

"All your meals you can take here. If you're worried about my pots and pans, I can cook on aluminum foil like I did when my uncle stayed with us a couple of days. He was as bad as you. And I got enough glassware, pie plates, custard cups, you could eat from them and not have to go hungry, or go to the grocery and get something to eat from a paper bag like an animal."

"Sure. I don't mind if it's not too much trouble for you. And if Dad doesn't mind my eating separate food while he's eating. You know how he is."

"Yes, I know how he is." She sat down across the table from him. "I know how he is, but do you know?"

"What do you mean?"

"I mean, do you know that your father is sixty-two years old already? And every day, winter and summer, in some of the worst storms, he goes to the store. He opens every day. And he works long hours. Even when it's McLane's day, your father opens and then instead of coming home as soon as McLane gets there, he's apt to hang around all morning. Then he goes at night to close. Ross McLane works a forty-hour week, but not your father. The other stores in the area close at eight or nine, but your father keeps open till ten every night. And you know why? Because he feels it's his duty, his responsibility. The others close earlier and earlier because they're afraid—so many holdups by these dope addicts—"

"Has Dad ever been held up?" he asked quickly.

"Once, but they caught them. Your father feels he's safe because we're on the Salem Road and lots of traffic. He never asks how I feel."

"Well, gee, I don't see what I can do."

"You don't see what you can do? Well, to start with you could go in and give your father a hand while you're here, just so he can feel you're still his son and a member of the family. Then you could come and live here in

36

Barnard's Crossing. The same job you're working at in a stranger's store, you could do in our store. And then, in time, you could take over the store the way your father did from his father. That's what you could do."

"I'm not coming back to Barnard's Crossing. That's definite," he said stubbornly. "I've made a life for myself in Philadelphia. My friends are all there."

"But before that, your friends were all here. You were born here. You grew up here."

"That doesn't mean I have to die here."

"Living in Barnard's Crossing is like dying? It's so bad here?"

"That's not what I meant. Look, Ma, in Philly I got a job. I work forty hours a week, and the rest of the time is my own."

"But you're working for somebody else and just for wages."

"So what? But when I'm through for the day, I'm free."

"Listen, Arnold, a nurse takes care of children and a mother takes care of children. When she's off duty, the nurse is free, but the mother is never free. So is it better to be a nurse or a mother? Here, you'd be working for—"

"Here, I'd be working for the store. When I was home, Dad cared a lot more about the store than he did about me," he said bitterly.

She nodded. "It seems that way sometimes. That's because a store, if you take care of it, it takes care of you. Your father lives from that store, and your grandfather before him. You remember him, your grandfather?"

"I was just a little kid when he died, but I remember him."

"He was quite a man, your grandfather. He was a pharmacist in the old country, and when he came here, he was highly respected. Do you have any idea what it meant in those days to be a pharmacist, and even more, to have been one in the old country? All the other immigrants were tailors and cobblers and peddlers, ignorant men, most of them. But your grandfather had been to the *gymnasium* and to a technical college. Nowadays, to own a drugstore, maybe it isn't so much. People think of it like any other business. How much does it take in? What's the net profit? But in those days it was a profession like a doctor. You stayed open till midnight every night, not so you could make a few more sales, but because you had a responsibility to the community. Your father was brought up with that idea. The store isn't just a store to him. That's why he stays open later than any other drugstores in the area. And on Wednesday nights, when all the other stores close early on account the doctors take Wednesday afternoons off, he keeps open till his regular time."

"Yeah, I know, sixty, seventy hours a week," he said bitterly. "And he expected the same of me. And when I took time for a little fun, wham! he fell on me like a ton of brick."

"You also took money from the cash register, Arnold," she said sorrowfully. "That's one thing a storekeeper can't allow, not even from his own son. It's like making a hole in the bottom of a boat."

"I was going to put it back."

"That kind of money you never put back. You lost it gambling and spending on your fancy girlfriends. Those were not nice people you were running around with over in Revere. It would only have got worse."

"I never spent more than I could really afford. That IOU Kestler kept pressing me for, that had been hiked. All I owed was fifty dollars and they made it a hundred and fifty—"

"You see the kind of people you were mixed up with?"

"All right, so what could I do? I was in a bind. Would you have felt better if I'd had both arms broken?"

38

"You should have told us. Your father would have taken care of it."

"Oh sure!"

"Yes, sure. The day after you left, Kestler came in looking for you. Your father asked him what he wanted and he showed him the IOU. Your father paid him and then told him never to come into the store again."

He crashed a fist down on the table and jumped up from his chair. *"I* paid him a week later, with my first pay check. I paid him off."

"You paid him a hundred and fifty dollars?"

"I paid him fifty. That's all I owed him. Oh, that bastard, I'll kill him."

"That's nice language you use in front of your own mother. This is what your new religious friends teach you?"

"But Ma, he took the money from me after he'd already got paid off. I'm going to see him—"

"You're here for a couple of days and you want to stir up trouble. Then you'll leave and—"

"But I can't let him get away with it."

"It seems to me you should be thinking of what you owe your father."

"All right, I'll send him a check as soon as I get back to Philly."

"He doesn't want your check."

"So what does he want?"

"I told you what he wants. That's too much? So the least you can do is while you're here, go in the store and help out."

"All right. I'll go over right now."

She considered. "No, better you should go tonight when Ross McLane will be there, too. The first day, it would be better if you were not alone, the two of you."

"So I'll go over right after the evening service."

39

"And Arnold, don't ask your father what to do. Go in like you owned the place. See what has to be done and start working."

"Okay, okay."

8

Morton Brooks, the principal of the religious school, knocked and, without waiting for an invitation, entered the rabbi's study. He was forty and hence a year or two older than the rabbi. His long hair, artfully combed from the side across the top of his head, accentuated rather than concealed his baldness. For a short time during his youth he had had an office job with a Yiddish theater in New York which was always on the verge of bankruptcy and which occasionally called on him for walk-on parts to save the salary of an actor. As a result, he regarded himself as of the theater primarily. He had been teaching in Hebrew schools for the past fifteen years while awaiting a call from the producer.

"What's the point of knocking if you don't wait for me to say come in?" the rabbi asked peevishly.

"Oh, I knew you were alone," said Brooks airily. "I listened at the door before I knocked." He perched familiarly on the corner of the rabbi's desk and lit a cigarette.

Inasmuch as they were of an age and Brooks was actually the elder, it was hard for the rabbi to put him in his place, especially when he was not sure what his place was. Although it was generally understood that the rabbi had overall supervision of the education of the congregation in Judaism, the operation of the religious school was the responsibility of the principal, who answered not to the rabbi but to the school board, which was elected annually. Even in the matter of salary, the rabbi was not sure who was senior, since his own was voted openly by the temple's board of directors while the principal's and teachers' salaries were negotiated confidentially by the school board.

Morton Brooks blew smoke toward the ceiling and said, "You haven't forgotten about Sunday, have you, David?"

"What about Sunday?"

"It's Parents Visiting Day."

"Oh that? What about it?"

"Well, I wondered if we couldn't make some changes in our procedure."

"Like what?" the rabbi asked cautiously.

"Well, you remember when the school board set up Visiting Day a couple of years ago, the parent was supposed to discuss his kid with the teacher. Then if he wasn't satisfied, he could talk to one of us."

"What's wrong with that?"

Brooks's voice took on a complaining tone. "Well, it didn't work out that way. They'd see the teacher, then they'd see me and then they'd insist on talking to you. And sometimes you'd say things to them that didn't exactly jibe with what I said."

"I had no way of knowing what you'd told them."

"Of course not. But the school board's original idea was that we were to share the work. Instead, they go from me to you like going to a higher authority."

"I can hardly refuse to talk to them," the rabbi pointed out.

"Yeah, but suppose you weren't available." He leaned forward. "Now there's a board of directors meeting at the same time and you normally attend. Suppose when they say they want to talk to you, I were to tell them that you had to attend the board meeting because it so happens that it's a particularly important meeting."

"Then all afternoon they'd be calling me at my house." The rabbi shook his head. "Nothing doing. Besides, many of them would be wives of board members and they'd know that nothing much was going to happen at the meeting."

"Don't be so sure, David," Brooks said loftily.

"What do you mean?"

"Well, you'll admit I know a lot more about what's going on around here than you do."

"Do you?"

"Of course I do, David. I see the kids every day and sometimes they talk about what they've heard at home. Then a lot of them are delivered by their mothers or picked up by them. The mothers stand around in the corridor waiting for the classes to end, and plenty of times I hear them talking among themselves."

"And what did you hear about Sunday's meeting?" asked the rabbi with a smile.

Brooks temporized. "Nothing definite, you understand, but I got the idea that something is in the wind. I got the impression that some business is planned for this Sunday just because they know you're not going to be there."

"Any idea what?"

"Nothing definite. But if they are planning something, and I'm sure they are, this gives you a wonderful opportunity to turn the tables on them." He got off the desk and circled to the visitor's chair which he pulled forward so he could be closer to the rabbi. His voice became conspiratorial. "Right after the minyan Sunday, the board holds their meeting. Right? So instead of going to the boardroom, you say nonchalantlike, 'Well, I guess I got to listen to parents' complaints this morning,' like it's an awful chore. And you come right here to your study. Okay, so maybe a parent or two comes in to see you. Chances are they won't, because usually they go to the classrooms to watch first. But you stay here regardless.

"In the meantime, down the hall the board has started their meeting and they're listening to the secretary read the minutes and committee reports and maybe Old Business. I figure that will take until ten o'clock or so. You'd know that better than I do. I'm just guessing on the basis that the board meeting usually ends about the same time our classes do, at noon. So I figure the first hour must be mostly routine."

"Go on."

"Okay, then they get to New Business," Brooks continued. "The way I figure it, there'll be a group that is sold on the idea and they're going to have to convince the rest. Now they're afraid that if you were there, you'd throw a monkey wrench in the gears because it's something you maybe wouldn't approve of, or maybe you'd feel they ought to go slow on. Okay, so somebody gets up to make a motion." He got up and raised his hand to suggest the person making the motion. "Somebody else seconds it." He took a step to one side to indicate the seconder. " 'Discussion on the motion.' " He took a step back to represent the chairman. "So they discuss it for a while and maybe somebody calls for a vote." Brooks went to the door of the study, opened and closed it with a bang. He posed in front of the door, his arms outstretched. "At that point you enter—Ta-ra!" He frowned and reconsidered. "No, better to play it in a low key."

He opened the door again and this time shut it quietly. "You kind of sidle in. Get it?" He looked at the rabbi eagerly.

The rabbi's lips twitched. "Then what happens? Do I say anything?"

Morton Brooks frowned for a moment as he set the scene in his mind. Then his face cleared. "Sure, that's it. You're playing it cool, so you say, 'Would someone be kind enough to enlighten me as to the subject under discussion?' Then you kind of look around and you notice a lot of red faces and maybe some that are too embarrassed to look you right in the eye. So you focus on one of them and he starts to squirm. You let him stew for a minute, and then you say, kind of sharplike, 'Well, Mr. Meltzer?'" He looked expectantly at the rabbi who nodded and clapped his hands in applause.

"One of your best performances, Morton. Then I suppose Meltzer breaks down and confesses that they were just going to vote to convert the temple into a roller-skating rink. No, Morton, nothing is going to happen at the meeting Sunday that doesn't happen at any other meeting. If someone comes up with a new idea, they talk about it and then lay it on the table for the next meeting, and usually for the next and the next until they've talked it to death and finally put it to a vote. As for the parents, I'll see them because their kids are important to them, and what's more, because they're important to me, a lot more than the board meeting."

"If that's the way you want it—"

"That's exactly the way I want it," the rabbi said in dismissal.

"Okay, but don't say I didn't warn you."

9

Unlike his three colleagues, Dr. Daniel Cohen, the newest member of the Barnard's Crossing Medical Clinic, was a general practitioner. Actually, although Alfred Muntz was a heart man, Ed Kantrovitz an internist, and John DiFrancesca an allergist, they all did a great deal of general work, as is necessary in small-town practice.

With his close-cropped hair, bow tie and sports jacket, Dr. Daniel Cohen looked like a college senior of a generation ago. But he was not a youngster who had just completed his internship; he was thirty-two years old and had been practicing for some time. Previously, he had had an office in Delmont and then closed it after a couple of years to open another in Morrisborough, where he had been equally unsuccessful. Yet he was a good doctor who had received excellent training and who showed sound diagnostic judgment. And he was a sincere, friendly man.

Perhaps he was too friendly, a former classmate suggested. He was lunching with a colleague when Dan's name came up. "You take the average patient, he's not looking for friendship. He's hurting and he's worried. He needs assurance that his doctor knows just what's wrong with him and just what will cure him. I don't say a doctor has to be cold and aloof. Although you take a sonofa-bitch like Jack Sturgis—and you know how big his practice is—well, he's so downright nasty that it inspires confidence. They figure that nobody could afford to be so nasty unless he was also damn good. What I'm saying is, your patient has to look up to you. With Dan Cohen, he's like your uncle who tells you to rub yourself with chicken fat to cure your arthritis. See what I mean?"

"Yeah, but how about Godfrey Burke," said the other. "Now he's a real friendly guy, always laughing and joking with his patients, and look at the practice he's got."

"Jeez, Godfrey Burke, he's six four or five and he must weigh two hundred seventy or eighty. A big bear of a man like that, if he weren't friendly, he'd scare the pants off you. But he's friendly like he's sorry for you, like you were a puppy or something, and he's going to fix you up. I guess what I mean is, Dan is like the old-fashioned family-type doctor, the kind that used to sit up half the night with a pneumonia patient waiting for the crisis. Well, that attitude is out nowadays. People are suspicious. They think if you're too anxious, you must have some sort of angle, like maybe you don't know what's wrong and you don't want to admit it. Or maybe you made the wrong diagnosis and gave the wrong medication."

Dr. Cohen used to agonize over the question himself. There were reasons that he could adduce. In Delmont the medical fraternity was a closed corporation who had shut him off from the local hospital facilities, either because he was the stranger or perhaps merely to reduce competition. But why had he done no better in Morris-borough? He told himself it was because he was the only Jew in town. On the other hand, the townspeople, for the most part Yankees, had been friendly enough when he met them on the street. Why hadn't they come to him for medical treatment?

But that was all in the past. Now, he was doing well in Barnard's Crossing, where he had been for less than a year. It was an ideal arrangement. The clinic had excellent facilities with plenty of parking space. They had a bookkeeper who took care of the billing, a technician to do electrocardiograms, blood and urine analysis, and even a graduate nurse who gave flu shots and could assist in minor office surgery or therapy.

And the town, too, was a pleasant place to live, with a large active Jewish community. He was a member of the temple, his wife belonged to the Sisterhood and the two children attended the religious school. His colleague Al Muntz was a close friend of Chester Kaplan, the president. Muntz had even hinted that if he were interested, he would be made a member of the board of directors at the end of the year. "It's a good thing for your practice, Dan. Ed and I are both members of the board." He laughed. "Hell, if I could manage it, I'd get John DiFrancesca on."

"I'm not particularly religious, though."

Dr. Muntz was stout, with a fleshy face and pale blue protruding eyes. When he opened them wide, he gave the impression of being shocked or amazed. He opened them wide now. "And I'm religious?" he demanded as though the imputation were an insult.

"Well, I mean as a member of the board you're expected to go to services on Saturday, aren't you?"

Muntz laughed coarsely. "I don't know who expects it. Whoever he is, he's been waiting a long time. I go on the High Holy Days, of course, and to the Friday evening services pretty regularly, but Saturdays? Cummon! Now Chester Kaplan, he goes. He goes every day morning and evening."

47

"Well, he's the president," Dan said.

"It's not that. He's the first president I remember since Jake Wasserman who does. He went before he became president. He's that kind of guy. He likes it. He really does. If he had his way, he'd make a regular *shul* out of the temple. And that's another reason I'd like you to be on the board, to preserve some kind of balance."

"You mean you'd like me to be on the board so I could oppose your friend Kaplan who'd be appointing me?"

"Nah." With a wide sweep of the hand, Muntz made elaborate denial. "In most things you'll find yourself agreeing with Chet. But he's an enthusiast and he's got this bunch on the board that are the same way. Well, I say if a bunch of guys have a kind of religious hobby and they want to get together and pray and talk religion, it's all right with me. It's a free country. But that doesn't mean that everybody has to go along. Like I've got nothing against people who collect stamps, but I wouldn't want them running the post office. Now you're just the kind of man we want on the board to keep a sort of balance. I've been puffing you up to Chet. But of course you've got to show him you're interested. You're coming tonight, aren't you?"

"You mean to Kaplan's house? I don't know. I have a date with my wife. We're going to drive out to the western part of the state to look at the foliage. She has an aunt in North Adams and we were planning to have dinner there. You know, make a full day of it."

Muntz shook his head reprovingly.

"Well, I figured this invitation was sent to all the new members of the congregation—"

"Don't you believe it, Dan. It's open house, but not everybody gets a personal invitation."

Dr. Cohen considered. "I suppose we *could* get back

48

earlier. I mean, once it gets dark, you can't see the foliage anyway."

"I would if I were you," said Muntz. "You'll be doing yourself a lot of good."

10

Because his wife was not feeling well, Bill Safferstein had come home for lunch instead of eating in town. In return, Mona Safferstein decided she would keep him company and came down to the dining room in a housecoat over her nightgown.

"I don't want anything, Hilda," she said as the maid set a plate of soup before her husband. "Maybe a cup of tea."

"Aw cummon," her husband urged. "Have some soup. It'll do you good."

"No, Bill, it's hard for me to swallow, and I think I've got some temperature."

He reached over and placed his hand on her forehead. "You *are* a little warm. The hot soup will ease your throat. Bring her some soup, Hilda."

Bill Safferstein had a pleasing, coaxing manner that suggested that he knew exactly what was good for you and that he would like nothing better than to get it for you. He was tall and handsome with wavy black hair cut fashionably long at the nape of the neck. When he smiled, and he smiled easily, he showed even white teeth. His pleasant manner and tall good looks as well as considerable luck had made him an extremely successful real estate operator.

But his wife, for the moment at least, was impervious to his charm. Normally cool and svelte and sophisticated, with the long narrow head of a professional model, now her face was drawn and showed lines of pain. She shook her head crossly. "No, really. I'll just have some tea and go right back to bed."

"Maybe we ought to call the doctor," he suggested, concerned.

"Oh, I don't think so. Besides, where are you going to get a doctor on a Wednesday afternoon?"

"I'll call Al Muntz at home. Maybe I can catch him before he goes to play golf or whatever the hell it is that doctors do on their afternoons off." Abruptly he left the table and strode to the phone in the hallway. It occurred to him that his wife must be feeling really ill not to put up a fuss at his calling the doctor.

He was back shortly. "Al has gone to some conference in Boston and will be away all afternoon, but his wife promised to tell him. She's sure he'll be able to look in on you sometime this evening."

"I don't think I really need a doctor," Mona said, but without conviction.

"Maybe you don't, sweetheart, but I'll feel better if Al Muntz checks you out." He went to the hall closet for his coat.

"Do you have to go now?" she asked plaintively.

"I got an appointment at the bank. Look, I'll try to get home early."

"Yes, but then you'll be going to Chet's for the evening," she complained.

"No, I'll stay in tonight."

Instantly, she was remorseful. "Oh, you don't have to because of me."

"But I want to."

"But you enjoy the Wednesday evenings at Chet's," she insisted, "and you say they help you. I want you to go."

"No. Chet will tell them about my offer for the Goralsky Block tonight, and it would be better if I weren't there. Besides, I've got a hunch that Aptaker will call tonight and I'd like to be around so that I can run right over and get his signature on an agreement."

"You and your hunches! How about his son?"

Safferstein laughed joyously. "His son is like my brother-in-law."

She managed a smile. "But he *has* got a son."

"Sure, but he's in Pittsburgh or Philadelphia or someplace. If he were interested in the store, he would have come back long before this."

"But if he does come back?" she persisted.

"He won't. This is the biggest thing I've ever tried. It's got to work."

"It isn't too big for you, is it, Bill?" she asked anxiously. "You're not overextended, are you?"

"Don't worry about that," he said, a little too quickly. "I've got a hunch, I tell you."

11

Akiva spent the afternoon tramping from one end of the beach to the other, renewing his acquaintance with the shoreline. The tide was out and after a while, he took off his boots and socks and slung them over one shoulder by their tied laces. He walked along the water's edge, wriggling his toes in the wet sand, luxuriating in its soft coolness. He came to the rocks of the Point, smooth rounded loaves of pudding stone split here and there by deep narrow channels where the water, even at low tide, rushed in and then was sucked back reluctantly by the receding ocean. The water left little pools in the rocks' depressions where a tiny minnow might be entrapped and dart from side to side until a wave came that was high enough to free it.

Akiva sat at the edge of one such pool and dabbled his feet in the water to wash off the sand. Then he held them straight out in front of him so that the sun could dry them and he could put on his socks and boots. As he leaned back on rigid arms, staring out at the horizon, he felt a peace that he had not known for a long time. As far as he could see, he was alone on the beach.

It occurred to him that it was a good time to practice meditation, undisturbed as he was within and without.

He sat up and maneuvered his legs into the lotus position. It was not easy for him, but with a little trouble he succeeded in tucking in his feet against his thighs. With arms outstretched and thumbs touching forefingers, he let his eyes fall closed. Images came flooding into his mind, and then as his breathing became slow and regular, he saw nothing except a kind of warm luminosity, the effect of the bright sun on his closed eyelids.

"Hey, whatcha doing?"

He opened his eyes and saw a small boy—five or six years old?—standing in front of him, a sandpail in one hand and an old spoon in the other.

Akiva smiled. "Just thinking," he said.

"Whatcha have your hands out like that for?"

"I guess it's because it helps me think. You live around here?"

"Uh-huh, over there," with a nod at one of the houses on the other side of the road that paralleled the beach. "Say, will you take me across? I'm not allowed to cross alone."

"Sure. You just wait a minute while I get my shoes and socks on. How'd you get across in the first place?"

"My mommy brought me."

"And what would you have done if I hadn't been here?"

"Oh, my mommy comes and gets me after a while."

Booted once again, Akiva stood up and held out his hand. "Come on, let's go."

The boy took his hand confidently and together they clambered up the rocks to the side of the road, where they waited as a succession of cars whizzed by. Then, during a lull, they started to cross the road just as a woman came out of the house opposite.

"Why didn't you wait, Jackie?" she called. "I was just going to get you."

"The man said he'd take me across," he shouted back.

Releasing Akiva's hand, he ran across the road and up the porch steps. Akiva lounged after him.

The woman looked at Akiva in momentary suspicion, then she smiled absently. Turning to the boy, she said, "All right, dear, thank the man and go inside and take some milk."

The youngster held out his hand and Akiva mounted the steps to take it. "Thanks," the boy said, and turned and ran into the house.

"He's very well behaved," said Akiva.

"Yes, well—"

"You're Leah Kaplan, aren't you?" he said wonderingly.

"Oh, do I know you? Kaplan was my maiden name."

"We were in school together," Akiva said. "One year I sat beside you in French class."

She looked at him uncertainly. "Oh, are you—you're Aptaker, Arnold Aptaker."

He smiled. "That was *my* maiden name," he said. "I'm Akiva Rokeach now."

"That beard, I would have recognized you right away if it weren't for the beard. What are you hiding?"

"Who's hiding anything? A beard is the natural thing; it's shaving that's unnatural." It was as though the years had fallen away and they were back in high school where derisive sallies were the pattern for conversation.

"Just because it grows doesn't mean you don't have to cut it," she said tartly. "How about toenails and fingernails? I always feel that a man with a beard is hiding something, either a weak chin or a scar, or an inferiority complex."

"Well, I'm not. It's—it's religious."

Then she noticed the yarmulke he was wearing. "Oh, you're one of those." She looked him up and down, taking in the boots, the patched jeans and the denim jacket. "The rest of you doesn't look very religious."

54

"Religion isn't a matter of costume," he said loftily.

"Just of hats, eh?"

"That's different. It's a head covering. Any hat will do, but this one shows that it's for religion and not just to keep my head warm or the sun off it."

"I see. Well, I've got to see to Jackie. Come in, if you want to."

"Well I—" but he followed her into the house and on into the kitchen, where Jackie sat at the table drinking a glass of milk. "Taste good, Jackie? You like milk?" he asked, making conversation.

The youngster nodded shyly and drained his glass as if to prove it.

"Now upstairs for your bath," she said. Obediently, the boy rose from the table and started for the stairs. "Aren't you going to say good-bye to the man?" she called after him.

He came back and went over to Akiva. He held out his hand again and said, "Good-bye."

"Gee, you sure got him trained," said Akiva admiringly.

"I do my best. Say, would you like some coffee? It's all ready. I usually have it while Jackie is having his milk." She brought two cups to the table along with a plate of cookies. "Go on, take one," she urged. When he seemed reluctant, she smiled and said, "It's all right. They're kosher. I made them myself."

"Oh yeah?" He reached for a cookie. "How come you keep a kosher kitchen?"

"Because it's the way I was brought up."

"So why did you find this funny?" he asked, touching the crocheted yarmulke on his head.

She grinned. "I wasn't brought up that kosher."

He grinned back at her, not in the least offended. "You been living here in town all along?" he asked.

"All except when I was at school."

"Your husband local? Anybody I'd be apt to know? I mean, one of the guys at school?"

She poured the coffee. "He's from Boston originally. Goldstein, Fred Goldstein. Know him?"

He shook his head.

"I was divorced last year," she said easily.

He had been seeing her as he remembered her in high school. Now he looked at her appraisingly. She was not particularly good-looking, he decided, just short of being plain, in fact. But her face showed a self-possession and assurance that he found oddly attractive. She had a high forehead and widely spaced cheekbones, but her brown eyes were also widely spaced, so that the face was not disproportionate. It struck him that there was nothing feminine about her features except for the soft rounding of the jawline, ending in a firm chin. She stared back at him and he lowered his eyes.

"Gee, that must have been tough on you," he said, "with the boy and all. I'm sorry."

"It happens all the time," she said with a shrug. "Half the girls I went to school with who got married are either divorced or separated. At least it seems that way. It's the times. People don't need each other anymore."

"What's that supposed to mean?"

"It's the truth. Men used to marry because they needed a woman—to cook for them, to clean and mend for them, to have sex with. Nowadays, it's no trouble to cook for themselves. You just have to heat something that you buy already cooked in a store. And no one mends anymore. You don't have to. Who darns socks these days? And sex is pretty readily available, too. So why should a man get married?"

"How about women? They still need to, don't they?"

She shook her head. "No more than men. They used to need a man to support them while they kept house. Now they can get jobs. And housekeeping is so simplified that

56

they can cook and clean for themselves even with a nine-to-five job. When people needed each other, they tended to stay together. Nowadays they marry because they just want each other. And when they stop wanting, there's no real reason to stay together, especially because when you stop wanting one person it's usually that you've started to want another."

"Is that what happened to you?" he asked.

She smiled sourly. "What do you think? He remarried as soon as the decree became final."

"And the boy, does he miss his father?"

"Of course he does, but he'll get over it. His father was away a lot on business, sometimes a week at a time, so it isn't as though he was accustomed to seeing him here every day. Children are flexible. Or do you have children of your own?"

He shook his head. "I'm still single." Then he laughed. "Up until eight or nine months ago when I came to Philadelphia I wasn't in one place long enough to get married."

"A hobo."

"Yes, I guess you could say so."

"And what made you stop in Philadelphia?"

"That's where I went to school. I stayed there because I came in contact with Reb Mendel's chavurah."

"And got religion."

"I found what I'd been looking for," he said simply. "I got an idea of the meaning of my life, a sense of purpose, a sense of destiny."

She was pleased that he had not responded in kind to her sarcasm. Yet she could not resist another sally. "And now that you've found the meaning of life, you've come to spread the gospel here?"

"Oh no, I'm just a beginner with Reb Mendel. I wouldn't presume to be an expert. I'm only here for a few days visiting my folks."

They talked—of people they had known at school, and

of what had happened to them; of her plans to get a teaching position next year "so I won't be dependent on Fred for support"; of his life on the road before settling in Philadelphia and the various religious disciplines he had sampled before he met Reb Mendel's chavurah. "You come to a new town and the quickest way to meet people is to go to one of these religious meetings."

Then Jackie called from upstairs. "I've had my bath, Mommy."

"I'll be right up, dear."

"I better be running along," said Akiva.

"Oh, all right. It was nice talking to you." She started for the stairs. "You don't mind if—"

"I'll find my way out."

As he trudged along the beach to where his car was parked, Akiva thought about the visit, mildly disappointed that she had not suggested that he call her and yet relieved, too. He told himself there was no point in establishing any more ties in Barnard's Crossing than he had to.

12

The noon broadcast had been almost entirely devoted to news of Hurricane Betsy. There were pictures of the havoc the storm had already caused along the Carolina shore and satellite photos of the eastern coast which indicated that southern New England would not entirely escape the storm. But no one was concerned, since it was not raining and the air, save for occasional gusts of wind, was balmy. And while there were now thick heavy clouds in the sky, the sun would occasionally peep through for a few minutes at a time, shooting golden shafts of light made visible by the dark clouds behind them.

In the early afternoon, the tide was unusually high, although not yet at peak, and cars lined the shore as people came to watch the majestic fury of the surf. At various points along the sea wall, where the land jutted out into the water, the surf was apt to be especially strong, and here young teen-agers gathered to brave the elements. As a big roller broke on the rocks and then receded, they would venture out to the very edge to challenge the next big wave, racing back to avoid the spray when it broke. Sometimes they waited too long, or the force of the wave was stronger than expected, and they would be drenched, while their more cautious friends jeered from a safe vantage point.

Jonathan, the rabbi's five-year-old son, had been playing in the yard most of the afternoon. Now he came running into the house to relate that his friend next door had been taken to the nearby shore to watch the surf and that he wanted to go, too. He appealed to his mother, of course, and she suggested to her husband that he could do with a little fresh air after having spent the afternoon in his study. So the rabbi, with Jonathan's hand firmly held against his ecstatic tugging, sauntered along the shore, stopping now and then to watch as a particularly big roller marched toward them to strike and disintegrate against the rocks.

The rabbi heard his name called, and looking around, he saw Akiva Rokeach waving to him. He waited for him to come up to them. "With the help of my wife," he said, "I finally remembered, or rather figured out, who you are. You're the druggist's son, aren't you? Mr. Aptaker? It's late in coming, but I want to thank you for what you did for us one night a few years back."

Akiva smiled and shrugged.

Rabbi Small continued, "You can understand that I was pretty much confined to the house for the next day or two taking care of Jonathan here, but then I went down to the store to pay for the medicine and to thank you properly. But you were gone."

Akiva grinned. "Yeah, the very next day as I remember it."

"Nothing to do with what you did for us, I hope."

"Oh no. My father asked me to. He gave me good marks for *that*."

"I see. So I gather you left because of a disagreement with your father."

"You might call it that." Akiva began to laugh. "Gee, you're just like my rebbe. You guys are all alike, I guess. I say something, and from just one word, or maybe from the tone of my voice, he infers a whole book."

"I'm sorry. I wasn't trying to pry."

"Oh, that's all right, Rabbi. As a matter of fact, I had a hellova fight with my father and I left. And I wasn't planning to come back."

"But you have."

"Just for a couple of days. And that was because Reb Mendel—that's my rebbe—told me to." He went on to describe Reb Mendel and the chavurah.

"You do everything he tells you?"

"I try to. I had a week's vacation and I wanted to spend it at his house. He has this big ark of a house and his chasidim sometimes stay there for a few days for intensive study. But he told me to go home instead, to my parents. So I did."

"Just like that."

60

"Uh-huh."

"Doesn't it bother you that someone is directing your life, making your decisions for you?" the rabbi asked.

"No. Because he has the Insight. He can see clearer and further than I can. It's like if a bunch of guys were wandering in the desert and they didn't know which direction to go, and one had a telescope and said he could see a village due west. Wouldn't they accept it and go in that direction?"

"I would probably ask if I might take a peek through the telescope," the rabbi said dryly.

"All right, say he didn't have a telescope, but he just had keener vision?"

"I'd want proof of it before I started walking," said the rabbi, with a smile.

"Oh, I know, you regular rabbis always sneer at the rebbe, but—"

"We regular rabbis are presumed to be merely experts in the Law," Rabbi Small interjected, "not miracle workers like a rebbe. My sermons are essentially explanations of the Law and our tradition. Nevertheless, if you had come to me as a friend and asked my advice, I, too, might have suggested this would be a good time to see your parents and make it up with them. But I would have suggested it as a friend, not directed you because I'm a rabbi. The decision would have been entirely yours."

"But suppose you knew, knew absolutely?"

"No one knows absolutely, Mr. Rokeach. Your rebbe, you say, is a psychologist. In my experience this does not necessarily confer expertise in understanding the motives of men, only some skill in designing explanations of their behavior, which may or may not be true and which can't be proved one way or another anyway. Your rebbe is probably a bright man and so has the insight that any intelligent man has. That's all."

"But if he's right every time?"

"No, he's not right every time. When he's right, you're likely to hear about it. And when he's wrong, you are apt to attribute it to your own failings. Just as, if some unforeseen good comes of your visit here, you will attribute it to your rebbe's ability to see into the future. If nothing much happens, you will probably believe you neglected to perform some mitzvah. If you complain to him, he may tell you to be patient, that just as a stone dropped in a pool causes ripples which radiate to the shore, so your coming here is the necessary beginning of a train of events that will ultimately redound to your advantage. And you will believe him, especially if something happens afterward that you can connect, however remotely, with your visit."

"How about the evidence of my own feelings?" demanded Akiva. "How about the calm and certainty that I felt after I joined the chavurah and Reb Mendel? Before that I couldn't make up my mind—what to do, where to go—"

"That's the penalty of having a mind," said the rabbi. "We all suffer from it in some degree. The lower animals who operate on instinct don't have the problem. The impulse to do something automatically shuts off all other circuits. The myth of the donkey who starves to death because he finds himself equidistant from two equal bales of hay applies more properly to humans than to donkeys. It's people, not animals, who want to be in two places at the same time, who want to do two things simultaneously. That's normal, but sometimes it reaches the point where it paralyzes action and decision, and the result is frustration, mental distress, sometimes complete inability to function. When you assign responsibility for a portion of your decisions to someone else, as you do to your rebbe, it's not surprising if the immediate effect is one of calm and relief. Some claim the same effect when they surrender their souls to Jesus, according to an acquaintance of mine who had been in the Jews for Jesus movement. Others invoke the Virgin Mary or a special saint, or the latest popular guru out of the East."

"But if it works—"

The rabbi shrugged. "The stress involved in struggle always ends when you surrender."

Jonathan tugged at his father's hand. "I'm hungry, Daddy. I want to go home."

"All right, Jonathan, we'll go home." To Akiva he said, "He's my rebbe, you see. When he commands, I obey."

"Will you be going to the service tonight, Rabbi? Will I see you there?"

"I expect to. Maybe you can meet our president, Mr. Kaplan. You might find him more sympathetic to your thinking."

"Kaplan? Has he a daughter Leah?"

"Yes, do you know her?"

Akiva smiled. "I—I went to school with a Leah Kaplan."

13

"Hey, where you been, Doc?" The voice over the phone was Joe Kestler's, and he was indignant. "I must've called your house a dozen times, and there was no answer."

"I take Wednesday afternoons off," said Dr. Cohen, and then was annoyed with himself for having bothered to explain.

"Well, my father is not feeling so good. He's awfully warm, like he's got a temperature. And he has to go all the time. And then when he does, he complains it like burns him. And then a few minutes later he's got to go again. He had the same thing a few months ago."

"I'm sorry, but—"

"Look, Doc, don't be like that. I know you got a right to an afternoon off, but he's really bad."

"Under the circumstances, I think it would be better if you called another doctor."

"Where am I going to get another doctor on a Wednesday?" Kestler demanded.

"You can take him to the hospital. I'm sure if you call the police, they'll send an ambulance."

"Sure, and if he passes out in the ambulance? And if he gets to the hospital and some young squirt of a student starts tinkering with him?"

"I'm sorry, but considering your father's action only last month—"

"Doctor, Doctor, that's business. You ran your fence over our land. So my old man filed suit. It doesn't mean anything. There's no hard feelings. It's just how you do things in business. The one thing has nothing to do with the other. And it's you he keeps asking for, because he's got confidence in you."

Dr. Cohen knew he should be adamant and refuse, but he could also picture the old man lying in bed, suffering. "All right," he said, "I'll drop by and take a look at him."

He hung up and said to his wife, "I've got to go out."

"But you were going to the Kaplans," she objected.

"Oh, I won't be long."

"Who is it?"

64

He hesitated, remembering how indignant she had been at the time. "It's Kestler, the old man," he said reluctantly.

"And you're going to see *him?*"

"Well, he *is* my patient."

"But a man who is suing you!"

"I suppose he feels one thing has nothing to do with the other. In a way, it's a compliment. Here, he's suing me and still wants me for his doctor."

"That's because he can't get anybody else on a Wednesday."

"So I guess that's another reason I've got to go."

"Well, if I were treating him, I'd give him something to remember me by. He wouldn't call me again in a hurry."

He smiled. "That's an idea."

When he was at the door, she called after him, "You going to want any supper?"

"Maybe something light. I expect they'll be serving at the Kaplans."

"Better take your raincoat," said Miriam. "If the storm should hit—"

"I was just out on the porch," the rabbi replied, "and it's positively balmy. Besides, I'll just be going from the car to the house."

"I don't see why you have to go at all. Kestler isn't even a member of the temple."

"That's why I make a point of visiting him regularly. To visit the sick is enjoined on all Jews, but the congregation palms it off on the rabbi and thinks of it as a special service they offer their members. 'Join our temple for free visits from the rabbi when you're sick.' So visiting a nonmember gives me the illusion that all my sick calls are purely voluntary. And Kestler is such an incorrigible old scoundrel that I feel it's a real mitzvah to go see him."

She laughed. "You coming right home afterward?"

"Yes—no, I think I'll stop at the Kaplans. He has an At Home Wednesday evenings, and I've never been."

"But—"

"Mort Brooks hinted this morning that Kaplan and his group were planning some skullduggery." He smiled. "Maybe I can get a clue."

Dr. Muntz ripped the sheet off his prescription pad and handed it to Safferstein. "It's a bacterial infection, I'm sure," he said. "I'm giving her penicillin, four times a day for five days. And I want her to take all of them. That's important. She may be all better by the second or third day, but she's to continue with the pills until she's finished the bottle. Understood, Billy?" The doctor's pale blue protruding eyes stared meaningfully at Safferstein.

"Oh sure, she's to take all of them," Safferstein said. "I'll get them right away."

Dr. Muntz glanced at his watch. "The drugstores are closed by now. Tomorrow will be all right."

"Town-Line Drugs is still open."

"Yeah, I guess they are at that. Then give her the first one tonight."

Safferstein helped him into his raincoat.

"You coming to Chet's tonight, Billy?" asked the doctor.

"Gee, I don't think I should with Mona feeling this way. You're going, I suppose."

"Oh sure. Chet expects me. I'm the official agnostic and cynic, you know. He needs my opposition to give some pep to the meetings." He chuckled. "Or maybe I'm the horrible example."

Safferstein grinned. "I always figured you were putting on an act."

"Oh, it's no act," said the doctor quickly.

Safferstein held the door open for him. "Then you're

66

missing something, Al," he said seriously. "I know since I joined, I got this feeling of certainty, like I can't go wrong. I've made some long-shot deals, and they've all worked out."

The doctor chuckled again. "If you say so, Billy. If you say so."

It was Mrs. Kestler, Joe's wife, who answered the doctor's ring. She was blond and fleshy and faded and reminded him of the little girl who had sat next to him in the third grade. She had been pink and white, and plump and blond, and he always felt a little sad at the thought that she probably looked like Mrs. Kestler now. She was gentle and slow, and he assumed as a matter of course that she was bullied by her husband and imposed on by her father-in-law. When she had last had a checkup, she had asked him to do a Wassermann, too, because "Joe was out of town on business and you know how it is when men go out of town."

"He's upstairs, Doctor," she said. "Joe is with him."

"All right, I know the way."

The examination did not take long, and when Dr. Cohen was finished, he nodded the son out of the room. As they proceeded down the stairs, Joe Kestler said, "Gee, that was quick. You guys got it made." He was a big powerful man with grizzled iron-gray hair covering a bullet-shaped head and with the flattened nose of a prize-fighter.

"Your father has a bacterial infection of the urinary tract," the doctor said, professionally impersonal.

"Sounds bad. What do you do? Can he take one of those wonder drugs like penicillin?"

"Your father is allergic to penicillin, so I'm giving him one of the tetracyclines instead. It works the same way. He's to take one four times a day. And he's to take all of them, even if the infection clears up after a day or two.

That's important. I'd like him to get started on them right away."

"You got samples with you, Doc?"

"Samples? No, I don't carry drug samples around with me. I'll write you a prescription."

"Where am I going to get a prescription filled this time of night? The drugstores are as bad as you guys. They all close early Wednesdays."

"I believe Town-Line Drugs is still open," said the doctor stiffly.

"I don't go in there."

"You mean you don't trade with them?"

"That's right. I wouldn't set foot in there," Kestler said doggedly.

"But with your father sick—"

Kestler shook his bullet head like a boxer clearing his brain of fog. "Makes no difference."

Dr. Cohen considered. "Maybe I've got some samples at home." Another idea occurred to him. "What if I called in the prescription and they delivered it?"

"So long as I don't have to go in there. But look, Doc, why don't you check first and see if you got the samples? I could follow you in my car."

"That won't be necessary. I'm going out a little later and I can drop them off here. If I don't have the samples, I'll call in the prescription."

"Okay, Doc, but first look and see if you've got the samples, will you?"

There were half a dozen cars parked along the curb in front of Town-Line Drugs. Inside customers were milling around, impatiently waiting for someone to take their money and wrap up their purchases. It was the approaching storm, of course, that everyone was concerned about. They were buying flashlights and batteries; small first-aid kits and aspirin; cigarettes and candy. The supply of candles—the store carried a line of fancy dinner table candles—was all sold out.

Marcus Aptaker was out front, the only one available to wait on trade, and he scurried from one part of the store to the other, smiling, courteous, brisk. Whenever he glanced to the back of the store, he was filled with a quiet joy, for he would catch sight of his son in a white tunic working at the prescription counter with Ross McLane. Earlier, a high school lad, Jimmie, had helped wait on trade, but he was out making deliveries now, the last of the evening, and would not be back.

Bill Safferstein entered, glanced around, and strode purposefully toward the proprietor, who was momentarily free. "Look here, Aptaker, I want—"

"I'm sorry, Mr. Safferstein," Aptaker said, gesturing to the customers in the store. "Not now, you can see I'm busy. This is no time to talk."

"Oh, I didn't come in about that. It's my wife. She's sick. Could I get this filled right away?"

Aptaker glanced at the prescription. "It will take a few minutes."

"I don't mind waiting." He looked around. "I see you've put on another pharmacist."

"My son," said Aptaker proudly, and hurried away as a customer called to him.

Jackie had gone to bed with little fuss and had fallen asleep almost before his mother had tucked him in. Leah looked around the room, adjusted the window and put out the light. Then she washed and put away the supper dishes and went into the living room. There she consulted the television column of the morning paper, and although no program held much interest for her, she turned the set on anyway. There was a lot of static, and the picture wavered and became snowy. She tried each of the other channels with the same result and finally turned off the set in disgust.

She picked up from the coffee table a book that she had been reading for the last several days, but she could not concentrate and found herself reading the same sentence over and over again. Realizing she was only looking at words, she closed the book and tossed it on the table.

She walked around the room, straightening a picture, moving a chair. She noticed that the barometer on the mantelpiece was low. She tapped it, and the needle moved lower still. She went to the window to stare out at the road and the sea beyond. She was restless and wanting to be doing something and didn't know what.

If it were not for Jackie upstairs, she would not be bound to the house. She could get into her car and drive along the dark country roads until perhaps she came to a diner where she might stop for a cup of coffee. There would be a truck driver who was a college graduate, with a blue denim shirt open at the throat and a cap perched jauntily on the back of his head, who would bring his coffee cup to her booth. . . . Or she could take a walk along the shore in the darkness, barefooted, and the water would be warm and she would slip out of her clothes and go for a long swim. She turned over on her back to float and she heard the splash of another swimmer. . . .

Suddenly, the room became daylight bright as a jagged bolt of lightning struck the water. The lightning was followed immediately by a crash of thunder, and the house was plunged in darkness. And then the rain came pelting down. Leah ran to the window and saw that the street lights had also gone out. She went onto the porch and looked up and down the street. All the houses were dark, but here and there she saw a flicker of light from a window as people lit candles. She went back inside and felt her way to the kitchen, where she found a stump of a candle. By its light she tried to dial her parents' home, but there was no dial tone, only a faint hum. Back in the living room, she dragged a hassock to the window and knelt on it with her arms resting on the sill, staring out at the raindrops bouncing off the road.

Ross McLane took the call, since his station at the prescription counter was nearest the phone. Because he was hard of hearing, he normally tended to speak loudly, but when he got on the phone you could hear him all over the store. "Town-Line Drugs . . . Who? . . . Oh, hello, Doctor. What can I do for you?. . . . Just a minute. All right, shoot. . . . Yup. . . . Yup. . . . Kestler, yup. What's the initial. . . J? Got it. . . . Minerva Road, forty-seven? . . . Uh-huh. . . . Okay. . . . Gee, I don't think so. The boy who makes the deliveries is gone. . . . I don't think so, but hold a minute and I'll ask." He cupped the receiver and called out, "Say, Marcus, it's Dr. Cohen on the phone. He wants to know if we can make a delivery tonight? Forty-seven Minerva."

"Tell him, no."

Into the phone, McLane said, "Look, Doctor, I don't see how we can. We're awfully busy and we'll be working late. We got a stack of prescriptions for the nursing home. There's just no one here to . . ." He cupped the receiver again. "He says it's very important, Marcus."

"Look, I'll deliver it if you like," Safferstein volunteered.

"You know him?" Aptaker asked.

"No, but if he needs it . . . and I live on Minerva. Forty-seven is on my way home."

"It's coming down in buckets," Dr. Cohen said, staring out of the window. "I wouldn't be surprised if the Kaplans called it off. I mean with a hurricane—"

"I got the news broadcast while you were out," his wife told him. "They said the storm was going out to sea

71

and we're just getting the edge of it, a kind of backlash. They expect it'll be over in an hour or so."

"Whether it's the real thing or just the backlash, it's pretty bad. I think I'll pass up Kaplan's meeting and stay home."

His wife was doubtful. "I don't know, Dan, Al Muntz seemed to think it was important, from what you said."

"Well, what if they called it off? I'd feel like an awful fool coming there in this kind of storm and there's no party."

"Wouldn't they have phoned?"

"Sure, but they may have called earlier, and we've been away all day."

"So why don't you call them?"

"Yeah, I guess I will." He picked up the phone. "No dial tone," he announced. He tried dialing anyway, but there was no answer. He jiggled the hook and then dialed the operator. He listened intently with the instrument pressed tight against his ear. Finally, he replaced it on its hook. "Out of order. Funny, it was all right a few minutes ago when I called the drugstore. Maybe that last lightning bolt hit a transformer, or the line may be down."

"I'll tell you what you do, Dan. Drive over there. If the place is all lit up and there are a bunch of cars outside, you'll know it's all right and you'll go in. If it's dark, or just ordinary lit, and there are no cars, you'll know it's been called off and you'll come home."

"Yeah, I guess that's what I'll do."

Safferstein carefully tucked the two small manila envelopes, each with its bottle of pills, into the pocket of his raincoat. It was raining now, so he put up his coat collar and dashed out to his car. No sooner had he set the car in motion when a lightning flash momentarily made everything bright as day. A crash of thunder followed immediately. And then the skies opened and the rain came pelting down in large drops that danced on the black asphalt road. A continuous sheet of water coursed down his windshield, and his wipers were powerless to clear the glass. The windshield began to steam up and he put on the defroster, but to no avail. He pulled up under a lamppost and shut off the motor. This can't last long, he thought.

"Well, that was quick," Mrs. Cohen said as her husband opened the door and wriggled out of his coat. "The place was dark, huh?"

"I didn't get to it. There's a tree lying across the road, right at the corner. I had to back up all the way to Baird Street to turn around."

"Oh, that big old elm? What a shame! Maybe you ought to call the police and tell them."

"And how am I going to call them? With smoke signals?"

"What I'm trying to get is a consensus," Chester Kaplan urged. "Now are we all agreed that it's pointless for the temple to retain and operate the Goralsky property?"

The response was general and immediate.

"Oh, sure. Who wants to be bothered collecting rents?"

"Or making repairs, or renting a vacant store."

"You can always get some real estate company to manage it for us," Abner Fisher pointed out.

"Yeah, and they take ten percent of the gross."

"Five percent," Fisher corrected.

"So five percent, and they don't do a damn thing except collect rents. I know. I'm with you, Chet, that we should sell the property, but can we, according to the terms of Goralsky's will?"

"Believe me, it's okay," Kaplan said quickly. "The will reads—and I'm quoting it exactly—'To the temple I bequeath the store block known as the Goralsky Block with the land thereunto adjoining.' Then he goes on to give the boundaries and then he says—now get this—'. . . so that the temple may derive therefrom an annual income to help meet the ordinary expenses of operation, or for the purpose of erecting a building such as a religious school or a permanent residence for the incumbent rabbi, or for any similar purpose that will be to the interest and advantage of the temple.' Now as far as I'm concerned, that last clause does it. We can use the property any way we want as long as it is to the interest and advantage of the temple. Right, Paul?"

Paul Goodman, who was also a lawyer, nodded. "That's the way I read it."

"And I'd say selling it and using the money to buy a place for a permanent retreat is definitely to the interest and advantage of the temple," Kaplan pressed on. "And the time to sell is now, because we've got an offer that we won't see again in a hurry."

"Well, what I want to know is why is Bill Safferstein offering such a high price for the property?" asked Abner Fisher, who frequently played devil's advocate to the group.

Kaplan turned toward the questioner, his face full of candor. "I don't know, Abner. All I know is what I said to some of you already. I was telling Bill Safferstein about the last retreat. He wasn't at that one, see? The monsignor came down and we got to talking and he said how the church was willing to sell the property. Now, the price he mentioned seemed to me like a steal. I told Bill that for a hundred grand we could buy it and fix it up. So he said, 'Tell you what, I'll give you a hundred grand for the Goralsky property.' I thought he was kidding, but he wrote out a check right then and there for a thousand dollars as an earnest against his offer to buy. Now that's all I know. Maybe that's his way of making a contribution to the temple."

"Cummon!" Abner Fisher was derisive. "Billy Saffer-stein is a nice guy, and generous, but paying that kind of money for a block of crappy stores, and with one of them vacant yet—"

"I got a letter the other day from the drugstore asking for a renewal on his lease," Kaplan interposed.

"All right, so there's one good store in the block, but it still doesn't explain—"

"That's how Bill operates," Paul Goodman said. "You ever play poker with him? When his luck is running, he plays it to the hilt. Say, the betting is going a chip at a time, he'll say, 'Let's drive out the buttonhole makers,' and kick it up five. And he buys real estate the same way. When I was liquidating the Harrington estate, he bid seventy-five grand for the land when the other operators were offering bids in the low fifties. Naturally, he got it. And then he split it up into about a hundred lots and peddled them off for an average of three thousand apiece and made himself a sweet little bundle. After he bought it, I told him he could have got it for twenty thousand less, and you know what he said? 'I never try to buy a property as cheap as possible. That way you're in competition with the other operators. They keep kicking each other up and before you know it, you're paying more than you intended and more than it's worth. I always figure what a property is worth to me, and that's what I offer. That way you discourage the competition. It takes the heart right out of them.'"

"Well," said Kaplan, "all I know is, it's one hellova good price, and if we don't take it, we all ought to go see some shrink and have our heads examined."

"I admit it's a good price and I think we ought to sell," said Fisher. "But I want to know if the place up in Petersville is a good buy and is it the place we want for a permanent retreat."

"You've been up there, Abner. You've seen it."

"Yeah, but I was there on a retreat. I saw it but I didn't check it over like I would if it were a place I was going to buy."

"Well sure, Abner, that's why I'm arranging for a retreat for this weekend. It'll give us a chance to look over the place. We can decide while we're up there and then come back and vote on it formally at Sunday's board meeting."

"It'll be a regular retreat?"

"You bet. Rabbi Mezzik will be there, and the rebbitzin to serve the Sabbath meal and bless the candles. Then Saturday, we can take a real good look at the place and come to a decision—"

"How about transacting business on the Sabbath, Chet?"

Kaplan grinned. "I figure this is holy business, so it's all right."

A police cruiser passed, slowed down and parked just ahead of him. The patrolman in a yellow slicker got out and came over. He shone his flashlight through the window.

"Why, it's Mr. Safferstein? Anything the matter?"

Safferstein lowered his window. "No, nothing wrong, officer. It was just coming down so fast that my wipers couldn't handle it. And then the windshield got steamed up. I thought I'd pull up here and wait a little while."

"You want to leave your car here and we can drive you home in the cruiser?"

"No, it's letting up a little now. I'll be all right."

"Anything we can do for you?"

"No, thanks just the same—well, maybe you can at that. I promised to deliver these pills . . ."

Mrs. Kestler peered anxiously out the window and said doubtfully, "It's let up some, Rabbi, but it's still coming down pretty hard. Hadn't you better wait a while?"

76

But he was anxious to get to the Kaplan At Home. "No, that's all right," he said, "I'll make a run for it. My car is right in front of the house."

The rabbi opened the door, momentarily stood in the protection of the porch and then dashed down the stairs and along the front walk to his car. He had intended to get in on the passenger side, which was next to the curb, and then slide over behind the wheel, but the door was locked. As he fished for his keys, a sudden gust of wind shook the branches of the trees, showering him with the water from their rain-laden leaves. Now thoroughly drenched, he remembered that the lock did not work well and required considerable jiggling of the key to open from the outside. In racing around to the driver's side, he stepped into the deep puddle that had formed along the curb and he uttered an unrabbinic and uncharacteristic oath.

At last behind the wheel, but soaked and uncomfortable, he thought, "I'd better get right home and get out of these clothes or Miriam will have a fit."

Although the force of the storm had lessened considerably, the rain continued in a heavy downpour. Safferstein had to drive almost to the end of the street before he could find a place to park, a good fifty yards beyond the Kaplan house. But he turned up his collar and, with hands thrust deep in the pockets, he trudged back along the line of cars. Arriving at the house, he quickly mounted the steps to the sanctuary of the porch. He paused, listening to the sounds from within. Noticing that the door was ajar, he pushed it open and entered.

Instantly, he found himself in an atmosphere of masculine gaiety and good fellowship. The large reception hall, the adjoining living room and the dining room beyond were full of men standing around in groups, talking, laughing, arguing. When they caught sight of Saffer-stein, they hailed him jovially.

"Hi, Billy."

"Hyuh, Billy, old boy."

"Hey, there's Bill Safferstein."

From the tone of their greeting, he suspected that Kaplan had already told them of his offer to buy the Goralsky property and that they approved.

He took off his coat and looked around for a place to put it. There were large piles of coats on several chairs in the reception hall, but since his was wet, he hesitated to place it on top of them.

Kaplan greeted him and then whispered, "It's all set." Taking his coat, he said, "It's wet, I better hang it up in the closet." Kaplan draped it on a hanger and then pushed the mass of coats along the closet rod and in-sinuated Safferstein's. "How's Mona? She okay now?"

"I went to get her some medicine and the driving was so bad I thought I'd stop here till it lets up a little."

"You bet. Come and have a glass of beer."

"Coffee would be better if you've got it."

"Sure. One coffee coming up."

"Say, can I use your phone?"

"Right there."

He dialed his house. It was the maid who answered. "Hilda? How's Mrs. Safferstein? . . . Oh, good. If she wakes up, tell her I stopped off at the Kaplans because of the storm, and I'll be along later."

Mrs. Kestler leaned over the banister and called down to her husband below. "Joe, come quick. Your father— he sounds terrible."

He ran up the stairs. "Hey, Pa, what's the matter? You all right?" To his wife he snarled, "Don't just stand there, dummy. Call the doctor."

She hurried downstairs. He could hear her dialing and

78

then talking but he could not make out what she was saying. He went down to join her, and she turned to him, her hand cupping the receiver. "It's the answering service. She wants to know what's the matter and she'll notify Dr. Cohen."

Grabbing the phone out of her hand, he shouted into it, "Look, lady, my father is acting up from some pill Doc Cohen gave him. You get hold of him and tell him to get his ass over here right away. Understand?" He banged down the receiver.

"Oh, Joe, I don't think you should have talked to her like that. You know, out of spite they can—"

"She better not. I could sue her for everything she's got down to her panties. You go and stay with him. I'll wait here by the phone."

"Oh, Joe, I'm afraid."

"Afraid? What's to be afraid of?"

"I don't know. He looks so—so funny."

"Go on. I want to be here to answer the phone when the doc calls. You, he could give fifty-seven varieties of crap."

Reluctantly, she started for the stairs. The phone rang, and she paused.

"Yeah. Who?"

"I'm Dr. DiFrancesca," said the voice over the phone. "Dr. Cohen can't be reached. His phone appears to be out of order. I'm standing in for him. What's the matter?"

"Well, he gave him this pill, and now he's having trouble breathing."

"I see. I think we'd better get him to the hospital. I'll call the police, and they'll send the ambulance. I'll alert the hospital that he's coming."

"And what happens if he gets worse on the way to the hospital?"

"Well . . . well, all right. I'll have the ambulance stop and get me and I'll come by with them."

"Hey, Chet, got an extra one of those maps?"

"Sure, Howard, plenty. Help yourself." Chester Kaplan held out a sheaf of Xeroxed sheets showing the route to the campsite where the retreat was to be held. "Now you're coming for sure, aren't you?"

"Would I give you my check for twenty-five bucks if I didn't plan to make the scene?"

Since the rain had let up a little, many of the guests began to leave, taking advantage of the lull in the storm. With much jovial humor, they moved toward the hall to get their hats and coats.

"While you're at it, Bert, pick out a good one."

"Hey, you sure you wore a coat?"

"Now remember, you guys," Kaplan called out to them, "we start out from here at half past two sharp. But if you should miss us, you'll have no trouble getting there by just following the map."

As Safferstein rose, Dr. Muntz called out to him, "You going now, Bill?"

"Well, I— You staying?"

"Sure. Stick around for a while."

Kaplan approached. "What's your hurry, Bill? Edie is fixing some sandwiches. We'll have another cup of coffee and shmoos a little."

"Well, all right. How does it look?"

"In the bag, I'd say. I figure there'll be no sweat voting it officially Sunday."

"Fine."

"I got a couple of letters from people interested in the vacant store. One is from a paint and wallpaper—"

Safferstein shook his head.

"And there's a letter from the drugstore about his lease."

80

"What about it?" Safferstein asked quickly.

"It seems his lease was expiring, so he wrote to Goralsky for a renewal. The old man agreed and had the forms drawn up. But he died before he got around to signing them."

Safferstein smiled broadly. "Is that so?"

"What do you want me to do?"

"Why don't you just write Aptaker and tell him I'm taking over and to see me about it."

Marcus Aptaker turned the key in the lock and then jiggled the knob to make sure the door was locked. "Good night, Ross," he said, and to his son, "Coming, Arnold?"

"You go ahead, Dad. I got my car here. I'll be along a little later."

The rain had stopped but it was misting, and as Akiva drove along the shore road he encountered patches of heavy fog that his headlights could barely penetrate. As he approached the house by the shore he saw that the entire area was dark, not only the houses but the street lights as well. He began to have doubts. Leah might have taken the boy to her parents' house at the approach of the storm and was there with him now. Or if they had remained, then they could be asleep, and if he rang the bell . . .

Then he saw her silhouetted in the window, looking out at the turbulent ocean. He parked his car and walked across the street, hoping she would recognize him as he approached.

She opened the door before he could reach for the bell. "What are you doing here?" she asked. "What do you want?"

"I tried to call you a couple of times, but I guess your line is dead. I was worried. You're right on the water. I thought I'd run out and see if you were all right."

"The electricity is out," she said, "and I used up the one candle I had." She stood aside for him to enter.

He found his way into the living room and sat on the sofa. A moment later he felt it give as she plumped down beside him. Her thigh was tight against his, and he thought she had misgauged the distance in the darkness. But she leaned against him. And then she was on top of him, her mouth pressed hard against his.

Later, when they were lying close together on the narrow sofa, she murmured, "It's been so long."

"For me too," he said huskily.

The phone rang, and Chester Kaplan called from across the room, "Take it, will you, Al."

Dr. Muntz picked up the phone and said, "This is the Kaplan residence. . . . Who? . . . He's not here. Just a minute, hold on." He cupped the instrument and called out to Kaplan. "It's for Dan Cohen. Was he here tonight? I didn't see him." He spoke into the phone again. "No, he didn't get here. Say, who is this? . . . Oh, it's you, John. I thought I recognized your voice. What's up? . . . What! . . . Just a minute." He raised his head and said, "Hey, pipe down, you guys, will you? I can't hear."

The room immediately got quiet, all eyes turned toward him.

"So they called you? . . . M-hm . . . M-hm . . . M-hm. . . Well, I guess it's one of those things. I'm sorry you got mixed up in it. . . . Yeah, bye."

"Was that John DiFrancesca?" asked Dr. Kantrovitz. "What happened?"

"One of Dan Cohen's patients died. They couldn't get hold of Dan, so the service called John. He says it was probably a reaction to medication that Dan ordered and—"

"Who was it?"

"Old man Kestler."

"Oh my God!" The cry came from Safferstein.

All turned to him. His face was ashen.

"What's the matter, Billy?" Kaplan asked.

"Maybe it was my fault. I might have switched the pills."

"What are you talking about?"

He explained how he had volunteered to deliver the prescription to the Kestler house. "So I had these two envelopes, one that Al prescribed for Mona and one for Kestler. Maybe the one I gave the cop for Kestler was Mona's."

"How about it, Al?" asked Kaplan. "Could what you prescribed for Mona have hurt Kestler?"

"It was penicillin," Dr. Muntz replied. "If Kestler was sensitive to it—" He broke off as another idea occurred to him. "You gave Kestler's pills to Mona?"

"No, I came right here because of the storm."

"So you've still got the other one," Muntz pointed out. "All you have to do is look and see if the pills you still have are Kestler's or Mona's."

"Yeah, that's right. They're in my coat pocket." Safferstein immediately went to the hall closet where Kaplan had hung his coat. The others followed. He picked up a coat and thrust his hand into the pocket. "It's gone," he exclaimed in dismay. "The pills are gone."

"Look in the other pockets."

"I remember putting them in this pocket." But he began to search nevertheless. He drew out a pair of gloves and stared blankly at them. "These aren't mine. Say, this isn't my coat. Somebody must have switched coats with me."

14

Marcus Aptaker stirred uneasily and then came awake. He rubbed his eyes and yawned mightily. His wife, in her bathrobe, was sitting on the rocker, staring out the window.

"What's the matter? Can't you get to sleep?"

"It's a quarter of two," she said, "and Arnold's not home yet."

"So what? He's a big boy now."

"But the storm—he may have—according to the broadcast a lot of trees blew down, and some telephone and electric-light poles."

"Good Lord, why do you want to imagine such things?" But he got out of bed and put on his bathrobe. "Let me make you some hot milk. Then you'll be able to sleep."

She followed him into the kitchen. "I don't want any hot milk. I think we ought to call the police."

He stared at her. "What for?"

"Well, you could ask if—"

"Look, Rose, if he's been in an accident, if that's what's bothering you, believe me, they'd let us know."

"So where can he be?"

"How do I know? He probably went to visit a friend and they didn't notice the time passing."

"Who would he go see? What friends does he have around here?"

"I don't know. All I know is he was on the phone a couple of times."

"I think we ought to call the police," his wife insisted.

"I'm not calling no police. What could I say to them? That it's almost two o'clock in the morning and my twenty-eight-year-old son isn't home yet? I'd never hear the end of it. Chances are he had a flat tire or something and he'll be along pretty soon."

"So why wouldn't he have called? He'd know we'd be worried, wondering what might have happened to him in a storm like this."

"How the hell do I know why he didn't call? Maybe he didn't have a dime."

Grumbling, Marcus Aptaker wandered into the living room and his wife followed after him. He turned on the TV to "The Late Late Show" and stared unseeing at the screen.

"Why don't you go to bed?" she urged. "You've got to get up in the morning."

"I don't feel sleepy." He was as worried as she was but he could not voice his fears lest he increase hers.

At three o'clock, Akiva came home. He was happy. He was euphoric. He was uneasy. "Gee, the house is lit up like a Christmas tree," he said gaily. "Don't you folks ever go to bed?"

"Oh, Arnold, we were so worried," his mother wailed.

"Where in hell have you been?" Aptaker demanded, his worry instantly converted to dark anger.

"Didn't you know we'd be worried?" his mother sobbed. "Where were you?"

"I— I went to see a girl."

"In Revere, I bet," his father shouted. He turned to

his wife. "One of those floozies he used to hang around with. You wondered who he knew around here, who he could go see. I'll tell you who. One of those nice girls in Revere you don't have to know personally, that's who. He's religious now. Goes to the synagogue. Won't eat your food because it isn't holy enough for him. And he's home one night and he goes chasing after whores."

Akiva lost control. "You can't talk to me that way," he shouted. "I don't have to take that from you."

"As long as you're under my roof—"

"Then Goddammit, I'll get out from under your roof," and he flung out of the room. He was back almost immediately with his suitcase in hand. He tossed the house key they had given him onto the coffee table. "There, I'm getting the hell out of here." He started for the door.

"Please, Arnold, please," his mother begged. "Where are you going?"

"Back to Philly. I shouldn't have come." He banged the door behind him.

Unbelieving, Mrs. Aptaker stared at her husband, who glowered at the floor. "Oh, Mark, you shouldn't—"

"Let him go. Who needs him?"

"No!" She pulled at the door and ran out onto the porch. She called to him, but he had already backed out of the driveway and was turning into the street.

As Akiva drove through the night, he took on passengers: his mother first, with whom he was contrite. "I knew all along it wouldn't work, Ma. That's why I didn't come back before. Dad is not a bad guy, but our chemistries don't mix, our vibrations don't harmonize. It's not his fault and it's not my fault; it's just one of those things."

Then Reb Mendel, with whom he was inclined to be jocose. "I guess, Rebbe, this is one time the Insight was a bit faulty. A little grease on the telescope lens, perhaps?"

And Leah, with whom he spoke seriously. "It's probably for the best, dear. I'd be leaving in a few days anyway. Of course, if you were to come down to Philly, and get a job there, or even in Washington, where I could visit on a weekend—"

His reverie was shattered by the unmistakable sound of a policeman's whistle. Since his car was the only one on the road, he knew it applied to him. Resigned, he slowed down and stopped. In the rear-view mirror he watched the policeman dismount from his motorcycle and stroll leisurely toward him. He turned on the overhead light and began to fish through the glove compartment for his registration.

The policeman bent down and glanced inside the car. "Hopping right along there, weren't you, mister? You going to a fire?"

"Look, officer, I'm driving down to Philly—say, you're Purvis, aren't you? Joe Purvis?"

"Yeah. You know me?" The policeman peered at him. "You're not—"

"Arnold Aptaker."

"How about that? How are you? What's with the whiskers?"

"Oh, you know, just thought I'd try it. Saves on razor blades."

"How about that? You been in town? I didn't see you around."

"Just visiting my folks for a couple of days. I live in Philly now. How long you been on the cops? I thought you were a carpenter."

"I *was* carpentering till a couple of years ago. Slim pickings during the winter, so I took the police exam. I still do some carpentering when I'm off duty, you know, for old customers."

"You got a brother, haven't you?" Akiva asked, anxious to keep the conversation going on friendly lines.

"Caleb? Yeah, he was a year behind us."

"I remember. He was in my English class. What's he doing? He on the cops, too?"

"Naw. He's with the *Courier,* circulation manager. He writes to all the Crossers who've moved away, like to Florida, and asks them to subscribe so they can keep in touch with the town. Does pretty good, too."

Inspiration came to Akiva. "Say, that's an idea." He searched in the glove compartment and found pencil and paper. He scribbled his name and address and handed it to the policeman. From his wallet he drew a five-dollar bill. "Here's five bucks. Give it to your brother and have him send me the paper."

"Well, gosh, why don't you write him yourself and he'll send you a form. I'm not sure how much it is."

"So when he sends me five bucks' worth, he'll send me a notice to renew. You know how it is, if I have to sit down and write a letter, I won't get around to it."

"Well, all right." The policeman folded the bill inside the address and inserted them into the sweatband of his cap. "Look, next time you come up this way, come see me. And say, take it easy for the next couple of miles. There's branches down all along the road."

Rabbi Small heard about Kestler's death the next day at the morning minyan. Although shocked that the man he had visited only the night before had died, he was not too surprised. Kestler had been over eighty and each time he had been to see him, he had seemed weaker and more fragile.

"You going to the funeral, Rabbi?" asked Chester Kaplan. "It's over in Revere at half past ten. He was a member of Bnai Shalom."

"I don't think so."

"Well, I suppose I'll have to go. I've done some legal work for the Kestlers over the years."

"It's a mitzvah to go," the rabbi observed.

Kaplan brightened. "Yeah, that's right, it is."

When next he saw the rabbi at the evening minyan he reported on the event. "You should've been there, Rabbi. There was quite a crowd. I wouldn't have thought he was that popular." Kaplan laughed. "But when I overheard some of the remarks, I figured they had come to make sure he was dead."

The rabbi raised his eyebrows. "So?"

"You know what he was, don't you?"

"Small-loans banker?"

"He was a usurer. He lent money on high-risk items. He gave second and third mortgages, chattel loans, that sort of thing. His prime rate of interest was somewhere around twenty-five or thirty percent. But you should have heard the eulogy. This Rabbi Rogin who officiated went on and on about how Kestler had loaned money, 'not to the financiers or the captains of industry, but to the poor and the humble.' I suppose he asked the son about his father and then dressed it up."

The rabbi nodded sadly. "We used to eulogize only great men, but nowadays the family expect it and appreciate it even when they know better. And afterward they tend to think of him the way the rabbi eulogized him. Maybe it's not a bad thing if it helps a son to think a little better of his father. Historians do the same for the statesmen and heroes they favor. And you lawyers, don't you do the same thing when you make your pitch to a jury?"

"Yeah, I guess we do," Kaplan said. As Rabbi Small was about to turn away, Kaplan had another thought. "Say, Rabbi, you used to visit the old man. How did he look to you?"

"What do you mean? He looked like a sick old man."

"Because afterward people went up to talk to Joe Kestler and offer him condolence. One woman, family I guess, went on about how surprised she'd been when she heard the news. She said when she last visited him he seemed so spry and alert. And Joe said he'd been getting along fine until he took this pill the doctor prescribed."

The rabbi looked sharply at Kaplan. "And what do you make of that?"

Kaplan grinned. "Speaking as a lawyer, I'd say Joe Kestler was laying the groundwork for a malpractice suit."

Although the telephone-repair crews worked through the night, it was not until he arrived at the clinic the next morning that Dr. Cohen heard from Dr. DiFrancesca that his patient had died.

Cohen shook his head sadly. "Gee, that's terrible. He

was a sick old man, but I didn't think he was in any danger of going. Maybe I should have had him come to the hospital."

"You can always second-guess yourself, Dan," said Dr. DiFrancesca. He was blond and blue-eyed, with the build of a football tackle. Although only a couple of years older than Cohen, he had the easy, comfortable look of a man who had found his niche and was sure of himself. "He may have reacted to the medication," he added. "That's the way it looked to me."

"Really? Gee, I had him on the same medication some months ago, and he took it all right. What were the indications?"

"Oh, the usual—inflammation, engorgement, evidence of difficulty in breathing. He could have developed a sensitivity, you know."

"There's always that danger, isn't there? How can you know in advance? Way back, he showed a reaction to penicillin, so I switched him to tetracycline and it went all right."

"What did you use, Dan?"

"Limpidine 250's. Pierce and Proctor. Same as I gave him last night. I've had good luck with it."

"Well, I guess this time you didn't." DiFrancesca hesitated. "Er—the son was pretty upset and carried on quite a bit."

"I suppose that's to be expected."

"No, I mean about the treatment, Dan. He claimed that his father was all right until he took the medication."

"He wasn't all right, believe me. He was running a temperature and was in considerable distress."

"It wouldn't surprise me," DiFrancesca went on, "if he brought a malpractice suit."

"What makes you think so?" Cohen asked quickly.

"Well, partly from just knowing the type. He's the sort

of guy who automatically looks around for someone to sue when anything happens."

Cohen nodded grimly. "I know what you mean. He comes by it honestly, though. He inherited it from his father."

"He kept insisting his father was all right until he took the pill you prescribed."

"If he was all right, why did he call me in? What did he need a doctor for?"

"Of course, but—"

"Look, John, the guy was eighty years old or more. He had a hundred and two temperature. He was having difficulty in urinating and when he passed he complained of a burning sensation. So it sounds like a bacterial infection. Right? It could have been viral, in which case the medication wouldn't have done any good, but it wouldn't have done any harm either. Now get this: he had much the same symptoms about six months back. I gave him the same medication, and it cleared up right away. So naturally, same person, same symptoms, I gave the same medication. It's good conservative medicine. Ninety-nine doctors out of a hundred would have treated him the same way. Maybe they would have used some other tetracycline, but essentially they're the same thing. So where's the grounds for a malpractice suit?"

"You don't have to convince me, Dan. But you know how it is, he can always get some shyster to bring suit. I tried to talk to him, explained that with a man that age almost anything could happen, but that kind—" He shook his head. "That's why I suggested that the police sergeant who came along with the ambulance should take charge of the pills, to make it part of the official record."

Cohen nodded. "That was good thinking. And if he does sue, well, that's why we carry insurance."

DiFrancesca hesitated. "It could be a little stickier than that. For one thing, this Kestler is the sort of guy

92

who shoots off his mouth. That could do you some damage."

"Yeah, I see what you mean."

"And Al Muntz is quite upset. Of course he called me at the house when he got home from Kaplan's. He wanted all the details."

"How's he concerned?"

DiFrancesca was embarrassed. "He seems to feel that in a matter of this kind, the clinic could be hurt; that if there's mud flying around, some of it could stick to the rest of us. As a matter of fact, Kestler accused me of trying to cover up for you because we were from the same office—you know, colleagues."

"That's a crock, John," Cohen said hotly. "How about the doctors at the hospital? They're my colleagues, too. Are they affected?"

"You know how it is, Dan. When you've worked yourself up to the kind of spread Al Muntz has on Beachcroft Road and you drive a Cadillac that you trade in every couple of years, you get awfully sensitive, maybe even a mite paranoid."

"Well, he has no cause," Cohen said shortly. But he was worried.

Both Muntz and Kantrovitz were at the hospital all morning, but they got back in time for lunch. The four doctors went out to eat together, but no one alluded to the case, neither on their way to the restaurant nor while they ate. However, when they were sipping their coffee, Muntz began. "About this Kestler business, Dan, John thinks there might have been an allergic reaction. What did you prescribe?"

"Limpidine. 250's. Four times a day for five days."

"Is that what it said on the bottle, John?" Kantrovitz asked.

"Uh-huh."

"For infection of the urinary tract?" Kantrovitz considered and nodded. "Did you ask if he was sensitive to it?"

"Aw, come on, Ed."

"Well, did you?"

"No, I didn't," Cohen said. "I didn't have to. I'd treated him with it some months before."

"Still, it's always a good practice to ask, just for the record."

"I wasn't interested in a record," Cohen retorted. "I was just interested in taking care of my patient."

"No need to get hot about it, Dan," said Muntz soothingly.

"We're just trying to help," Kantrovitz chimed in.

"Help how? The man is dead. Don't tell me you haven't ever lost a patient."

"Of course. That's over and done with. We're concerned about you now. According to John there's a good chance of a malpractice suit."

"So I'm insured for it."

Muntz nodded. "Naturally. But John here feels that Kestler might do a lot of talking. In fact, Chet Kaplan was telling me he did a lot of yakking at the funeral."

"So?"

"So that could be bad for all of us."

"How?"

"Oh, you know, a lot of people have funny ideas of how a clinic works," said Muntz vaguely.

Ed Kantrovitz was a thin, serious man, who did not so much speak as make pronouncements. "Look at it this way, Dan," he said. He pursed his lips while organizing his thoughts. "Somebody tells somebody that somebody died. The first thing that's likely to be asked is who was his doctor. So suppose he says it was one of the men at the clinic. Now the person can go away thinking it might be Al or me, or John—"

"Or me," said Cohen. "And if they said it was one of

94

the doctors from the hospital, it could be any one of a hundred doctors."

"Let's not get too hypothetical," Muntz suggested. "Right now we're concerned about Kestler."

"Sa-a-y." Kantrovitz snapped bony fingers. "Isn't Kestler the guy you were telling me about a while back, Dan, the one who brought suit against you?"

"Yeah, that's right. When I put up my fence, he claimed part of it was on his land."

Dr. Muntz stared, his blue eyes protruding as though they would pop out of his head. "And you treated him?"

"Well, he couldn't get another doctor, and that was just business."

Dr. Muntz shook his head slowly from side to side. "You ought to know better than that, Dan."

"Well, what's wrong—"

"You don't treat someone that you're emotionally involved with," Muntz said flatly.

"You wouldn't treat a member of your own family if they got sick, would you?" demanded Kantrovitz.

"What's wrong is that it doesn't look good," Muntz said. "Here's a guy you got a right to feel sore at, and you give him a pill that maybe results in his death. What's more, you don't just give him a prescription. No, you call it in to make sure he gets it right away. Now that just doesn't look good, not to the man in the street. And if there's a trial, he's the guy that's going to be sitting on the jury."

"But the guy was sick, and I thought— I could help him," said Dr. Cohen. "Could I just turn away—"

"That's exactly what you should have done," Muntz interrupted. "He was not your responsibility. You should have told them to call the police and they would have sent an ambulance and taken him to the hospital."

"And if he'd got worse on the way, or even died—"

"He wouldn't have died. And if he had, it wouldn't have been your fault."

They argued at length, keeping their voices low since they were in a public place, looking around every now and then to see if anyone was listening. And they got nowhere. Dr. Cohen insisted that it was his duty to treat anyone whom he had the knowledge and skill to help if they asked for his aid, and Muntz and Kantrovitz maintained with equal stubbornness that his first duty was to himself, that he had the right to refuse treatment if his own standing in the profession and community was thereby jeopardized. DiFrancesca remained silent for the most part, except when it looked as though the argument might become personal. Then he would shift uneasily in his seat and say, "Aw, fellers."

When they finally rose to return to the office, there was a distinct coolness in the manner of the two older men toward Cohen, and even a cool civility toward DiFrancesca for not having supported them.

That evening, Mrs. Cohen found her husband unusually silent. She naturally attributed his unease to the death of his patient and wisely made no attempt to cheer him up. The next morning, however, when she noticed that his mood continued, she said, "Why don't you go to that retreat this afternoon, Dan? It will do you good to get away for a couple of days."

"I don't think I can. They leave early in the afternoon, and I'd have to postpone a couple of my patients."

"I'll tell you what, put a bag in your car anyway. Then if you decide to go, you can just take off. Have Madeleine call me and say you're not coming home."

17

"Just happened to be passing and saw your car in the driveway, David." It was Hugh Lanigan.

"Come on in," Rabbi Small said to the stocky man with the broad red face who was Barnard's Crossing's chief of police. The two men had been friendly from the first year of the rabbi's incumbency, reason enough for the casual call. But from long experience, the rabbi had learned that there was usually some official reason for these visits, and he wondered what was in back of the police chief's mind.

"We were just having a cup of coffee," said Miriam. "You'll join us, won't you? I'm taking a little breather from preparing for the Sabbath."

"Don't mind if I do," Lanigan replied. He set his uniform cap on the floor beside his chair and ran thick, stubby fingers through his hedge of short white hair.

"Try one of these," the rabbi urged. "It's called *kichel*. It goes well with coffee."

"Mmm, very nice. What do you call it? *Kichel?* You're right, it does go well with coffee. Maybe you could give Amy the recipe."

"Glad to," Miriam said.

The chief sipped at his coffee and sighed contentedly.

"This is the first restful moment I've had in the last forty-eight hours. We were all day Wednesday preparing for the storm, and all day yesterday cleaning up."

"Isn't it mostly the town repair crews that are involved?" asked Miriam.

The chief laughed shortly. "Sure, they do the actual work—clearing away a fallen tree or fixing a water main. But it's the police who are notified what roads are blocked. We check them out and tell the department that's going to do the repair work. Say a store window gets broken. We've got to stand by and guard it until they can get it boarded up. Take the harbor, we had the two police boats working around the clock checking moorings and chasing boats that had broken free. There are auto accidents, and people get hurt and we have to get them to the hospital. Take old man Kestler, who was buried yesterday. Well, it was the officer in the cruising car who delivered his medicine to him. And late that same night we had to send the ambulance to take him to the hospital. So you had two police services there for that one man. By the way, just as a matter of idle curiosity, why did they bury him yesterday? I mean, he dies Wednesday night, and you bury him the next day. Was there any special reason they couldn't wait?"

The rabbi shook his head. "We always bury the dead the next day, or as soon as possible. We don't embalm, you see. It's traditional, because the land of Israel is tropical or semitropical, I suppose. So it would be for a special reason if we waited."

"You don't hold a wake? You don't let him lie in state for the family and friends to take a last look at him?"

The rabbi went to the bookcase and reached for a dictionary. He thumbed it, found the word, and read, "Here it is: 'Wake—to keep a watch or a vigil, as over a corpse.' It comes from an Old English root that means to watch. Well, we do that. It's considered a good deed, what we call a mitzvah. In most communities there's a sort of society, Chevurai Kedusha, that undertakes to wash the body, dress it in grave vestments and then sit with the corpse all through the night reading from the Book of Lamentations. Normally, we do not arrange to view the body. That's contrary to our tradition, which holds that once the spirit is gone, the body is just clay."

"And yet," Chief Lanigan interjected, "according to Sergeant Jenkins, when the doctor suggested an autopsy, Joe Kestler made an awful fuss about it, claimed it was against his religion."

The rabbi nodded. "I didn't think Joe Kestler was overly concerned with religion, but it's in keeping with our general tradition. We don't approve of autopsy unless there is a clear indication that from an examination of the remains, someone else's life can be saved or that something specific can be learned. Man is made in the image of God, so to cut up the body is to desecrate the image."

"That doesn't seem to square with the idea that the body is just clay once the spirit is gone," the chief pointed out.

"No, it doesn't." The rabbi grinned. "Our attitude is a little ambivalent there. Our tradition isn't a planned system, you know, where every item jibes with every other. It developed over the centuries. The aversion to cutting up the body, or to cremating it for that matter, is bound up with the idea that some Jews have of the resurrection that will take place when the Messiah comes. They mean resurrection of the body as well as of the spirit. So it's important that the whole body be there in the grave, ready to spring back to life."

"That seems kind of hard on those who died some time ago," Lanigan observed, "or those who lost limbs in battle."

"It does, rather."

"Was there any reason why you didn't do the honors on old Kestler?" asked the chief.

"Only that he came from Revere originally and was still a member of the synagogue there."

"What a subject for conversation," Miriam exclaimed. "And over coffee!"

"I imagine the chief is working around to something," her husband said with a smile.

Lanigan gave him a quick look from under bushy eyebrows and emitted a short laugh of embarrassment. "Well, there is something."

The rabbi nodded encouragingly.

"Do you want to speak to David alone?" Miriam asked.

"Oh no. Nothing like that. Please stay." Chief Lanigan leaned back in his chair. "I've been doctoring with Dr. Daniel Cohen practically ever since he came here about a year ago—well, because I like him. Besides, he's a general practitioner, practically the only young one in town, and I like the idea of having a family doctor. Everybody else around is a specialist. So I go to him for most things, and so does Amy. I'm sure if anything really serious happened to either of us and he didn't feel he was quite up to treating it, he wouldn't hesitate to have us call in a specialist."

Miriam nodded sympathetically.

"Today, I went to see him for a checkup. Nothing the matter, you understand. I try to go about once a year. It's a good idea."

"You ought to do it, too, David," said Miriam automatically.

"So I'm sitting there in his office, and the phone rings," the chief continued. "It's the switchboard operator, and she says she's got someone on the line who insists on talking to him right away. He says to put him on, and immediately I hear, because he's shouting at the top

100

of his voice, 'You got a hellova nerve sending me a bill.' Well, it was sort of embarrassing and if it weren't that I was in my undershirt and shorts, I would have eased out so he could have his conversation in private. But I couldn't very well go out in the corridor where other patients were waiting so I stayed, and I could hear as plain as the doctor was hearing. It was Joe Kestler, and he was mad because he'd just got a bill for services. You see, these four doctors, they each have their own practice and their own examining room, but they share a bookkeeper as well as a nurse and technician. It's like a clinic. And it's the clinic that sends out the bills."

"I know the general arrangement," said the rabbi.

"Yeah, it's a common setup these days. Well, Kestler got his monthly statement and was full of indignation, because he felt the doctor's treatment had resulted in his father's death. I gathered he figured what happened to his father canceled all the family's debts to the doctor. He went on to say that he was going to sue him for malpractice—'for every cent you've got' is the way he put it and that he had absolute proof because Rabbi Small was there when he gave him the pill—"

"I see. That's how I come into the picture."

Lanigan nodded. "That's right. Well, I didn't say anything to the doctor when he hung up. I could see he was embarrassed. But I thought I'd look into it a little." He laughed apologetically. "It's not really a police matter, I suppose, because no one has reported anything to us. If Kestler wants to bring a malpractice suit against Dr. Cohen, that's a civil suit, and it's his right. On the other hand, hearing Kestler on the phone and knowing him a little, he's apt to go shooting off his big mouth, and that could ruin a doctor, especially a man like Cohen who is shy and being new in the area hasn't built up a following as yet."

"I see."

"The police are also involved in another way," Lanigan continued. "It was the officer in the cruising car that delivered the pills—"

"Yes, I saw the cruiser drive up. How did that happen?"

"Well, the doctor called the prescription in to the drugstore and one of their customers, a Mr. Safferstein—" he cocked an eye at the rabbi.

"Yes, I know him. Nice fellow."

"Yes, well, Safferstein agreed to deliver the medicine because they were busy at the store and Kestler's house was on his way home. But then the storm started and Safferstein stopped under a lamppost because the rain was coming down so hard. The cruising car spotted him and stopped to see if everything was all right, and he asked the officer to deliver the pills."

"I see."

"Then the police were involved again when the ambulance crew came to take the old man to the hospital. Kestler began his accusations right there in the bedroom where his father lay dead. He insisted it was the pill that had killed him. So the doctor who came with the ambulance suggested that the police should take charge of the pills." Lanigan reached into his back pocket for his wallet and drew from it a slip of paper, which he tossed on the coffee table. "That's a copy of the receipt the sergeant wrote out for him."

The rabbi picked it up and read aloud, " 'Received from Joseph Kestler for official custody a bottle containing eighteen pills.' " He broke off and looked at Lanigan. "Eighteen?"

"You caught that, I see."

"Chai," Miriam murmured, and her husband smiled.

The chief looked at them inquiringly.

The rabbi proceeded to explain. "Chai means eighteen in Hebrew, and it also means life. It's a sort of numerology some of the old rabbis used to play with. You see, the Hebrew alphabet is also a number system, like A is one, B two, C three and so on. So AB would be twelve and BC twenty-three and ABC would be a hundred and twenty-three."

"I understand."

"Some of the numbers spell out words, which gave rise to a lot of involved and mystical biblical interpretation. Some of those word-number relationships stuck and came into common usage. One of them was *chai*, eighteen, which is also the word for life. People frequently make charitable contributions in eighteen or multiples of eighteen." He smiled. "And it's useful. If someone offers, say, fifteen dollars for charity, it's easy to jack up the contribution by suggesting they make it *chai* dollars, which would be eighteen, a net gain of three dollars and practically painless."

"What if he planned to give twenty? Mightn't he then reduce it to eighteen for the same reason?" asked the chief.

Miriam laughed. "A good fund raiser would try to jack him up to thirty-six, double *chai*." She took the receipt from her husband and studied it. *"Chai* seems kind of inappropriate in this business, though. What's so special about eighteen pills?"

The chief looked at her fondly. "Well, if there are eighteen and he took one, that would mean there were nineteen originally, and that's a funny number to prescribe. As a matter of fact, the label on the bottle said they were to be taken four times a day, so nineteen—"

"I see," said Miriam excitedly. "You think they gave him two and that may have done it."

"How about it, David?" The chief turned to the rabbi. "You were there."

The rabbi's brow furrowed as he strove to remember. "Let's see. I heard the doorbell and I looked out the window and saw the cruising car. Then Mrs. Kestler came up with the pills. I remember her twisting the cap off the bottle and teasing out the cotton-batting plug." He shook his head. "That's all. I turned my head at that point."

"Why? Did something happen?"

The rabbi shook his head. "Nothing special. You see, he was an old man and his hands shook, but more when someone was watching him. So I turned away when she handed him the glass of water."

"Then you didn't see whether she gave him one pill or two?" the chief asked.

The rabbi shook his head regretfully. "What did you have in mind?"

"Well, I haven't checked it out with the doctor yet," said Lanigan, "but it occurred to me that while one pill might be harmless, two might not be. From what the sergeant told me, it seems that the old man had an allergic reaction. Now you know that people who are sensitive to certain things can go for years taking them and suffer no bad effects. And then they take a little more than normal and they get a reaction."

"I see." The rabbi nodded. "And why would Mrs. Kestler give the old gentleman two pills when the prescription called for one?"

Lanigan sat back expansively in his chair. "Now there you enter the realm of possibilities, and I see two. The first and most likely is that she gave him two because she thought two was better than one. My father was apt to do something like that. He always took a little more than the doctor prescribed on the general theory, I guess, that the dosage was the minimum that a patient could be expected to take. In those days all medicines tasted anywhere from bad to horrible. He wanted to show, as a lesson in character for my brother Pat and me, he could take it."

"No bad effects, I trust?" said the rabbi, smiling.

Lanigan chuckled. "My guess is that as bad as they tasted, medicines weren't so powerful in those days, except maybe for castor oil."

"And the second possibility?"

"I get the feeling that the care of the old man rested largely on his daughter-in-law's shoulders. Suppose she gets tired of being the drudge. Suppose she gets tired of waiting on the old man hand and foot. A sick old man can be troublesome, demanding. So what if she gave him two pills with the idea of getting rid of him?"

The rabbi shrugged. "And how would she know that two pills would do it?"

"She could have assumed it. Possibly the doctor might have cautioned them not to give him more than the prescribed dose."

"But that would be murder," exclaimed Miriam.

"If it were proved. A good lawyer could make it manslaughter or a mercy killing," said Lanigan. "But you'd be surprised at the number of those kind of killings that are committed, a nitroglycerin tablet knocked out of a man's hand while he's having a heart attack, a piece of candy withheld from a diabetic going into insulin shock, that business a few years back with Isaac Hirsh here in town. Very few of them ever come to the courts, but we hear about them in the police."

"Do you check the possibilities of murder every time someone dies even though it's almost certain to be death from natural causes?" asked Miriam.

"Of course not. But if the death is awfully convenient for someone, or if someone is going to get badly hurt by it as Dr. Cohen might be in this case, I can't help wondering. And sometimes I inquire around a little."

"And those are your two possibilities?" asked the rabbi. "Surely, there are any number of others."

"Like what?"

Again the rabbi shrugged. "The most likely is that the

drugstore put only nineteen pills in the bottle. Or Joe Kestler might have told his wife to give his father a couple of pills."

"Why would he do that?"

"For the same reason you suggested she might have done the same thing. And that could account for Joe Kestler making a fuss about the autopsy. Of course, two pills would probably have done him no great harm in the first place."

"I think you're right," said Lanigan regretfully. "It's just that Dr. Cohen is in a jam and I'd like to help him."

"Well, if you're considering possibilities—"

"Go on."

"The pharmaceutical house that manufactured the pills might have made a slight change in the formulation. Or that particular batch could have gone bad. Or the pill could have interacted with something the old man took unbeknownst to Dr. Cohen. Want more?"

"No, I get the point." Lanigan grinned sheepishly. "I wasn't trying to pin a murder rap on the Kestlers. It just occurred to me that I might be able to use it to keep Joe Kestler from shooting off his big mouth and hurting a nice fellow like the doctor."

The rabbi considered. "Well, you could still use it for that purpose. But the danger is that if you pointed out there was a pill missing and it suggested that old Kestler might have taken two, contrary to the doctor's orders, Joe might wonder about his wife. It could go hard with her."

"You're always so damn helpful, David," said Lanigan ruefully as he lounged to his feet.

When he left, Miriam asked, "Do you really think he happened in just because he was in the neighborhood, David?"

"Not if he went to the trouble of making a copy of the
106

sergeant's receipt. And that suggests that Lanigan is suspicious of Kestler's death."

"I don't see—"

"My car has been in the driveway ever since I returned from the morning service around half past seven. All right. Lanigan goes to Dr. Cohen's office in Lynn. Say he had the first appointment, which I suppose would be around nine. Why didn't he stop by on his way back? Instead he went to the police station, and then came here."

"How do you know? Maybe his appointment was for later. Maybe he *had* just left the doctor's office and *did* stop here because he saw the car."

"Then he wouldn't have had a typed copy of the sergeant's receipt with him," said the rabbi triumphantly. "No, there's something bothering Lanigan. And it's not just that Kestler might gossip about Dr. Cohen. All this questioning about burying the old man the next day suggests that he thinks there's something wrong."

"You mean he believes the old man was murdered?"

The rabbi pursed his lips and considered. "Lanigan has been a policeman all his life. When you've been practicing a trade or profession for a long time, you develop a sixth sense about things that relate to it. A little warning bell goes off in your mind. Yesterday, for example, Kaplan was telling me about the funeral and how Joe Kestler acted. His lawyer's sixth sense told him that Kestler was planning to institute a malpractice suit. Something he said tripped that warning bell. Well, it's my opinion that Lanigan heard a bell, too."

18

Friday noon, Chester Kaplan called Safferstein. "That guy that took your coat, Billy, he just brought it back. It was the fellow who came with Cy Perlow. I took the liberty of going through the pockets and I found the envelope with the bottle of pills. You'll be glad to know that the envelope had your name on it, and the label on the bottle also had your name on it, or rather Mona's. So you worried for nothing."

"Thanks, Chet, that *is* good news. Actually, I figured I had given the cop the right envelope because if the name had been wrong, he would have noticed it. Then yesterday morning I went into the drugstore to get a refill for Mona. I saw that they put the patient's name on the bottle itself, so I figured even if the Kestlers hadn't looked at the envelope, they'd certainly notice if there was the wrong name on the bottle. I felt pretty sure, but still I was a little uneasy. Believe me, I appreciate your calling me. It's a big relief knowing that I had absolutely nothing to do with Kestler's dying."

"Naturally," said Kaplan. "I'm glad I happened to be home when the coat was delivered. I'm sure Edie wouldn't have thought to look through the pockets. And I was in the house because we're going up-country to the retreat.

How about coming along? I should think you'd be in the right mood for it."

"Gee, I don't think so, Chet, not with Mona sick."

"I understand. Remember me to her."

"Will do. By the way, I didn't get a chance to ask you the other night, how does it look, the retreat business, I mean?"

"It looks fine, Billy, just fine. We've got a good majority. Not all of them are interested in the temple acquiring a retreat, you understand, although it's in style these days. But even those who don't like the idea are interested in a campsite where they can come up for a weekend or where their kids can go camping in the summer. Actually, the only opposition as far as I can make out is the rabbi."

"Why is the rabbi against it?"

"Well, you know, he's a conservative type guy. Who knows, maybe he's a little jealous of Rabbi Mezzik."

"Yeah, but if Rabbi Small should start arguing about it at the meeting—"

"I doubt if he'll be at the meeting."

"Why not?"

"Because this Sunday is Parents Day at the school, so he'll be busy with parents most of the morning. Now, what I'm planning is to hold our meeting at the camp. You know, get everything ironed out. Then when we hold our regular meeting Sunday morning, we just put the matter to a vote because we will already have had our discussions. Then, we adjourn."

"Gee, that's slick, Chester. I got to hand it to you."

Friday started out badly for Dr. Cohen. Not only was he subjected to Kestler's phone call but he had the embarrassing experience of knowing that Chief Lanigan had overheard the conversation. The day did not improve when his next patient was late, thus disrupting his morning schedule. As a consequence he was still closeted with a patient at noon, and his colleagues went off to lunch without him.

He lunched alone at a nearby diner on a stool facing the wall. No sooner had he returned when the hospital phoned to tell him that a coronary patient he was treating had suffered a relapse and he had better rush over. He stopped just long enough to tell the switchboard operator to call his afternoon patients and reschedule them for next week. As an afterthought, he added, "And Madeleine, call my wife and tell her I won't be coming home."

It was half past two before Dan Cohen was able to leave the hospital. He drove straight to the Kaplan house. But when he arrived, he found no cars in the driveway or parked in front of the house. He had come too late. It seemed a fitting conclusion to the day. Nevertheless, he mounted the steps and rang the bell.

Mrs. Kaplan answered. "Oh, Dr. Cohen, isn't it?"

"That's right. I guess they've left already."

"About fifteen minutes ago. Do you know how to get there?"

He shook his head.

"Just a minute. Chet had some maps Xeroxed." She left him and reappeared a moment later. "You won't have any trouble following these directions. It's really quite clear. You might even catch them. They sometimes stop for coffee on the road."

19

They had settled in by the time Dr. Cohen arrived at the camp, a large frame building in a clearing in the woods. Through a corridor in the trees, he could see a lake some fifty yards beyond the building. Hearing a car, Chester Kaplan came bustling out. "Oh, it's you, Doctor. Gosh, I'm glad you could make it. We got more people this time than we have rooms prepared, so we're doubling up. Isn't it wonderful?" He consulted a clipboard. "Let's see, there are two cots in Room Twelve. I'll put you in there. You'll be in with Matthew Charn. Know him?"

Cohen shook his head.

"He's from Salem, but he's been to most of our retreats. Wonderful man, very sincere, and he'll be able to show you the ropes. Why don't you go up and introduce yourself. We don't stand on formality here."

He tucked his hand in the doctor's arm and, gesturing with the clipboard that he held in the other, he led him up the stairs to the porch. "If the weather is nice, we sit out here a lot. Of course, at night if the bugs are bad . . ."

Kaplan steered Cohen inside the house and with a wide sweep of the clipboard he introduced him to the room in which they found themselves. "This is our chapel, meeting place, assembly hall, recreation room, you name

111

it. This is where we hang out most of the time." The room was bare except for a table at one end and a number of folding chairs scattered about. It ran the full two stories of the house and above could be seen the peaked roof with slanting joints that met at the rooftree.

"Like a church, huh?" Kaplan commented. "I mean the roof—it's almost Gothic."

"Yeah, very nice," said the doctor.

Another sweep of the clipboard at a balcony railing that ran along one side of the room. "The bedrooms and bathrooms are up there on the mezzanine. You just go up those stairs and Room Twelve is at the end. But first," he pointed the clipboard to the back of the room, "the dining room is beyond those folding doors. If we need to, we can push them back and make one big room. The rebbitzin is in there right now preparing for the Sabbath meal. Come and meet her." He steered the doctor to the partition and the clipboard hand somehow managed to turn the knob and open the door. "Mrs. Mezzik," he called out cheerily, "we'll need another place setting for Dr. Cohen here. Dr. Cohen, Mrs. Mezzik, our rabbi's wife."

She was a short dumpy woman in her midthirties. She acknowledged the introduction with a sad, tired smile. To Kaplan, she said, "No trouble, and there's plenty of food. You want to arrange the place cards?"

"You're going to have a Sabbath meal that you'll remember for a long time, Doctor. Wait till you taste the rebbitzin's gefilte fish—just like your mother used to make."

"I chop it. I don't grind it," she admitted shyly.

Still clutching his arm, Kaplan turned him around and moved him toward the door. "Why don't you go up now and get acquainted with Matt Charn? I've got to arrange about the meeting."

Dr. Cohen mounted the steps and made his way along the balcony until he came to Room Twelve. Although the door was ajar, he knocked and in response to "Yeah" from within, he entered. Save for two cots and a painted bureau, the room was bare. In the middle of the ceiling, dangling by its own electric cord, was a single fly-specked light bulb. A heavyset man with a big belly and pinkish jowls lay on a cot. He was dressed only in socks, underpants and undershirt.

"Matthew Charn? I'm Dr. Cohen. I guess I'm supposed to bunk with you."

The other man pushed himself up to a sitting position and held out his hand. "Glad to know you, Doctor." He explained his state of undress. "I always change in honor of the Sabbath. My mother made me when I was a kid." He had a guttural raspy voice, as though it needed clearing.

"You a regular medical doctor? Reason I ask, I got a nephew that's a doctor, but he isn't worth a damn if you got a bellyache, because he's a doctor of economics." He laughed heavily. "And he ain't much good on the stock market either. This is your first time here?"

"That's right."

"Then let me tell you, you're going to get a real religious experience. I've been to almost every one Chet has organized. The first time I came here I was all broken up. I'd just lost my wife, see. I guess the Man Upstairs wanted her more than He thought I needed her, and I tell you I just couldn't function. But I was glad for her sake because it was the big bug that got her."

"The big—"

"CA," Charn explained. "Bad medicine. Bad, bad medicine. With what she went through for almost a year, and then the end, I just couldn't cope. Then Chet decided he was going to have this retreat and he asked me if I was interested. Well, you want to know the truth?"

Cohen nodded politely.

"I *wasn't* interested. That's the truth. I wasn't interested in anything. But I came anyway, and that first Friday night service, well, it made a difference. You know you're supposed to greet the Sabbath like it was a queen and rejoice over it like a bridegroom over his bride. That's what it says right in the prayerbook. Well, I've been to any number of Friday night services in a lot of temples and synagogues, but this was different. In the synagogue, maybe there's one or two who really mean it, religious types like Chet or the rabbi of the congregation, but you take the rest, and they're just going through the motions. But here we mean it. That first time when we greeted the Sabbath, I got so worked up that when we turned around to face the door it was like I was expecting some high-class broad to come sashaying into the room. Right then, I knew she was still there, my Charlotte. She'd been with me all along, but I hadn't felt her presence because, because I hadn't tried."

Cohen nodded sympathetically.

"The big thing," Charn went on, "is to let yourself go. The first time I cried like a baby. I still do sometimes, but nobody notices. You're all alone and yet the whole damn world is with you. And say, Doc, when you go downstairs, pick out a seat near a window. That way you got the sill to lean on, because if you don't have something to lean on, that meditation can be a sonofabitch."

A bell rang, and Charn said, "Uh-oh, that's the signal for the first meditation. Why don't you go down now? No sense waiting for me. I might be a little late, but it makes no difference because Rabbi Mezzik begins with a little talk and I've heard it before."

The others had evidently not waited for the bell, since they were all seated when Dr. Cohen entered the assembly room and, mindful of Charn's warning, made his way to a chair near a window. He was surprised to see that they had all brought prayer shawls. Standing behind the table was Rabbi Mezzik, a theatrically handsome man

114

with a Guards moustache and a Vandyke. Cohen thought he might be a little younger than the rebbitzin. He was resplendent in a high velvet cantorial yarmulke and a long silk prayer shawl draped over a black academic robe. Rabbi Mezzik called them to attention by rapping on the table, which served as the reading desk.

"I want everybody to put on his *tallis*," he said. "Those of you who didn't bring one, we've got some spares that you can use."

Dr. Cohen took one and draped it around his shoulders, but he wondered about it, since he had always thought that the prayer shawl was used only for morning services.

As if to answer his unspoken question, Rabbi Mezzik went on, "We don't usually wear the *tallis* except in the morning service. The reason for that is a lot of halachic tomfoolery that we don't have to go into at this time. Take my word for it, it's all right to wear it here and now. What's more, we're going to wear it every time we come together as a group, day or night. And even when we go for this walk through the woods that Chet has planned for tomorrow afternoon, you'll put it on. Because the *tallis* is really a cloak like the toga that the Romans used to wear, except that ours has fringes to distinguish us from the other nations.

"Now before we start our program, I want to give you some idea of what it's all about, especially the new people. Those who've heard it before, well, it won't do them any harm to hear it again. What this program is all about is religion. And what's religion all about? Any religion? It's about God, about the effort of people, all kinds of people, since the beginning of time, to make contact with God. That's religion. What's not religion is gathering together in a special place, a synagogue or church or mosque, to say certain words in an old-fashioned archaic language. That's socializing. That's making contact with your friends and neighbors and with society. It's not a bad thing in itself, but it's not making contact with God, so it's not religion.

"Now I'll tell you something funny," Rabbi Mezzik went on. "At one time that *was* religion. When? Back when they first made up those prayers, when the language in which they were set was not archaic, when it was the normal way of talking. But now, it's just the preservation of tradition, also not a bad thing in itself, but not religion, because it's not making contact with God. So what happens? The need to make contact with God is there, but we're not getting through. And what's the result? I'll tell you: our people, especially our young people, are going elsewhere in an effort to make contact. They go to Zen Buddhism, to Meher Baba, to Krishnamurti; some go to Chabad, and some try to do it with drugs. That's the result."

He paused and looked about triumphantly, as though they had been arguing the matter with him and he had just presented the clincher. "And does it work?" he asked. And he answered himself. "Of course it works—for some of them. They don't just tell you this is right and this is wrong the way the traditional religions do. They provide a method for acquiring the one and scorning the other. In other words, they don't just tell you where the place is; they tell you how to get there.

"And each has a different way of getting there. Is that so strange? If you wanted to go to Chicago, is there only one way? It would depend on how you wanted to travel, and where you came from, wouldn't it? Well, we all come from different traditions and different societies with different lifestyles. We dress differently, we eat differently, we live differently, so why shouldn't we pray or meditate or make contact with God differently? In India, they sit on the ground to eat, and to show respect they get down as near to the ground as possible—" To illustrate, he suddenly crouched down beside the lectern as though

116

about to receive a cut from the whip of a master. He sprang to his feet once again. "So it's only natural for them to meditate in the lotus position. But it doesn't have the same effect with us, because it's alien to our tradition and lifestyle. We don't touch our foreheads to the ground the way the Muslims do and we don't kneel like the Christians, to show respect. We stand. Nor do I believe in the rocking and shaking of the Chasidim—their interpretation of 'Love your God with all your heart and all your might'—I think that's alien, too.

"The main prayer in our liturgy, the *Shimon Esra,* the eighteen blessings, that is part of every service, is also called the *Amidah,* the Standing, because we always stand to say it. So to make contact, we stand in silent meditation, each one making his contact direct, without channeling through some saint the way the Christians do, or for that matter through a rebbe like the Chasidim do. We stand, in token of our manhood, in token of our superiority to the lower creatures, in token of our having been created in His image. As it is unthinkable for Him to kneel, so we must not.

"Now, while an adept *can* make contact, *can* meditate, almost anywhere, under almost any circumstances, most of us need the support of others. And that is why we pray in a group, as individuals but in a group, a minyan, a congregation of ten or more adult males, with no women or children to distract us. There's nothing puritanic about it. It isn't another example of male chauvinism. It's as natural as life itself. You all know that children have a short attention span. After a few minutes, they begin to fidget and ask questions and want to go to the bathroom. And just as you don't want them around when you're computing your income tax, so you don't want them around when you're trying to make contact with God. And women are distracting in another way. It doesn't mean you're a sex maniac if you get a little warm thinking

117

about a woman. That's natural. That's the way God made us. And if we weren't that way, the race would die out. He wants us to react like that. It's what He meant when He told us to be fruitful and multiply. But when you're trying to make contact with Him, it gets in the way. And pretty soon, you're thinking of *it* rather than of Him. Some of the very pious, especially the Chasidim, wear a girdle around the waist to separate the upper part of the body from the lower. Personally, I don't think it's any more help than the belt you wear to keep your pants up. The best way is not to have them around." He smiled at them. "Now, I ask you, is it male chauvinism to admit you think so highly of women that you confess they can distract you from God Himself?

"All right, then, I want you all to rise now and cover your heads with your prayer shawls. That's the idea, get it right over your head. That way, you shut out everything and you can be alone with your thoughts. You're shutting out the world, you're isolating yourself in order to make contact with God. You're going to stand in silent meditation for half an hour. If you get tired standing, then sit down and rest for a while, but keep it up as long as you can. And don't look at your watches. I'll tell you when the time is up. Then we'll have our regular Friday evening service and then the delicious Sabbath meal that Mrs. Mezzik has prepared."

20

Friday afternoon Rabbi Small paid his condolence visit to the Kestlers. Over the years he had performed this melancholy parochial duty many times, but he had never grown sufficiently accustomed to it to be anything but uncomfortable for the half hour or so that it usually lasted. If the deceased had been young, a child perhaps, the grief of the immediate family was apt to be overwhelming, and he always came away with the feeling that he had obtruded. On the other hand, if it were an old person, like an aged parent, the atmosphere was more subdued than sad. He knew that before his arrival, conversation had flowed easily as at any other social occasion, with perhaps an occasional joke offered. He had indeed heard the muted laughter as he approached the door which was kept ajar so that the family would not have to respond to the constant ringing of the doorbell. As soon as he entered, however, faces became sober and conversation was reduced to philosophical platitudes, as unruly schoolchildren quiet down when the teacher appears. And he resented this dampening role in which he was cast as the professional condolence purveyor of the congregation. In his own mind, he was never at ease with it. While it was only fitting and proper to grieve over the dead, the mourning period was also intended to help the bereaved overcome their grief, and he was perhaps doing them a disservice by plunging them into it again by his very presence. Moreover, he believed that it was wrong to simulate a grief that one did not actually feel. Nevertheless, he was taken aback when he entered the Kestler house and found Joe and his wife playing cards.

"Oh, it's you, Rabbi," Joe Kestler said. "Come right in." And then embarrassed, he explained. "The wife was kind of low, and I thought a couple of hands of gin would get her mind off—well, off things."

"I understand," the rabbi replied.

Christine Kestler seconded her husband with, "I was like all edgy. It was such a shock."

"Still, he was a very old man, and sick," the rabbi murmured.

"He could have gone on like that for years," Kestler asserted, "if Cohen hadn't fed him that pill."

Mindful of his conversation with Lanigan, the rabbi responded sharply. "Are you suggesting that the doctor deliberately gave your father medication that would harm him?"

"I'm not suggesting anything," said Kestler doggedly. "All I know is Cohen was sore at my old man on account he sued him about a fence he put up. Maybe that's why he didn't take too much time to think it out. He was in and out of here in a matter of minutes. I even complained about it, didn't I, Chris?"

"That's right," she nodded vehemently. "Joe was real sore about it."

"If the diagnosis is obvious . . ." the rabbi suggested.

"Then it wasn't, or my father wouldn't have died. He was sick, but all right. You saw him. Then he took that pill and in less than half an hour he was dead. You saw him take the pill. You were a witness to it."

"I saw your wife administer a pill," said the rabbi

120

coldly. "I have no way of knowing what kind of pill it was."

"Oh, that's all right," said Kestler confidently. "It was the cops in the cruising car that delivered the pills. You must have heard them drive up. In any case, they'd have a record of the time, and it was while you were here. A minute later, the wife comes up to give it to him. Then when the police ambulance arrived they took the whole bottle of pills. So we got everything nailed down evidencewise."

"But I have no way of knowing that the pill that Mrs. Kestler received from the police was the one she gave your father."

"Are you saying she could have switched them, Rabbi? That my own wife would want to hurt her own father-in-law?" Kestler was aghast.

"I'm not saying anything except that the chain of evidence is not as complete as you seem to think. The discrepancy that I pointed out is what any lawyer would be certain to seize on. He might also think it strange, as would the court, that you would engage a doctor with whom you had quarreled."

"I didn't want to call Cohen. It was my father who made me. I begged him not to. But he said that suing him was just business and had nothing to do with calling for doctoring. So say he was wrong, that still don't give Cohen the right to give him the wrong medicine."

"And you think because he was angry with your father, he prescribed the wrong medicine?"

Kestler's face took on a look of great cunning. He smiled. "Oh, I'm not saying he did it deliberate. That would be murder, and I'm not accusing him of murder. All I'm saying is that because he was sore at my old man, he didn't take the time to make a careful diagnosis, so he made a mistake. That's negligence, and that's malpractice. And I'm going to sue him for it."

"When you called Dr. Cohen, he immediately agreed to come over?" asked the rabbi.

Kestler's eyes narrowed as he thought about the question, suspicious that the rabbi might be laying a trap. "Oh, I wouldn't say he agreed right away."

"And yet you persisted."

"Well, it was Wednesday," Mrs. Kestler offered.

Her husband glared at her. "The old man had confidence in him as a doctor."

"I see. So even though it was Wednesday, his day off, he came to see your father. And your point is that he just took a quick look at him and then handed you a prescription to—"

"He didn't give me any prescription," said Kestler. "He called it in when he got home."

The rabbi showed his surprise. "When he got home? Why didn't he call it from here or just give you a written prescription?"

"Joe thought he might have some samples," Mrs. Kestler hastened to explain.

Joe Kestler shot her a venomous glance. "It was kind of late," he elaborated, "and all the drugstores were closed except Aptaker's, and I don't go in there. So I asked him if he had any samples, and he said he'd drop them off to me if he had. And if he didn't, he'd call in the prescription and they'd deliver it."

The rabbi nodded as he considered. "So here's a doctor," he said, as though he were trying to reason it out for his own understanding, "who is called on his day off by someone who has brought suit against him. And he not only comes, but offers to drop off samples of the medication he prescribes or make arrangements for it to be delivered. And this is the man you've been slandering and are planning to sue?"

"He made a mistake," said Kestler, "and my father

122

died. So that's malpractice. I got nothing against the doctor personally, but I got a right to sue, same as I would if my best friend rammed into me with his car."

"It's the insurance that pays," his wife added.

The rabbi rose to go. "The doctor may have made a mistake," he said, "as any man can make a mistake. Or he may have prescribed the correct medicine. If you bring the matter to court, it will be the court that will decide. But to speak evil of a man is considered a very grave sin by our law, Mr. Kestler. In our tradition, it is thought to bring on the most terrible punishments."

Remembering the disapproving looks from her husband, Mrs. Kestler feared that she would receive a torrent of abuse as soon as the rabbi left. But Joe Kestler maintained a dour and gloomy silence as he paced up and down the room in deep thought. Finally he stopped and faced her. "You know what he was trying to say?"

"Well, Joe, I think—"

"Shut up and listen. This guy Cohen is a member of his congregation, see. So he's got to take care of him. He knows I'm going to call him for a witness, and being a rabbi, he's got to tell the truth. But he's smart and can shade it which way he wants. So I think it's time I saw a lawyer. In the meantime, I don't want you shooting off your mouth about Doc Cohen. Understand?"

"But I never—" She saw his annoyance and said, "Oh, I won't, Joe. I won't say a word."

21

Once again, as he had half a dozen times during the weekend, Daniel Cohen covered his head with the prayer shawl. It was Sunday morning and the last scheduled meditation of the retreat program. But the hope that he had had at the beginning that perhaps, just perhaps, there was something in it was gone. And he now felt only a kind of embarrassment that he, a doctor, a man of science, should have come here in the woods to commune with The Almighty in order to—to what? To ask for a special suspension of the universal law of cause and effect for his personal advantage?

True, when he went to the synagogue on the High Holy Days, or even to an occasional Friday evening service, it was ostensibly for the same purpose. But that was different. In actuality, it was more of an affirmation of his connection with the group in which he had been born. One did not so much pray as recite set prayers more or less by rote. It was a social obligation, one of the things that Jews expected of each other.

This was different. He had really tried. During the traditional prayer services, while his lips moved in recitation of the Hebrew prayers, his mind asked earnestly in English for help. During the meditations, he had remained standing until time was called, not once sitting down to rest or even leaning against the windowsill. And in the discussions, he had actively participated.

"Why can't we sit down and relax for the meditation, Rabbi?"

"Because you might fall asleep, for one thing. In Transcendental Meditation, which was popularized by the Maharishi, they do sit in a comfortable position—"

"And does it work?"

"Oh, sure, as a means of beneficial relaxation. There's a doctor from the Harvard Medical School, I believe, who's even done some scientific experimentation with it, controls and all that sort of thing, and found that it actually reduces high blood pressure. You may have heard of it, Doctor. But that's just a technique for relaxing; it's not religion. Remember, we're after a religious experience. And for that you need a state of tension, balanced tension. The Buddhists use the lotus position; in Zen they kneel. But I'm convinced that the Jewish tradition calls for standing."

"How about this business of saying a word or a phrase over and over again?"

"The mantra?" Rabbi Mezzik nodded his handsome head. "Some find that it helps their concentration. There's some evidence that our ancestors made use of it. At the end of the Yom Kippur service we recite *Adonai Hoo Elohim*—the Lord, He is God—seven times. That suggests to me that the phrase may have been used as a mantra and not just the seven times ordered in the prayerbook."

"But what's supposed to be the effect of the meditation?"

"It's hard to say, because it differs for each individual. You may feel that everything is connected to everything else, what I call the Universal Relationship. Or you may

125

sense the basic unity of the universe. Or you may experience a great serenity."

Dan Cohen experienced none of these. What he had experienced, he told himself grimly, was tasteless food, a hard lumpy mattress on a narrow cot with a too-thin blanket against the night chill and the constant dull companionship of Matthew Charn. Of Kaplan, he had seen very little outside the group sessions, for he had been largely preoccupied with a special circle, all of them members of the board of directors of the temple, who had kept apart from the rest. And this morning, when he came down for the first service, they were gone.

"Chet and some of the others had to return early this morning," Rabbi Mezzik explained. "There's an important board meeting they've got to attend. However, we still have a minyan, so it's all right."

No one seemed to mind, but for Dan Cohen it was one more annoyance to be added to those he had suffered during the weekend. As he stood there with the prayer shawl over his head, he asked himself just why he had come. Of course, he had wanted to get away from Barnard's Crossing and from his practice. But why here, and why did he need to get away at all?

The death of a patient, while always traumatic, was to be expected in medical practice. Nor was he overly concerned about a possible malpractice suit; he was sure his treatment had been correct and certainly defensible.

The reaction of his colleagues, especially the two older men, had been unexpected and disturbing, but surely the way to deal with that situation was to stay and fight it out rather than to run away. Conceivably, it might get to the point where they might ask him to leave the clinic. That *would* be disturbing, he admitted. It would not happen immediately because he had a contract, and if he were to hold them to its terms, it would be a year or more before they could force him out. By that time, he might be able to build up a clientele and open his own office in Barnard's Crossing. And he didn't have to come all the way up here and stand with a prayer shawl over his head to arrive at that conclusion.

So why then was he here? Once again, he remembered his embarrassment during the telephone conversation with Kestler, all the more acute because it was overheard by Lanigan. He wondered uneasily if the police chief knew about the lawsuit over the fence. Were the police notified of such things? It suddenly came to him that what really bothered him was the repetition of his failures. He had failed in Delmont, and again in Morrisborough. Was the same thing going to happen in Barnard's Crossing? Was he failure-prone, as some people are accident-prone? Taking the experience in the three towns together, did it mean that he was unsuited to the practice of medicine?

Was he losing faith in himself as a doctor? An uneasy thought occurred to him which he tried to put out of his mind: was it possible that the first time he had prescribed Limpidine for Jacob Kestler, there had been an allergic reaction? He had not consulted his case records before going to see him the night of the storm, relying on his memory. He was sure there had not been but it had been months before and he might have forgotten. And now, standing there alone, he admitted that when he first heard of Kestler's death, the idea had crossed his mind. He had not bothered to verify it, because he was so sure. Or was it because he was afraid?

Although the retreat program called for Sunday dinner and a meeting afterward, he decided not to wait but to leave immediately after the meditation. He must check his records; he would hesitate no longer.

To his roommate, he lied that he had a patient whom he had promised to visit before noon. And he used the same excuse in saying good-bye to Rabbi Mezzik.

"And how did you enjoy your experience?" Mezzik asked.

"All right, I guess. I think the rest did me some good."

"And the religious experience, did you profit from it?"

He was on the point of making polite acknowledgment, but he still felt aggrieved. "I'm afraid not, Rabbi. It didn't touch me at all. To be perfectly frank with you, I thought it was a lot of nothing."

Surprisingly, Mezzik was not offended. He even smiled. "That's the way it frequently strikes people at first."

"What do you mean, at first?"

Mezzik looked off into the distance. Then he eyed the doctor speculatively and said, "When you treat a patient, Doctor, when you give him medicine, is he healed immediately?"

"Sometimes he is. Most of the time not immediately."

"Well, that's the way it is with a religious exercise. Sometimes there is a great and sudden cognition, a revelation, a sudden awareness as though someone had snapped on the light in a dark room. And sometimes it takes a little time. And of course sometimes, as with your medicines, nothing happens. Now you prayed and meditated. I watched you and I think—I have some experience in these matters—that you prayed honestly and sincerely. Believe me, something will come of it. Maybe tomorrow, or next week, or even next year, but something will happen, I'm sure."

As he drove home Dan Cohen thought of what Mezzik had said, and his face relaxed in a wry grin. It was the old hokum. The fakers who operated medicine shows probably used the same spiel. It gave them time to get out of the county before the wrath of their dupes caught up with them.

Home at last. He had no sooner parked his car when his wife called to him, "Dan? Telephone. It's Chief Lanigan."

22

"Hello, Dr. Cohen? . . . My sacroiliac kicked up, but real bad. I was just able to make it back to my desk."

"It's happened before, has it?"

"I can count on an incident about once a year or so. But usually, it's just a gnawing kind of ache like I'm carrying a hundred pounds of lead strapped around my waist. This time, I got a shooting pain and I just couldn't straighten up. I'm down at the stationhouse. At home I got a special belt that I put on when it happens, but I sure can't drive home now."

"Maybe I'd better come and have a look at you. I could at least strap you up."

"I'd appreciate it, Doctor. I know that about all I can do is live with it until the pain wears off, but I've never had it so bad before."

"Well, maybe I can give you something. I'll be along in a few minutes."

A little while later, the doctor was looking at the woe-begone face of the chief and nodding as he explained, "I wouldn't mind, Doctor, if I had done something foolish like trying to push a car out of the snow. I did that once and my back kicked up. I deserved that, and it was only a mild case as these things go. But here I just leaned forward to return a folder to the file cabinet and, wow! I couldn't move."

Dr. Cohen nodded. "It goes away after a while, doesn't it? Two or three days?"

"It gets easier in a few days, but it lingers on for a couple of weeks usually. But I've never had anything like this. Usually, it's a kind of ache, if you know what I mean. This was a sharp shooting pain, and I couldn't move at all for the first few minutes. Then I managed to work my way over to my chair by holding onto the cabinet and then the desk."

"I think maybe I'd better give you something," said the doctor. He fished in his bag and came up with a small bottle. "Luckily, I had some samples at home. This is a muscle relaxant. It may make you drowsy, so I wouldn't take a long auto trip if I were you. I've had pretty good luck with these pills, although some of my patients said that they didn't help at all." He went to the little sink in the corner of the office and drew a glass of water. "Here, I'd like you to take a couple of these now, and then a couple every four hours. By the way, are you allergic to anything?"

"Not that I know of," the chief replied as he took the pills from the doctor's outstretched hand. He looked at them curiously for a moment and then popped them into his mouth, and swallowed them with the aid of the water.

"Why do you ask if I'm allergic to anything?" Lanigan asked. "My back problem couldn't be the result of an allergy, could it?"

"Of course not. I was thinking of the medication. There's always a chance of an allergic reaction, sometimes quite severe, from almost any medication you might take. It's especially true these days when we use such highly sophisticated formulations."

"Is that so? Say, is that what happened to old man

Kestler? He got an allergic reaction to the pills you prescribed?"

The doctor shrugged. "It's possible. My associate, Dr. DiFrancesca, was inclined to think so. Where there's a known allergy to a particular medicine, of course we don't prescribe it. That's why we always tell patients what the medicine is and ask about their allergies, if any. Normally, for instance, I would have prescribed penicillin for Kestler, but I knew he was allergic to it, so I prescribed one of the tetracyclines. He could have been allergic to that, too, but it was a lot less likely. I mean, a number of people are allergic to penicillin, but not too many to tetracycline. And I'd had him on it before. But even there you can't tell. Sometimes, it's sort of cumulative."

"Any chance the drugstore made a mistake?"

The doctor shook his head. "No, I shouldn't think so. They're terribly careful these days because of this sophisticated formulation I mentioned. A mistake on the part of the druggist is highly unlikely. And the manufacturers cooperate by putting out their pills in all different shapes and colors instead of just round and white the way they used to do years ago. The pill I prescribed for Kestler, for example, was kind of pink oval—"

"Orange, I'd say," said the chief.

"No, pink. Well, maybe you could call it salmon-colored. How do you know?"

"I looked at them. I've got them right here. I'm sure they're orange. Just a minute." He pulled open a desk drawer and took out the envelope that contained the bottle of pills. He uncapped the bottle and shook a few pills out on the desktop. There was no mistake. Oval they were, but they were also unmistakably orange. "Now wouldn't you call them orange?" he asked.

"Let me see that bottle." The doctor read the label aloud: "J. Kestler, Limpidine two hundred fifty, one tablet four times a day, Dr. D. Cohen."

"That's what you prescribed?"

The doctor nodded.

"And those are the pills? What did you call them—Limpidine?"

"I always thought they were pink. Look, I've got a book at home that the pharmaceutical industry issues every year to all doctors. It has all the information on the medicines they manufacture as well as colored plates of the pills. I could swear that Limpidine is pink but I'll look it up as soon as I get home."

"You do that, Doctor, and call me back. I'll be here for a little while."

Dr. Cohen managed to observe the speed limits all the way home, but just barely. He parked his car in the garage and then hurried to his study without bothering to take off his coat. He opened the *Physician's Desk Reference* and stared at the colored plate. He was right! The Limpidine was pink. The orange pill was actually a form of penicillin put out by the same house. Somehow Aptaker had made a mistake and issued the penicillin pill. And of course the old man had reacted to it, since he was sensitive to the medicine. So the mistake was the druggist's, and he was in the clear!

His heart sang within him. It had happened! He had gone to the retreat; he had prayed, truly prayed perhaps for the first time in his life; and the very next day, this great depressing weight had been miraculously lifted.

He reached for the telephone.

The problems of parents with their children, all seemingly requiring nothing less than a rabbinic decision or at least an opinion, were many and various. Rabbi Small saw each parent in turn while the rest waited outside on a settee near his study.

". . . I know it isn't terribly important, but kids are sensitive, and when Malcolm Studnick was given the part

132

in the play, where everybody said my Ronald was so much better in the tryouts, he was hurt. . . ."

". . . You know how it is with girls, Rabbi. Being popular is important to them. It can affect their whole personality. So dancing class and tennis lessons, they're part of her necessary development as a woman. . . ."

". . . It isn't that my Sumner is not interested, Rabbi. It's just that he hasn't got the time. . . ."

". . . Right now, Rabbi, where he's been sickly almost since he was a baby, my husband feels, and I do too of course, he should be outdoors as much as possible. I thank God for Little League. If it weren't for Little League, he'd be moping around the house all the time. That's why I was so interested in the camp when my husband came home and told me about it Wednesday night. Now if he could get his Judaism there during the summer—"

"What camp is that, Mrs. Robinson?"

"You know, the place up in Petersville. As I understand it, it's to be used not only as a retreat for adults, but there'll be opportunity for the children to go up there for a couple of weeks in the summer."

"But that's not for the immediate future, Mrs. Robinson, it's just being discussed."

"Oh no, Rabbi. According to my husband they discussed it thoroughly at the retreat yesterday, and they were going to vote on it today."

"Oh, I see." Rabbi Small managed to curb his impatience and gave no indication that he was anxious to get rid of her, but when the conference was over and he saw Mrs. Robinson to the door, he said to the woman who was about to enter, "I'm sorry, Mrs. Kalbfuss, but I have to go to the board meeting."

"But it's over, Rabbi. They all left a little while ago."

He looked down the corridor, and sure enough, the door to the boardroom was open and the room was empty.

As he was driving home, Chester Kaplan spotted Dr. Cohen raking leaves on his front lawn and drew up to the curb. "Hi, Doctor," he called. "Sorry I had to rush off this morning without saying good-bye."

"Oh, that's all right," said Cohen, approaching the car, rake in hand.

"How was it? Did you like it?" Kaplan asked eagerly.

"It was fine," said the doctor, his face expanding in a broad grin. "Real fine, kind of wonderful, in fact. Reminds me, I haven't paid you yet. If you've got a minute, I'll go in and make out a check, or come in if you like."

"No, that's all right. You send it to me. I've got to run along. I'm glad you had a nice time."

"Oh yeah, it was a real experience."

When he got home, Kaplan immediately went to his study and typed a letter on temple stationery to Marcus Aptaker, Town-Line Drugs, informing him that the board of directors of the temple had voted unanimously to sell the Goralsky Block and the adjacent land to William Safferstein, 258 Minerva Road, Barnard's Crossing, and that he should address his request for renewal of his lease to him.

23

"Don't do it, David," Miriam urged. "Kaplan put one over on you. Don't give him the added satisfaction of showing him that you're hurt."

134

"I can't just let it pass," the rabbi said, but he took his hand off the telephone.

"But you don't know what happened. All you know is what some woman told you they were going to do at the meeting. You don't know if they actually did it. Why not wait until they tell you officially?"

Her husband sat down, and since he appeared receptive, she continued. "You think they voted to buy that place up in Petersville. Well, what if they did? They have a right to, haven't they? They don't need your permission. You're just invited to attend board meetings as a guest. You weren't elected to the board."

He nodded. "No, of course not. And if they want to buy a piece of land up-country for some ordinary purpose—"

"Like what?"

"Well, even for investment. I might have some thoughts on the wisdom of the move, but no real interest as rabbi of the congregation. But on the basis of what Kaplan has let drop the last couple of months, I am reasonably sure they plan to use the place as a retreat. Now that *does* concern me."

"Well, I suppose since it's a religious thing—"

He looked at her in surprise. "It's more than that. It's not just something that I feel they should have asked me about, like—like whether to buy a new Scroll of the Law. This retreat idea involves a change in the direction that the temple is taking. Suppose they're considering doing away with the Bar Mitzvah at the age of thirteen in favor of a confirmation at fifteen or sixteen as is the case in many Reform temples. Or suppose they decided to institute a new seating arrangement where women would be separated from men as in Orthodox synagogues. Those are not the kinds of things where just my opinion or advice is involved. In matters of that sort which indicate a basic change in the temple, it is my consent that they must get."

"And if they refuse?"

"Then I resign, of course," he said simply. "I say, in effect, I am a Conservative rabbi and as such accepted a position with a Conservative congregation. Now you wish to become a Reform congregation or an Orthodox congregation. Very well, it is your right, but I cannot continue to serve."

Miriam was troubled. "Aren't you overreacting, David?" she hazarded. "If a few members of your congregation want to go into the woods and pray on their own—"

"It's not a few members. It's the president and the board of directors of the temple, presumably acting for the congregation as a whole, and using congregation monies. And they're not just going into the woods to pray. They're setting up a branch of the temple and are engaging this rabbi, of whose views I know nothing, to guide them." He got up and went to the telephone.

Miriam tried once again. "Well, even as a matter of tactics, wouldn't it be better if the board notified you about what happened at the meeting? I mean, wouldn't it be better if they came to you, instead of you going to them? For all you know, Kaplan plans to call you sometime this afternoon or even to come over to explain it."

He considered. "I doubt if he will. He probably expects to see me at the minyan this evening."

"Same thing."

He was silent as he thought about it. Finally he said, "Maybe."

He was moody all afternoon and spent most of it in his study. Miriam realized that her husband was deeply hurt and did not disturb him. But in the evening, she entered his study and was surprised to see that he was standing in the corner praying, his lips moving rapidly as he recited the *Shimon Esra*. She waited until he was finished and said, "Aren't you going to the minyan, David?"

136

He shook his head. "No, I'm not. And I don't think I'll go for the rest of the week."

"They'll think you're sulking."

He grinned. "Let them. Maybe I am, at that. I haven't decided just what I'm going to do, but I am *not* going to argue this issue in the corridor with Kaplan and whoever else might decide to join in. I'll wait until Sunday and then when the minutes of the previous meeting are read, I'll know exactly what they did and act accordingly. If they have passed a motion to buy the land in Petersville for a retreat, then I'll ask for reconsideration."

"And if they reconsider and end up voting the same way?"

"Then I shall ask that they call for a general meeting of the membership where I can state my views and ask for a vote by the congregation as a whole."

"And if they refuse?"

"Then, of course, I will resign."

24

On the spur of the moment while on his way home, Lanigan parked his car at the corner instead of entering the street. He winced as he always did when he saw the neon sign, YE OLDE CORNER DRUGGE STORE, JOS. TIMILTY., REG. PHARM., PROP., but he went in nevertheless. Timilty, a short, dark, stout man, came hurrying over. His Russian-style tunic of pale green nylon with Ye Olde Drugge Store stitched on the pocket in dark green had short sleeves, exposing hairy forearms. He was bald, but as though to compensate, he had bushy black eyebrows accentuated by the heavy dark frames of his eyeglasses. Even immediately after shaving, his jowls were bluish; now, late in the afternoon, they were blue-black.

"What can I do for *you?*" he asked, to emphasize the importance of the customer, as taught in the salesmanship course he was taking. He was new in the area, having bought the store less than a year ago from the Brundages, who had operated it as far back as Lanigan could remember.

Somewhat taken aback at the directness of the approach, Lanigan cast about for something to buy. His eye swept along the displays, the salted nuts, the boxes of candy, the perfumes; the dog collars, leashes and rawhide chewing bones; canary and lovebird supplies; the children's toys. But he had neither dog nor pet bird, nor child at home and he knew that if he brought home a box of candy or perfume, Amy would think he had been drinking. Then he thought of the tiny sample bottle of pills Dr. Cohen had given him and drew it out of his pocket.

"A funny thing happened to me this morning," he said. "I was in my office down at the stationhouse looking over some files, and I bent over, and by God, I couldn't straighten up."

Timilty nodded knowingly. "Sacroiliac," he said positively. "First time it's happened?"

"No, but never like this." He went on to tell of calling Dr. Cohen, ". . . and these pills he gave me, well, they worked like magic. A half an hour later, I was as good as new." Timilty nodded, smiling the superior smile of the professional at the layman's marveling at the wonders of science.

"Usually it takes me as much as a couple of weeks to get over an attack, but here, in half an hour—nothing. So I was wondering if you had these pills—they are just a sample that Doc Cohen had in the house—well, I could keep a supply of them handy. Then if it happened again, why, I'd have them."

Timilty glanced at the little glass bottle the chief held out to him. "Sure, we've got them. There are a number of preparations that do much the same thing, muscle relaxants we call them. But you want to be careful about driving when you're taking them. They can make you drowsy."

"Do I need a doctor's prescription? Because if I do—"

"No, *you* don't need a prescription. How many do you want?"

"Gee, I don't know. A dozen?" the chief suggested.

"Sure. You can always get more if you want them." He went to the prescription room in back of the store, and Lanigan followed.

"Gosh, how do you keep track of all these medicines, Joe?"

"Oh, there's no trouble if you have a system." He laughed. "Old Man Brundage used to do it by instinct, I guess." He selected a plastic tube and typed a label. "You understand, I can only put the trade name of the medication on the label," he said. "*You* can write in the doctor's name and the dosage yourself if you want to. I can't without a prescription."

"Oh, that's all right," Lanigan said easily. "You do a lot of prescriptions?"

"Fifty, sixty a day."

"You pour them out of the big bottles into the little bottles, eh?"

Timilty was about to explain haughtily that there was a great responsibility involved, but he remembered that Lanigan was an important man in the town, so he winked and said with a grin, "That's just about it."

"You never actually have to make up something?"

"Oh sure. Liquid medicines, salves, suppositories, sometimes even pills. Some of the old-timers have their special prescriptions even for pills and I compound them and put them up in plastic capsules. By the time I came into the drug business, the drug houses had got it all organized."

"Ever make a mistake?"

Timilty shook his head gravely. "Never on a drug. No druggist does. He'd go out of business."

"But some pharmacists—"

Timilty shook his head stubbornly. "I'm not one to go around boosting the competition, but no druggist can afford to make a mistake on a prescription. Sometimes, a doctor will specify the drug of a particular pharmaceutical house, say Squibb's, and you're out of it. But you've got the identical formulation from, say, Parke-Davis. Well, I've known of druggists who'll give the Parke-Davis. Now that's not really a mistake. It's what you might call unethical. And some doctors will overlook it, while some will raise hell. My rule is that we always contact the doctor and ask him if we can make the change. Otherwise, I just don't dispense it."

"You mean, you just hand the prescription back to the customer and tell him you can't fill it?"

Timilty winked again. "The usual thing is to tell him it will take a little time to fill, and we offer to deliver it."

"I see." Lanigan grinned. "It's happened to me. Then I've wondered when I got the pills what there was about them that took time since they were obviously manufactured. I mean the druggist hadn't rolled them himself."

140

"That's business. A good businessman tries to hold on to his customers."

"Yeah, I guess so. But look here, some druggists must be more reliable than others."

"Not on filling prescriptions accurately," the druggist said. "Not if they're still in business."

"Then how do you people compete with each other?"

"On service, price, location, personality. Just like grocery stores. The Campbell's soup in one store is the same as the Campbell's soup in the other. But one store is cheaper, or it's nearer or cleaner. So you go to that one."

"Or maybe one gives a little more than the other," Lanigan suggested.

"How do you mean?"

"Well, you come in with a prescription for some pills, say. So one guy will fill the bottle and another guy maybe stuffs in a lot of cotton batting."

Timilty shook his head vigorously. "The doctor indicates on the prescription how many he wants, and that's what we give him. There are a lot of medicines where he wants you to take just so many pills and no more. Or he wants you to take the full dosage, no matter how good you feel after you've taken half of them. So we give exactly what the doctor calls for, no more and no less. Besides, with some pills costing seventy or eighty cents a piece, nobody is going to give any extra."

"How about the pharmacists who work for you?"

"They wouldn't be any different when it comes to filling a prescription."

"I suppose each one initials or signs the prescriptions he fills."

"What for? What would be the point?"

"Well, say something went wrong?"

Timilty looked at him in astonishment. "What could go wrong?"

25

Chief Lanigan pushed the *Physician's Desk Reference* over to his lieutenant and said, "Now here is what Doc Cohen prescribed, and this is what Old Man Kestler received and took."

Lt. Eban Jennings focused watery blue eyes on the small colored plate, then turned to the pill lying on the desk. His prominent Adam's apple wobbled and he said, "Not the same at all. The druggist must have made a mistake."

Lanigan shook his head. "According to Dr. Cohen, that's most unlikely. I checked with Timilty, who took over Brundage's store at the foot of my street, and he says druggists just don't make mistakes on prescriptions. Now, he's one of those eager-beaver business types and if he could give the competition the leg, I'm thinking he'd do it. But he agreed with the doctor—a druggist just doesn't make that type of mistake."

"Then what's it mean?"

Lanigan leaned back in his chair. "Well, I'd say, if it wasn't a mistake, and yet it happened, that it must have been done on purpose."

"But that's murder," Jennings objected.

"Or manslaughter. And why not? Murders are not all

142

committed with guns or daggers, you know. Most folks don't have guns, or daggers either. Except for the professionals, it's usually done by what's at hand. The sharp instrument usually turns out to be something familiar, like a steak knife. How about Millicent Hanbury, who used a knitting needle? And how about Ronald Sykes who killed Isaac Hirsh by just closing the ventilator of his car while the motor was running? Think about it. What's handy would be the natural thing to use. Here's a druggist with a store full of chemicals. If he wanted to kill someone, he might try to get hold of a gun. But more likely, the first thought that would come to mind would be the things he has right on his shelves."

"Yeah, but—aw, that's crazy. Look, Hugh, since we sold the house and took the apartment on Salem Road, I've traded with Town-Line Drugs. I stop in there almost every evening for the paper and some cigars, and a nicer guy than Marcus Aptaker you wouldn't want to meet. Not that he's one of these glad-hand boys. Kind of conservative, as a matter of fact, you know, with a sense of responsibility. A man like that wouldn't go around dispensing stuff that would kill people."

"I've known Marcus Aptaker longer than you have," Lanigan said. "When I first came on the force, I had the night beat in the Salem Road area. Drugstores used to keep open till midnight those days, and Aptaker's was where I'd stop in to warm up. He had a hot plate, and many a cup of coffee I had courtesy of Marcus Aptaker, while we chewed the fat. I like Aptaker, but he's one of those rigid, straitlaced types. That kind sees everything as black or white, nothing in between. And when he thinks someone has wronged him, I can imagine him feeling he's judge and jury—and maybe even executioner. You remember his son, Arnold?"

"Yeah, seems to me he used to work for him."

Lanigan lay back in his swivel chair and brought his

heels to rest on the open bottom drawer. With his head cradled in his interlaced fingers, he stared up at the ceiling and said, "That same boy, Arnold, he kicked him out two, three years ago, for pilfering the till."

"Oh no!"

"Oh yes. The boy was playing around in the nightclubs and gambling joints in Revere, and he'd run up a bill that he gave an IOU for. They were pressing him for payment and threatening him, I suppose. With those boys you don't pay up, and you get your arms and legs broken. So I guess Arnold dipped into the till, and his old man caught him at it and kicked him out."

"How come I never heard of it?"

"Because you were in Washington taking that FBI refresher course that I euchred the town into putting up the money for."

"Oh. And what happened? Did Aptaker come to you?"

"Not then. Marcus Aptaker paid the IOU and told the collector he didn't want him to set foot in his store again." The chief lowered his feet to the floor and sat bolt upright. "But that kind, they never let well enough alone; they can't stop pushing. The collector laughed at him and said the store was a public place and he'd come in any time he felt like it. That's when Aptaker came to see me. He wanted me to warn him off. Said he'd kill this guy if he didn't stop bothering him."

"What could you do if this guy was from Revere?"

"He'd just moved into town. It was Joe Kestler."

"Joe Kestler?" the lieutenant said. "I didn't know he was in the rackets. I thought he was in business with his old man, mortgages and such."

"I don't know that he *is* in the rackets," Lanigan said mildly. "He told Aptaker he'd bought that IOU, or discounted it."

"So what did you do?"

"Oh, I went to see Kestler."

144

"And what did you tell Kestler?"

Lanigan grinned. "It wasn't so much what I told him as what he thought I told him. All I said was that I didn't want any trouble in the town, that he was new here and if he wanted to live nice and peaceful, he wouldn't go starting fights. I suppose in other places that kind of warning by the chief of police meant that if he didn't keep his nose clean, he'd have all kinds of trouble with the authorities, that his property was likely to be reassessed, or that the building inspectors would be down to condemn his wiring or his plumbing. As far as I know, he stayed away. At least, Aptaker never complained to me again. Too bad Kestler didn't continue to keep his distance, but I suppose with his father sick—"

"Hey, just a minute, Hugh, are you saying—why, that was all of three years ago."

"Yeah, but some things get worse with time," the chief said. "Aptaker's boy never came back. The longer it lasted, the more it would hurt. Besides, if Kestler did stay away, this was the first chance Aptaker had to get back at him."

"But the medicine wasn't for Joe, the one he'd had trouble with. It was for his father," Jennings objected.

"Yeah, I thought of that," said Lanigan. "But all that appears on the medicine label is the initial J, and that applies to both the father and the son, because the father's name was Jacob. Now if the father was sick, wouldn't the son have come in for the medicine? So if the son didn't, maybe he was the one who was sick and didn't pick it up because he couldn't."

Eban Jennings shook his head slowly. "I can't believe it, not Marcus Aptaker."

"You can't tell what people are going to do, Eban, not by what they seem."

"But it doesn't add up," Jennings protested. "Aptaker

145

has a fight with Joe Kestler three years ago, so he kills his father three years later?"

"His son left home because of that fight, Eban, and Marcus had plans for him. The store isn't just a business with Marcus. It's a tradition that he meant Arnold to carry on. That makes a difference."

"Well, look here. How would he know that the new pills would do him any harm? Answer me that."

"He wouldn't, of course, not for sure. But according to Doc Cohen tetracycline was developed for people who are allergic to penicillin. So, being a druggist, Aptaker would know there was a good chance that it was being prescribed because the patient was allergic to penicillin. In that case a penicillin pill would do a lot of harm even if it didn't actually kill the patient. One thing is sure—Town-Line Drugs made a mistake in a matter that drugstores never make a mistake on—"

"So what do you plan to do?"

"Well, I guess I should ask Mr. Aptaker a few questions."

"But how do you know it was Marcus Aptaker that made the switch?" Jennings asked. "How do you know it wasn't the other pharmacist, Ross McLane? Now there's a sonofabitch if ever there was one. He's grouchy and sarcastic and don't know how to talk to a person. Now get this, Hugh, when a customer comes in to buy something, it's Marcus that waits on him. Why? Because McLane don't know how to deal with a customer. He barks at you, 'What do you want?' like you're interrupting him and he's doing you a favor."

"What are you getting at, Eban?"

"What I'm saying is that when customers are in the store like there must have been Wednesday because of the storm coming, it's Marcus who's out front. So McLane is in back working on prescriptions."

"But McLane is new in town," the chief pointed out.

"About a year," said Jennings.

"And we don't know of any connection he had with Kestler."

"That doesn't mean there wasn't one. McLane used to have a drugstore in Revere. And that's where Kestler comes from."

"Well . . ."

"Look, Hugh, suppose you hold off talking to Aptaker for a couple of days, while I do a little snooping around Revere and see if I can come up with something."

Lanigan nodded. "All right. I guess it can wait a couple of days, but I don't want any long drawn-out investigation, because in the meantime Dr. Cohen is taking it on the chin."

Except for Dr. Cohen's certainty that Lanigan was his friend and wanted to help him, he could not understand why he had abjured him not to confront Aptaker about the mistake in the prescription.

"Let me check into it first, Doctor," Lanigan had said.

"I don't understand. What is there to check?"

"Well, a mistake was made. There's no question about that. It could be a matter of straight out negligence, or it could be something else—"

"Such as?"

"I don't know. That's what I want to find out."

"What's wrong with my going there and finding out for myself?" Dr. Cohen asked.

"Well, in a sense the police department is a party to this, because we have official custody of the pills. For that matter, we even delivered them. I'm not sure, for instance, that I should have shown them to you. I mean, if we're involved, then it's part of the official file on the case. If Kestler should bring a malpractice suit, a smart lawyer could make something of your being my doctor and my showing you evidence without the knowledge and not in the presence of the other party and his attorney. He could suggest, for instance, that we connived to switch them. Believe me, I've had plenty of cases go sour over something like that. I'd like to make some inquiries."

"How long would it take?" Dan asked.

"Oh, I don't know—a day or two," the chief replied.

"Well, I guess I could wait a couple of days, but I don't want it to drag along. It could hurt my practice."

"I understand. I'll get on it right away."

Cohen's first impulse on discovering the truth had been to call Dr. Muntz and the rest of his colleagues and tell them. On reflection, however, he decided against it. For one thing, he still resented the way they had reacted to the news of his difficulties, and for another, he did not want to suggest that he himself had had any doubts of the correctness of his treatment. He planned to tell them, of course, but only incidentally when the matter came up again in casual conversation.

But here it was Tuesday afternoon, and the occasion had not as yet arisen. It may have been his imagination, but he thought he detected a certain coolness toward him on the part of his associates. Yesterday they had gone to lunch without him. He had been closeted with a patient, but one of his colleagues could have called on the inter-office phone and asked if they should wait for him.

And for the rest of the afternoon, it had seemed that they had avoided him. To be sure, they had all had full schedules, but there were always a few minutes between one appointment and the next, even on the busiest days, when they would drop into one another's office for a cigarette and a little arm-stretching relaxation. Not once had one of the doctors so much as waved to him during the entire afternoon. Dan had expected that Al Muntz would at least have asked him about the retreat. After all, he had got involved with it on his urging. It would have given him an opportunity to tell of his experience of the weekend as a preface to what had happened subsequently in Chief Lanigan's office. But Muntz did not refer to it.

Tuesdays, both Kantrovitz and Muntz conducted clinics at the hospital, but they usually managed to get back to their offices before the noon hour. Today, however, neither returned by the time Cohen was ready to leave for lunch. And when he looked in on DiFrancesca, he was told, "Why don't you run along, Dan. The wife is picking me up. We're going to look at a new rug."

Was it all coincidence? Or was he being oversensitive, maybe even slightly paranoid? He phoned Lanigan in the hope that he might have news for him. But Lanigan was not in his office.

"Will you have him call me when he gets in?"

"Right."

All afternoon he waited for the call, and when it did not come by closing time, he decided to do something on his own. Surely there could be nothing wrong in just seeing Marcus Aptaker, in just talking to him. He would not mention Kestler's prescription. He could just stop by for—for some cigars. They could talk about—about any-thing, the way they usually did when he stopped by and

Aptaker happened to be free. Then if Aptaker should happen to mention Kestler . . .

27

The letter from the temple came in the morning mail. Except for a momentary tightening of the lips, Marcus Aptaker gave no indication of his disappointment, but he was abstracted all morning and had to force a smile when he faced a customer. He waited on trade, he checked in a shipment of merchandise, he answered the phone, he rang up sales and made proper change or recorded the amount on the customer's charge card, but it was all automatic, his mind elsewhere, wrestling with the problem.

There was no point in appealing to Safferstein for renewal of his lease as the letter suggested, since Safferstein had been trying to purchase the store for his brother-in-law. Now he would not have to buy; he had only to wait the few months for the lease to expire and then take it over. Safferstein had originally hinted that he was prepared to pay a good price, but obviously his purchase of the block changed that. Aptaker felt certain that if Safferstein were willing to go through with his offer to purchase—and it was doubtful that he would now—it would be on the basis of buying the stock as depressed merchandise and the fixtures for only what they would bring in the second-hand market. Goodwill was out of the question.

He toyed with the possibility of renting another store. It would mean a sizable investment in new fixtures, but if his son were with him, it would be a logical move. But that expectation, he now realized, had been little more than a daydream and even less likely now since his son's short visit home. It became clear to him that he was alone now, and sixty-two, too old to start a new business.

It flashed across his mind momentarily that he might speak to Kaplan and ask him to reconsider or perhaps let him make a plea directly to the board of directors of the temple. But why should they give him special consideration when he was not even a member of the congregation?

He faced the immediate problem of deciding what he was going to tell his wife. In his mind, he rehearsed the tone and attitude he might adopt. He must not let her know how much he was hurt. "I suppose it's just as well. I've worked hard all my life and it's time I took a rest. Maybe we could take a trip, and then with my Social Security and yours and with what I've saved up, we should be able to manage. Maybe I could get a part-time job just to keep busy. I'll admit I wouldn't have sold out, but now that it's happened, I'm kind of glad." But would she believe him?

McLane arrived a little after noon, and after giving him a few instructions, Aptaker went into the prescription room to eat the lunch which Rose prepared for him every day.

He ate quickly, as he invariably did in the store, taking large bites of his sandwich and helping it down with gulps of coffee. As had happened a couple of times before, when he finished eating, he felt a lump in his chest. He drank a glass of water slowly, and that gave him some measure of relief. He wanted to belch but couldn't. Finally, he yielded to the urgency of the dull ache and mixed a little bicarbonate of soda in a glass. That indeed induced a belch, but the relief was momentary, and almost immediately he felt the pressure in his chest again.

McLane looked at him with some concern. "Got a heartburn? Here, take one of these," he said, picking up a tin from the patent-medicine counter. "They're good. I've tried them."

Marcus chewed on the tablet and then took another, and again there was momentary relief; but the pressure came back again. It occurred to him that the pain and pressure might be from his heart rather than from indigestion. When McLane wasn't looking, he opened a small bottle of nitroglycerin tablets and put one of the tiny pills under his tongue. Almost immediately there was a sharp tightness in his head. It did not last long, and by the time it was over, the pain in his chest was gone.

For about an hour he felt quite normal, and then the pressure came back again. He grimaced with the pain and surreptitiously put another tablet under his tongue. Once more he experienced relief, but he was aware that he was perspiring and he thought his face must be pale.

Normally, Marcus would have left around two, but he was sure his wife would note that he appeared ill and become alarmed. Out of her solicitude she would bedevil him with interminable questions—Did anything happen at the store? Did you have a fight with McLane? Was there trouble with a customer? Then, if he were to tell her about the letter, and sooner or later he'd have to, her woman's logic would assume a connection with his present distress. He would be unable then to convince her that giving up the store did not matter to him. So he decided to remain in the store until dinner time, taking it easy. He would go to bed early, and he was sure that after a good night's rest he would be all right in the morning. Of course, it was impossible for him to remain seated in the prescription room while there were customers out front, and in spite of his resolution he waited on trade almost as much as he normally would.

Once, McLane asked him, "You all right? You look sort of pale."

"Sure, I'm all right," he asserted. "Maybe it's this new fluorescent tube. You look kind of pale yourself."

Shortly after five, Dr. Cohen came in, and Aptaker went over to wait on him. The doctor looked at him narrowly, and as Marcus grimaced from a spasm of pain, Dan Cohen said, "Hey, what's the matter?"

"Oh, just a little stomach upset, I guess. I feel like burping and I can't seem to get it out."

"You're perspiring," Cohen said.

"Yeah, maybe a little. It's warm in here, and I've been running around."

"How long have you had this upset?"

"Oh, just a little while."

"He's had it since lunch, Doctor," McLane volunteered.

"Any pain in the arm?" Cohen asked.

"No."

"Where do you feel it, Mark?"

"Right here," and he touched his chest.

"Any trouble breathing? Is it a squeezing type of pain?"

"No, nothing like that."

"Let me have your wrist."

"Aw now, Doctor, I know what you're thinking. It's nothing, I tell you." But he held up a limp wrist.

The doctor felt the pulse and then said, "Look, take off your jacket and shirt while I get my stethoscope from the car."

"I'm not going to take my shirt off in the store."

"Why not? There's nobody here now. We can go in the prescription room or the toilet. No, never mind. What you need is an EKG. Who's your doctor?"

"I don't have one," Aptaker said. "I'm never sick."

"All right then, I'll drive you back to my office and I

153

can do it there. Or better still, I could drive you to the hospital."

"I'm not going to any hospital. Rose is expecting me home in about an hour."

"Don't be a damn fool," Dr. Cohen said. "You might have to go home on a stretcher. Let me take you to the hospital."

"Go ahead, Marcus," McLane urged. "I'll phone Rose for you."

Aptaker hesitated, looking from one to the other, and read the urgency in the doctor's face. "All right," he said, "but I'll talk to her. Just get the number for me."

When she answered, he said, "Rose? I had a little stomach upset and Dr. Cohen happened to come by. He wants to give me a checkup."

Later, during the evening visiting hours, Rose Aptaker sat by her husband's bedside. He was in a hospital johnny, and his bed was raised so that he could face her without discomfort.

He explained how they would manage. "You can open in the morning, Rose, and McLane said he'd cooperate in any way necessary. He'll come in around ten and—"

"No." She shook her head in firm disagreement. "I'm calling Arnold to come home. He'll take your place until you get back on your feet."

"But he's got a job."

"So he'll quit or take a leave of absence."

"But if he won't come?" Marcus asked.

"He'll come."

Aptaker smiled wanly. "You know, Rose, this business—" he touched his breast— "it's nothing serious, you understand. It's a mild heart attack, and I feel fine, but it's still a heart attack, and that means it will take some time. According to Cohen, it may be three months before I can go back to work."

154

"Whatever time it takes, Arnold will stay, I can promise you. I know the boy. But maybe it would be a good idea if we called in a specialist, a heart man to—"

"No, no. If Cohen thought I needed one, he'd suggest it. I got faith in Cohen. I like the way he works. I feel he's concerned about me."

28

Chester Kaplan's closest friend in Barnard's Crossing was Al Muntz, even though the doctor was openly and argumentatively agnostic. They visited back and forth regularly, informal evenings in which the wives tended to talk together of clothes and cooking while the two men argued about the larger concerns of politics and religion.

Afterward, Kaplan might say to his wife, "I don't know how a smart guy like Al Muntz can be so dumb about everything except his own little speciality. Did you hear what he said about my going to the temple every morning?"

And at the Muntz household, Mrs. Muntz might say, "Gee, Al, why do you always argue with Chet, and always about religion? I think he was hurt by what you said about his going to the minyan."

"I said it because of what he said. He started it. If he says something that my common sense tells me is just plain superstitious nonsense, am I supposed to just sit there and say nothing?"

Tuesday evening, before they set out for their dinner date with the Kaplans, Mrs. Muntz adjured her husband, as she always did, not to spend the evening arguing about religion.

"Hell, religion is his bag, not mine. I don't talk about it. He does."

"Well, you don't have to answer."

"Sure, I'll just sit there like a dummy and nod my head."

And when they left their car and walked up the path to the front door, she reminded him, "Now, let's keep it light and pleasant. Let's have one evening without arguments."

"All right, all right."

And to be sure, all through dinner, under the watchful eye of his wife, Muntz resolutely refused every gambit offered by his host that might have led to argument. Even after dinner, when the women were in the kitchen loading the dishwasher, and Kaplan began to expatiate on the wondrous calm and peace of the weekend at the retreat, the doctor agreed that it certainly was nice up there. But, when encouraged, Kaplan went on to describe the positive physical benefits that some had experienced, the doctor could not help remark, "I'm willing to believe that Joe Gottlieb's sinuses may have stopped bothering him—temporarily—but don't try to tell me that God did it. Just don't try."

"I didn't say it was God," Kaplan said stiffly. "I merely said that he felt his head clear up right after the first period of meditation, and that it stayed clear all through the weekend."

"So what? I bet it's happened plenty of times. A lot of that is psychosomatic, and if you can kind of switch your mind off—Hell, it sometimes happens if you go to a movie or get absorbed in a book. But it doesn't last. Or, if it does, then you develop some other symptom. If you're trying to peddle this retreat as a cure for what ails you—"

"I am not trying to peddle anything," said Kaplan. "I

156

merely gave Joe Gottlieb as an example of the sort of thing that can happen when you succeed in shutting out the everyday world and concentrate on higher things. That's essentially the meaning and the effect of the Sabbath."

"So we've got the Sabbath. We've had it for a couple of thousand years. Why do you suddenly have to go off in the woods to celebrate it?"

"That's just the point," said Kaplan eagerly. "An institution that's as old as the Sabbath tends to become just a matter of form. The substance evaporates. It's the same with prayers. The people who wrote them, and maybe for some time after, they really prayed just as they honored the Sabbath. And maybe while Jews lived in the close-knit community of the ghetto, and their lives were hard, they were able to retain the initial enthusiasm for prayer and the Sabbath, to really feel their meaning. I know when my father spoke of the Sabbath in the old country his eyes would light up as though it was a wonderful experience he was remembering. But nowadays, we just go through the motions. The prayers don't mean anything, and the Sabbath doesn't mean anything, especially here in America. So they have just become rituals. And because they don't mean anything, they don't have any effect on our lives. That's why it's necessary to go off into the woods, to a new place, to start all over again to recapture their essence."

"But why now, Chet? It was just as true ten years ago and twenty years ago."

"Because it's in the air. The young people sense it and show it in their dissatisfaction with the old ways. They are searching for something new. The time is ripe. You probably feel it too, but you won't admit it to yourself. Tell me, why did you vote to buy the retreat, if deep down—"

"Hell, I voted for it because you presented it as a sort of package deal: sell the Goralsky property and buy this place up-country. I'm all in favor of selling the Goralsky property because I know that if the temple retained it, the place would just go downhill and be worth less next year than it is this year and even less the year after. An institution can't manage commercial property, not even a bank can. Besides, Bill Safferstein was giving us a crazy price for it, maybe half again what it's worth on the market today. So I'd be a fool not to vote to sell it. As for the place up in New Hampshire, I figured we were getting a pretty good deal on that, too. We might develop it into a sort of camp where members of the temple could go for a week or two in the summer, or even as a kids' camp. But as far as anything else is concerned, don't expect me to go along. My training has been scientific. I've got to have proof, hard, scientific, mathematical proof before I believe something."

"How about your own colleague, Dan Cohen? He came. Now you've got to admit he's had the same training you have. His attitude is as scientific as yours, isn't it?"

"Well, I'm not so sure. He's a G.P. Some of them get into all kinds of things. I've known some of them to give advice on family matters, even legal matters. But all right, let's say he is strictly scientific in his thinking. What about Dan?"

"Have you talked to him?" Kaplan asked. "Since he went on the retreat, I mean?"

"As a matter of fact, no. I've been kind of busy the last few days, and we just didn't happen to get together. Why, what did he say?"

"I saw him Sunday afternoon, and he was positively euphoric. When I asked him how he'd enjoyed the retreat, he grinned from ear to ear and said it was a tremendous experience. He felt it might have changed his whole life. How about that?"

"Well . . ."

"Go on," Kaplan taunted him. "Go on and talk to him. You'll see what he says."

158

"Well, because a man has had scientific training doesn't mean he's going to be scientific all the time," said Muntz lamely.

29

Rabbi Small saw Marcus Aptaker in the course of his regular pastoral visit to the hospital.

"How do you do, Rabbi. It's nice of you to stop by," Aptaker said politely.

"How are you feeling?" the rabbi asked gently as he drew a chair toward the bed.

Aptaker thawed a little. "All right, I guess, but kind of weak."

"Was this something sudden, or had you been ailing for some time?"

Aptaker shook his head wearily. "I don't know. Maybe it was coming on and I didn't realize it. They say it's due to tension. Well, I guess a man in business these days has plenty of tension, especially in the retail drug business where you don't know when you open in the morning that some crazy hippy isn't going to come in and take a shot at you. You learn to live with it, but I suppose it's building up all the time. Of course, the letter I got from you people didn't help any."

"A letter from us?" the rabbi asked, puzzled. "You mean from the temple? What kind of a letter?"

"The letter from your board of directors. You're a member, aren't you?"

"I—I attend the meetings by invitation of the president. I'm not actually a member."

"You mean you don't vote?"

"Yes, when I'm present I vote, but—"

"Well, the letter said it was by unanimous vote of the board, so you must've voted for it."

"Believe me, I know nothing about any letter sent you, Mr. Aptaker. What did it say?"

"It said that you people couldn't renew my lease on account you were selling the block."

"I didn't even know you had asked for a renewal of your lease."

"Oh yes, Rabbi. See, when my lease was close to expiring, I wrote to Mr. Goralsky asking for a renewal. So he wrote back that I'd been a good tenant, and he was willing to give me a new lease on the same basis as the old one for five years and five years' option and that he'd send out the lease forms for me to sign."

"And he didn't?"

"Oh, he sent them out all right," said Marcus. "But there was this clause saying that I had to take out insurance for my plate glass. Well, we'd crossed out that clause on previous leases, because I always took care of the plate glass myself. So I wrote him and asked he should cross out that clause."

"And he refused?"

Aptaker shook his head grimly. "No. He died. I was going to write to his son, Ben, but then I got this notice from the lawyers saying the property had been willed to the temple, so I wrote to you people and I didn't hear a word for weeks. It didn't bother me, you understand, because where it's an organization I figure there's bound to be some delay. And besides, I had sent the temple a copy of Goralsky's letter. Then yesterday, I get an answer. It's from Chester Kaplan—he's your president, isn't he?—and he says the property has been sold to William Safferstein and I should contact him."

"And did you?" the rabbi asked.

"I only got it yesterday. Besides, what's the use where he's been after me to sell him my store?"

"Safferstein wants to buy your store?"

"He wanted to. Now he doesn't have to bother. He can just wait a couple of months for my lease to expire and just take it over."

"But why would Mr. Safferstein want your store? He's in the real estate business."

"Well, he does. The last few months he must have asked me a dozen times. See, he's got this brother-in-law who's a pharmacist, and he's always hitting him up for a loan which he never pays back. And being it's his wife's brother, he can't turn him down. So he got the idea of buying my store and setting him up in business for himself. Now, if he's hot after my store, why would he extend my lease?"

"But if you haven't asked him . . ."

Aptaker shook his head. "No need to. And if I did, it wouldn't be asking. It would be begging. He'd just turn me down."

"But if Safferstein came to see you several times when you'd refused the first time . . ."

Aptaker grinned. "That's different. That's business. Maybe you wouldn't know, being a rabbi, but it's like this. Suppose somebody says he wants to buy your store, you don't ask how much he's offering because you don't want to appear too eager. Besides, you wouldn't want it to get around that you were interested in selling because that might suggest that business wasn't too good and it could hurt your credit. So you kind of fence with him. 'Why should I want to sell a good business?' Or 'Why do you want to buy a drugstore when you're not even a pharma-

161

cist?' See, you don't talk serious at first. Well, every time he comes in, like to buy a paper or a pack of cigarettes, he raises the question. He doesn't mind my putting him off because he's a businessman, too, so he knows the score. But then he comes to see me at home. That means he's serious. So I've got to talk serious, too."

Aptaker had been lying on his back, but now he turned over on his side to face the rabbi directly. "I explained to him why I can't deal with him. You see, I don't think of it as my store to do with what I please. I got it from my father and I feel I should pass it on to my son. I mean, it's not a job that you can walk away from. Where you've got something you've worked for all your life and your father before you, and you've trained your son to take it over, you don't just sell it to some stranger because he offers you a few thousand bucks. It's a family thing. So I told him I'd have to talk it over with my son and see how he felt."

"And Safferstein would come in and ask if you'd heard from your son?"

"That's right, Rabbi. But a thing like this, you can't just write a letter. You got to sit down and talk it over."

"So when Safferstein would inquire, you'd tell him you hadn't heard yet."

"Uh-huh. Because what I had in mind was maybe to take a weekend off and go see Arnold in Philadelphia where he's working."

"But wasn't he here a few days ago?"

Aptaker's face reddened. "Yeah, but we didn't have a chance to talk. Something came up and he had to go back to Philadelphia."

"And now?"

"Well, now it makes no difference," Marcus said gloomily. "My lease will expire and maybe Safferstein will make me some kind of offer for my stock. More likely, I'll have to sell it to the auctioneers."

"Have you got the correspondence on all this, Mr. Aptaker? I mean the request for renewal and—"

"Sure. I'm a very systematic man, Rabbi. I got a file of all the letters I received and carbons of the letters I sent."

"Could I see it?"

"Why not? You think you can do something?" Marcus asked eagerly. Then regretfully, "Believe me, it's hopeless. It's all perfectly legal. It's just my tough luck that Goralsky died when he did."

"Still, I'd like to see the correspondence if I may."

"You're welcome to it, Rabbi. When I get out of here, remind me."

"Couldn't I see it before then? Perhaps your wife . . ."

"All right. It's in a folder in the store. When Rose comes tonight, I'll tell her to dig it out for you."

At noon, Dr. Kantrovitz stuck his head into his colleague's office and asked, "Lunch?"

"Right," said Muntz. "Let's get hold of Dan. How about John?"

"He's not back from the hospital yet."

Dr. Kantrovitz walked the short distance to Dr. Cohen's office and called, "How about lunch, Dan?"

And Cohen, who had spent the last ten minutes in his office wondering if they would ask him, answered with alacrity, "Yeah, I'm starved."

It was not until the three men were dawdling over their coffee that Muntz asked about the retreat.

Dan Cohen smiled broadly. "It was okay. You know, a kind of change of pace. All this prayer and meditation they go in for, well, that was all right, too. After a while, you kind of get into the spirit of the thing and it's kind of relaxing."

"Relaxing?" Muntz asked. "Is that all? According to Chet Kaplan—he said he bumped into you after you got back—you were practically euphoric."

"Oh, that!" Dr. Cohen chuckled. "Yeah, I guess I was. You see, this Kestler business had got me down, even though I was sure I had given the old man the right medication. Still, I was worried because, well, because Kestler is Kestler. And also because of the way you guys reacted about his suing me. As a matter of fact, that's why I decided to go on this retreat. I'm not religious, but I thought it would be a good excuse to get away from it all. Well, I'd just come home, and I get this call from Chief Lanigan."

He went on to tell of his meeting with Lanigan and finished with, "So it was right after that I saw Kaplan, and he asks me how I enjoyed the weekend. Well, naturally, I was feeling pretty good."

"Then Kestler didn't get the medication you prescribed?" Muntz asked.

"No, he got a pencillin tablet instead."

"And he was sensitive to penicillin?"

"Uh-huh. That's why I prescribed Limpidine."

"So he probably did get a reaction, and it could easily account for his death," said Kantrovitz.

"Yeah, but it was not from Dan's prescription," Muntz pointed out.

"So what did you do about it?" demanded Kantrovitz.

164

"Naturally, I was going to see Aptaker and have it out with him, but Lanigan said since the police were involved, he wanted to check it out first, so I didn't do anything. I expected he'd get on it right away. But when I didn't hear from him, I thought I'd stop by the drugstore on my way home yesterday—"

"And?"

"And nothing," Cohen said. "When I got there, Aptaker was having a heart attack, so I rushed him to the hospital."

"Aptaker is in the hospital with a heart attack?"

"That's right. He's my patient now. I certainly can't say anything to him now. It would kill him. Set him back anyway."

"But look here, you've got to do something about it," Muntz said. "You can't let Kestler go on shooting off his mouth about you, not when you've got the perfect answer. It won't do your practice any good, and it won't help the rest of us either."

"Do you know what you've got to do?" Kantrovitz said solemnly. "You've got to take yourself out of this case. You tell Aptaker you feel he ought to have a regular heart man, that you don't feel—"

"Competent?" asked Cohen. "Believe me, if I thought that, I'd turn him over to a cardiologist right away. But there have been no complications. I've got him on a low-fat, high-protein diet. I'm watching his daily EKG's and enzyme tests and—"

"I don't mean that you can't handle it," Kantrovitz said. "I mean that you could tell him that so you can get out from under. Then he's no longer your patient and you're free to act."

Cohen shook his head stubbornly. "Even if he were no longer my patient, I couldn't do it. If you took him over, Ed," he challenged, "would you let me tell him he'd made a mistake on a prescription and someone had died from it?"

"No, but—"

"So what do you intend to do?" Muntz asked.

"I don't know. Just sweat it out, I guess."

Al Muntz leaned back in his chair and thrust his hands into his trouser pockets. He shook his head slowly in a kind of wonderment. "You know what, Dan? You've done it again."

"Done what?"

"Got yourself a patient that you're emotionally involved with."

But later, when he was alone with Kantrovitz, Muntz said, "You know, Ed, he's a damn fool but I can't help admiring Dan. Here he is, taking a chance on wrecking his practice to avoid hurting one of his patients. Maybe that's been his trouble all along. He believes all that stuff med school deans dish out at commencement."

"But look here, if you were in Dan's position, would you tell Aptaker?"

"Of course not," Muntz said, "but I wouldn't have let myself get in that position in the first place."

31

Mrs. Aptaker entered the rabbi's study and sat down gingerly. She looked about her at the walls lined with large leather-bound books, two of which were lying open on the desk.

"I hope I'm not interrupting your work," she said.

The rabbi smiled. "Not at all, Mrs. Aptaker." He motioned at the books on his desk. "This goes on all the time. It can wait. And how is Mr. Aptaker?"

"All right, I guess."

"And your son? What do you hear from him?"

"Arnold? You know him? He's coming home. I called him when his father got sick. He said he'd come just as soon as he winds up things in Philadelphia. It could be a matter of months before my husband gets back on his feet, so Arnold has to make arrangements."

"Of course."

"Because even if we have to sell the store, we should have someone here from the family that knows about these things, about things in a drugstore."

"Maybe he'll decide to stay for good," the rabbi suggested.

She sighed. "I don't know. Arnold didn't get along so good with his father, especially in the store. Maybe like two women can't work in the same kitchen, so two men, a father and a son, they can't get along in the same business."

"And how are you managing?"

"Well, Ross—that's McLane, the other pharmacist, he's very cooperative, but he'd like me to get another pharmacist to help out. But then when Arnold comes, we wouldn't need him."

Rose Aptaker placed the cardboard folder she had brought with her on the desk and said, "These are the letters my husband said I should show you. I looked through them before coming here. I never saw them before. My husband, you understand, he didn't like to bother me with business matters. Maybe he thought I might worry. There's a letter here that my husband wrote to your temple, a copy I mean, asking to renew his lease. It was sent out more than a month ago, and there was no answer until—until a couple of days ago, telling him he should ask Mr. Safferstein. That was the day my husband got his heart attack, Rabbi. Is that the way a temple should act? Not answer his letter and then finally send him a letter he should get a heart attack? That's religion?"

"I know nothing about it, Mrs. Aptaker, but if you'll give me a chance to read it—"

"Sure, read. But I got to get back to the store."

"If you could leave it with me—"

"Why not?" She rose to go and then changed her mind and sat down. "When I went to see my husband at the hospital this afternoon, he seemed to have a little more spirit, somehow. He was even a little excited. I think maybe it was because of your visit, something you may have said." She looked at him questioningly, and when he offered no comment, she went on, "So what I wanted to say, Rabbi, is that when you read over these letters and you see it's hopeless, it would be better if you didn't tell him right away. I mean it could wait a little while until he got stronger."

"I said nothing to your husband, Mrs. Aptaker, only that I should like to see the correspondence he had on the lease. If he jumped to the conclusion that I could do something—"

"What difference does it make?" she demanded fiercely. "If he's kidding himself, at least he's getting stronger on it."

"But he'll have to face it sooner or later," the rabbi insisted.

"So better later than sooner." She made as if to rise and then thought better of it. "I don't know if you can understand what the store means to my husband. It's not just a living; it's like an institution to him, like a college or a bank. If he should sell it now, even at a good price, his whole life would be like a failure. Sure, we made a comfortable living, but if he sells the store, then he'll be balancing the accounts in his mind and he'll see that for

168

all the time he spent there, he was working at clerk's wages. But if he can pass it on to Arnold, then it's in the family and it's still his and it doesn't make any difference how many hours a week he puts in. You know we got customers who moved to Florida ten and fifteen years ago and we still send them refills on their prescriptions."

"I think I understand, Mrs. Aptaker," the rabbi said kindly. He accompanied her to the door just as Miriam, who had been out shopping, arrived home. He introduced the two women.

"I hope your husband is feeling better," said Miriam.

Rose Aptaker shrugged her shoulders and smiled sadly.

Later, as Miriam went about preparing the evening meal, she asked, "Can you do something for them, David? She looked so unhappy."

Her husband, lounging in the kitchen doorway, shook his head. "I doubt it. Not being a member of the temple, Aptaker has an exaggerated idea of the power and authority of a rabbi. I'm afraid he's caught in one of those situations, which probably happens quite often in business, where he suffers a sizable financial loss through nobody's fault. And yet . . ."

"What is it?"

"It's funny that Kaplan didn't mention receiving Aptaker's request for a renewal on his lease. He had it for some time. I'm sure he never raised the matter at any board meeting."

"It is curious. Can you make anything of it?"

"Well, at least I can call Kaplan and ask how it happened." The rabbi went to the phone. "He should be home about now."

"What can I do for you, Rabbi?" Kaplan asked jovially when the connection was made.

"I was talking to Marcus Aptaker, the druggist in the Goralsky Block. You may have heard that he's in the hospital now with a heart attack. He tells me that he

169

wrote to the temple asking for a renewal of his lease. I wonder why you didn't mention it at any of the board meetings."

"Because it was a minor administrative matter, Rabbi. I didn't say anything for the same reason that I didn't mention the minor repair that I had made to the roof above the tailor shop. If I brought up for discussion every little item that came to my attention and that I acted on, we'd never finish."

"It was no minor matter to Aptaker, and I intend to bring it up at the meeting."

"Ah, Rabbi, you're sore because I put one over on you."

"You railroaded through the sale of the Goralsky Block. I'm going to move for reconsideration."

"What? Because I didn't happen to mention Aptaker's letter to the board?" Kaplan was incredulous.

"For that, and because it has always been the practice on important matters, especially where they involve large sums of money, to hold over the final vote on a motion for at least a week."

"You know, Rabbi, I never considered you a sore loser. You go right ahead and make a motion to reconsider. All that will happen will be that I'll beat you again."

Thinking it over, however, Kaplan decided he ought to alert Safferstein to the rabbi's intention. He called and told him of the conversation he had just had.

"What does it mean, Chet?"

"Not a thing, Billy, believe me. I've got a real solid majority. I could even defeat him on the motion to reconsider."

32

The next day Rabbi Small was driving along Route 128, that linear suburb of research laboratories, electronics firms and automated industrial plants. As he passed Goraltronics, Incorporated, he was suddenly struck by an idea. Forgetting his reason for being on Route 128 in the first place—that he was on his way to the monthly meeting of the Greater Boston Rabbinic Council—he took the next exit and made his way back to the plant.

Unused to the ways of large corporations, he listened patiently as Ben Goralsky's secretary explained that he was busy and would be occupied for the rest of the week; that he would not be available for the following week either since he was going out of town; that if Rabbi Small would tell her the nature of his business she would see about the possibility of arranging an appointment some time during the week after that.

"Can't you just tell him I'm here now?" he asked plaintively.

Her smile at his naiveté was answer enough, and he was about to turn away when Ben Goralsky came striding out of the office and saw him.

"Rabbi Small, what are you doing here? Come in." And much to the chagrin of his secretary, he put a burly

171

arm around the rabbi's narrow shoulders and steered him into his private office. Ben Goralsky was a big man with a large nose and knobby cheekbones. Though he was in his midfifties, his thick black hair showed no touch of gray, even at the temples. Seated behind his desk, he beamed affectionately at his visitor.

"Tell me what I can do for you, Rabbi."

"Well, I wanted some information about the property your father willed to the temple."

"Oh sure, what do you want to know? I see where Bill Safferstein finally got it."

"The board voted—" the rabbi broke off as he got the implication of Goralsky's remark. "You mean he tried to buy it from you?"

"That's right, from my father. He told Billy it wasn't for sale."

The rabbi smiled knowingly. "So as not to appear eager?"

Ben Goralsky looked at him sharply. "Why no. My father really didn't want to sell." He canted his head and considered. Then he laughed shortly. "Maybe that's why Safferstein came to me—because he thought my father was just being cozy."

"And what did you tell him?"

"Oh, I said I'd talk to my father about it. I gave him a statement on the property—you know, income, expenses, what it's assessed for, lease obligations, the usual. On the basis of that, he made an offer a couple of days later. It was a very good offer, so I spoke to my father about it." He shook his head. "He said he didn't care to sell."

"Why not, if the offer was a good one?" the rabbi asked.

"Well, at the time I thought it was because my father didn't like to sell land. You see, we'd bought that property years ago because we had thought of building our plant there. It was right on the Salem Road with easy access for

172

cars and trucks, but then Route One Twenty-eight opened up, and this was a better deal. In all that time, I couldn't get my father to sell the Salem Road property. But now I'm inclined to think he didn't want to sell to Safferstein because he was planning to give it to the temple."

"But couldn't he have sold the property and then given the money to the temple?" the rabbi asked.

Ben Goralsky chuckled. "And pay a capital-gains tax on the sale? Oh no, my father was too good a business-man for that."

"You say it was a very good offer. Why do you suppose Safferstein was so anxious to get that property?"

Goralsky shook his head. "I don't know. There's talk of a big apartment complex for senior citizens going up on the Salem side. That would improve the block some, but not that much."

"And can you think of why Safferstein would offer to buy the drugstore?"

"Aptaker's? He did? Hm, now that begins to make sense."

"It does?" the rabbi asked.

"Sure," said Ben Goralsky. "It means he's planning to tear down the block. It's the land he wants, but I'll be damned if I see why. There's plenty of vacant land around there."

"I'm afraid I don't follow."

"Look, Rabbi, the drugstore has a lease, and a lease is binding on all succeeding owners. If Safferstein's going to tear the place down, he has to have it free of encumbrances. Any idea what he offered for the store?"

"Only that Aptaker said it was a good price. He said Safferstein wanted it for his brother-in-law."

Goralsky laughed.

"I take it you consider the brother-in-law a figment of his imagination," the rabbi said.

Goralsky shrugged. "What else? He had to have some reason for buying a pharmacy."

"How about the leases on the other stores? Wouldn't he have to buy those, too?"

"The other stores were tenants at will," Goralsky explained. "Only the drugstore had a lease. The old lease was about to expire, and Aptaker wrote to my father and he renewed it on the same terms, ten years. I thought it was a mistake tying ourselves up for that length of time—"

"But the tenant is equally bound, isn't he?"

"Not really, Rabbi. If the tenant is a large corporation or an individual of solid financial status, then sure, he's bound as much as we are. But if it's a small man, what can we do? Suppose the drugstore decided to go out of business tomorrow, would we sue him? Or would the temple—because the lease is binding on any subsequent owner—sue him for ten years' rent?"

"I see."

"But I didn't like to argue with my father about it. Toward the end he was pretty weak."

"Yes, I remember," the rabbi said. "When I'd come to see him—"

"Ah, but that was in the afternoon or the evening, Rabbi. In the morning he was apt to be pretty lively. Of course, that's when he'd conduct his business."

"You mean he actually was engaged in business even then, after he took to his bed?"

"Oh yes," Goralsky said proudly. "He'd dictate letters and instructions every morning until almost noon. He did that right up to a few days before his death."

"You mean he had a secretary at the house?"

Goralsky chuckled. "I guess she thought of herself as his secretary. Actually, she's one of the girls from our stenographic pool. I'd send her out to the house every morning, and even if my father didn't have any business, she was someone to talk to—Alice Fedderman. Her father

174

is a member of the temple. Would you like to talk to her?"

"Why yes, if it's all right."

"Sure." Goralsky spoke into the intercom. "Rabbi Small would like to talk to Alice Fedderman from the steno pool about my father. Would you have her go to the conference room. It's free, isn't it?"

"Yes, sir." And a few seconds later: "She'll be right down."

"I'll have someone take you there, Rabbi."

She was waiting for him when he arrived, a slim girl of nineteen or twenty, heavily made up with eye shadow, liner and mascara. Her lips were coated with a kind of white glaze. She was wearing high platform shoes and a very short skirt so that her crossed legs exposed considerable thigh. Rabbi Small had a vague recollection of having seen her at various young people's functions at the temple, but then perhaps not—they all looked so much alike.

"Hello, Rabbi. They said you wanted to talk to me about old Mr. Goralsky so I took along the notebook I used when I went to see him."

"I was interested in a letter he wrote to Mr. Aptaker who has the drugstore—"

"Oh yes, about the lease." She smiled. "I remember that very well."

"Is that so? Any particular reason?" the rabbi asked.

"Well, it was just a little before—that is, toward the end, for one thing. But this letter I had to do a couple of times. It was like this." She leaned forward confidentially. "He didn't talk so good, I mean grammarwise. So he'd tell me what he wanted to say, and I'd like reword it in a business letter."

"I understand."

"We got this letter from Mr. Aptaker asking if he could have his lease renewed. So Mr. Goralsky said since he was a good tenant, he'd give him the same lease he

175

had before without any increase in rental. So I wrote the usual business letter. You know, 'In reply to your letter of the twentieth, I am instructing our attorneys to draw up a lease on the same terms as the present one. When you receive the forms, please sign both copies and return them to me for my signature.' The usual. But when I typed the letter and gave it to him to sign, he was kind of put out about the way I'd written it. I guess he was having one of his bad days. He said"—and she mimicked his heavily accented English—" 'I want you should tell him because he was a good tenant and never caused me any damage to my property and always paid his rent on time and kept up the property, I'm giving him the same lease like before and not raising him the rent.' " She favored the rabbi with a self-satisfied wink. "I took it down just the way he said it. I was going to write it that way, too, because I was kind of annoyed with him. He was a nice man, but he could also be, you know, like gross."

"Gross? Mr. Goralsky?"

"Well, you know, like picky—picky. But by the time I got back to the office, I'd cooled down; so I fixed it up a little, but I still put in about how he was a good tenant and all. He liked it, so that's the way we sent it out."

"Mr. Aptaker wrote back—"

Alice Fedderman shook her head. "I wouldn't know anything about that. I only went there a couple of days more. See?" Between thumb and forefinger she held up a couple of pages of her notebook to show how little had been written. "I was told Mr. Goralsky had taken a turn for the worse and wasn't up to giving dictation."

"You're sure no other girl was sent out?"

"Oh no. He liked me. And I liked him."

"Even though he was gross?" the rabbi asked with a smile.

"Oh, you know. I didn't mean gross like gross. I mean he was like nervous, maybe because he was so old."

Rabbi Small thanked her and refused her offer to escort him back to the office. "I'm sure I can find my way back," he said.

He merely wanted to thank Ben Goralsky for his consideration, but after they shook hands and the rabbi had turned to go, he thought of something. "You said the lawyers went out to see your father about his will. Was that because he was confined to his bed?"

"That's right, Rabbi. It was just three weeks, maybe a month, before he died." His face grew somber and reflective as he added, "I guess he knew then he was going to die." He extended his hand again, "Well, good-bye, Rabbi. I hope we've been helpful."

The rabbi smiled. "You have, Mr. Goralsky. Believe me, you have."

33

Lt. Eban Jennings sat down heavily, pulled out the lower drawer of Lanigan's desk and then, leaning back in his chair, raised his legs to rest his heels on the edge of the drawer.

"Make yourself at home," said Lanigan.

Jennings ignored the sarcasm and focused watery blue eyes on his chief as he declared solemnly, "McLane had a drugstore in Revere, and Kestler, the old man, had a chattel mortgage on it."

"So?"

"So he lost the store when Kestler foreclosed," said Jennings.

"Mm—interesting."

"Yeah." The lieutenant waited for Lanigan to digest the information. "I've heard it both ways," Jennings went on blandly. "Some of those I talked to, women mostly, said he would have lost his business anyway. That after his wife died, McLane kept a dirty store and was nasty to customers. His wife was in the store with him, and I suppose she'd be the one who would be tidying up all the time. Then when she died—"

"Sure."

"And he was always having trouble with the people he hired. I talked to one of them, a pharmacist working for the new owner. He said he was a hard man to work for, grouchy and what you might call inconsiderate."

"What kind of store is it?" the chief asked.

"It's a small neighborhood store. My guess is that his real trouble began when the big cut-rate store opened half a dozen blocks away. If he'd been popular with the customers, they wouldn't have changed to the new store, especially where his was handier."

"Don't you believe it, Eban. People will go quite a distance to save a few pennies. And then criticize the old place to justify their disloyalty," he added reflectively.

"Yeah, could be," Jennings agreed. "That was pretty much the point of view of the grocer next door. Of course, he's suffering from some new supermarket competition himself. According to him, McLane kind of let go when his wife died, but he was sure he'd have snapped out of it in time. But"—he lowered his feet to the floor and sat upright to give additional emphasis to what he was going to say—"Jake Kestler called his loan and pushed him to the wall. Now that was about a year ago."

Lanigan sat silent, his fingers drumming nervously on the arm of his chair as he digested the implications of his lieutenant's report. Jennings broke the silence. "Look, Hugh, why don't I bring in McLane for questioning?"

Lanigan did not answer immediately. He tilted back in his chair and gazed up at the ceiling. Jennings' eyes were focused on him expectantly, his prominent Adam's apple bobbling in his scrawny neck. Finally, Lanigan spoke, his face still turned upward. "Maybe it was a mistake sending you to the FBI school and assigning you last year to that course in Boston. You've taken on big-city ways, Eban, and big-city attitudes. Something like this, if it had happened in Boston, I suppose they would immediately have brought Aptaker in for questioning. A couple of cops would have gone down to his store and taken him into custody right then and there. If there were customers in the store, too bad. If he was alone at the time, he'd have to close up for the day. And then, after they questioned him, if they found they couldn't charge him, they'd let him go. Maybe they'd say they were sorry. And the poor bugger would go back to his store, happy that he'd been cleared."

He sat up straight and looked directly at Jennings. "But then he'd find out that he didn't have a store anymore. Word would have got around. Dammit, it's a drugstore. If there was the slightest suspicion that he might have made a mistake on a prescription, who'd bring in one to be filled? But this is a small town, Eban. The people here are our friends and neighbors. What's more, they vote our salaries every year at the town meeting. We can't take a chance hurting the innocent while chasing after the guilty."

"But you said yourself you were going to talk to Marcus Aptaker."

"Sure, but I wouldn't have had him picked up and brought here. I planned to drop in on him when no one was around. We would have a friendly conversation and I would explain the situation to him. Then if he made an admission, I'd charge him. Or if he didn't, if he couldn't come up with an explanation, then I'd check the whole thing through first and make sure I had an iron-clad case before I'd go ahead. I wouldn't be afraid he'd leave town."

"Well, McLane—"

"McLane is different," the chief interrupted.

"Why?"

"Because he just works there," Lanigan said. "It's not his store. It's no skin off his nose if the store is ruined. He just gets a job someplace else. And if I were to have McLane brought in, or even if I went down there and spoke to him, even if he were cleared, he'd talk. He'd complain about dumb cops every chance he got. And that's the difference: because Marcus wouldn't talk, knowing it would hurt his business. And he knows me well enough to know that I wouldn't talk."

"So what are you going to do?" Jennings asked.

"Oh, I'll manage to see McLane, but I'll try to arrange it so that it's accidental-like," Lanigan replied. "In the meantime, I want you to go back to Revere and get whatever you can on McLane. Trace him back to his baptism. And the Kestlers, too. See Captain O'Day—"

"He's retired."

"I know," Lanigan said, "but he still hangs around headquarters and he can get a lot that you couldn't. As an out-of-town cop, all they'll give you is official stuff. With him in your corner they'll open up. Because I want everything—rumors, gossip, the works. I'll work this end. I'll see Safferstein—"

"Why him?" Jennings asked.

"Because he got the pills from the drugstore, and I

180

want to check the movement of those pills right back to when they were put up."

"But look, Hugh, you start asking him questions about the pills and he'll start wondering about Aptaker's. What's to keep *him* from talking?"

"You're right. I'll have to play it cozy. I'll have to figure out some reason for seeing him, something that has no connection with the drugstore."

"Is it that time of year again, Chief?" Safferstein asked, smiling as he reached for his checkbook.

Lanigan looked puzzled. Then he remembered the last time he had come to Safferstein's office. "You mean the Policeman's Ball? Oh, we won't be around selling tickets for weeks yet. No, this is a matter of personal business."

"Let me guess. Your wife is tired of taking care of a big house where there are only two of you now, and she wants to sell and move into a modern apartment."

"Wrong again," said Lanigan, grinning. "She wants to go into business, open a store, a card and gift shop. I can't say I'm crazy about the idea, but—"

"Why not? It will keep her busy, and it could net her a little income."

"Well, these days, any extra income—"

"Sure, and I've got just the place, or I will have in a couple of months. Market Street in Lynn. What's the matter?" as Lanigan shook his head.

"She's already picked the place," said Lanigan, "She's interested in the vacant store in the Goralsky Block. I hear the temple sold it to you."

"Why there, Chief? It's not much of a location."

"It's on the Salem Road and there's lots of traffic."

"Yes, but people on their way to Boston or in the other direction, up-country, don't usually stop to buy a greeting card or a gift item. For that type store you need a lot of local traffic," Safferstein pointed out.

"Well, Amy seems to think that a lot of people come there because of the drugstore. It's been there for over half a century and in the same hands. It's a kind of institution. Even folks from my part of town go there. You shop Town-Line, don't you?"

Safferstein shook his head. "Almost never. I was in there the other night, you know, the night of the storm, because I figured all the other places would be closed, but normally I don't trade there. By the way, I want to thank you for the courtesy your man in the patrol car showed me. You know what happened, don't you?"

"Oh sure, the sergeant reported it."

"I was planning to write a note complimenting the police force. Would it do you people any good?"

The chief grinned. "It wouldn't do any harm to have a letter like that in the files, especially come town-meeting time when our budget is up for review. You know, I never really understood how you came to have those pills."

"Just that I happened to be there talking to Aptaker when the doctor called in the prescription. The other pharmacist answered the phone and asked Aptaker if they could deliver it. Aptaker said no, but I'd heard the name

182

and address—you could hear him all over the store—and since it seemed to be an emergency, I offered to drop it off."

"You knew Kestler?"

"Never met the guy, but it was on my way home, so why not?"

"You heard what happened to him?"

Safferstein nodded. "Yeah, I was over to Chet Kaplan's. I thought I'd wait until the storm lightened instead of going straight home. The doctor called Al Muntz while I was there and he told us. Tough break!"

"Yeah, well it happens all the time," Lanigan said philosophically.

"Well, about that empty store. I don't think I can rent it to you."

"Why not?" the chief asked.

"I have other plans for it."

Lanigan had all the information he needed, but he felt he ought to pursue his original approach lest Safferstein, thinking it over, might decide it was Aptaker he was really interested in. So he said stiffly, "If you're worried about my wife paying the rent—"

And Safferstein, aware of how important it was for his business that he should remain on friendly terms with the town officials, raised both hands in protest. "Believe me, Chief, it's not that."

Lanigan pressed him. "Do you have another tenant for it?"

He could lie, of course, and say that he had in fact already rented the store, but then when it turned out that he hadn't, Lanigan might feel that he had not been candid. And why shouldn't he tell him? Everything was set, and it would be common knowledge in a few days anyway. He laughed shortly. "Look, Chief, can you keep a secret?"

"Sure."

"I mean even from your wife."

Lanigan chuckled, "That's a little harder, but I do it all the time. I don't ever tell her about anything that comes into the office unless it's already public information."

"Well," Safferstein confided, "the fact is I can't rent that store to you because I'm planning to tear down the building. I own or I've got options on all the land in the area. The Goralsky Block was the last parcel. I'm going to build the biggest shopping mall in New England right there along the Salem Road."

"I see," the chief smiled. "You know, another reason the wife was interested in that store was that she figured if you took it over, you'd improve it the way you have other places around."

Safferstein smirked with satisfaction. "Just luck, Chief. I've been lucky."

"Pretty consistent though," said Lanigan. "So maybe it isn't just luck."

35

Rose Aptaker was too tired to prepare a proper meal for herself, so she boiled a couple of eggs and afterward heated up the morning's coffee. She had opened the store at half past eight and operated it herself until nine, when Ross McLane arrived. Fortunately, no one had asked to have a prescription filled. If a customer had come for a prescription, she would have had to tell them that the pharmacist would not be in until later and that they would deliver it in the afternoon.

At noon she took half an hour off and went home for a sandwich and a cup of coffee; then back to the store, where she was on her feet all day until six; then to the hospital to see her husband and to assure him that everything was fine; then back to the store until they closed. She had not felt like eating at six, but had stopped off at a coffee shop for more coffee and a doughnut, and that sustained her until she returned home. But now she was too tired to broil the lamp chops she had bought for her supper.

She heard the car pull into the driveway but was too tired to move. Only when the doorbell rang did she go to the door. It was Arnold. He was flanked on either side by a large suitcase. "I'm here, Mom," he announced.

"So you're here," she said. She offered her cheek as he embraced her and then stood aside for him to enter.

It was not as he had expected it would be. As he drove through the night, he had imagined her hugging and kissing him, murmuring "Thank God, you've come back to us." He concealed his disappointment, however, and brought his bags into the hallway. It occurred to him that they had never been demonstrative with each other and that it did not mean that he was not welcome.

"How's Dad?" he asked.

"He's all right. Have you eaten?"

"Yeah, I ate on the road."

"So a cup of coffee, maybe?"

"All right."

"It's from this morning," she warned. "I cook up a whole pot in the morning and then—"

"Fine. As long as it's hot. This morning's coffee will be fine."

His mother turned up the flame. The coffee did not

take long to become hot, since she had heated it for herself only a little while before. She poured him a cup and sat down heavily opposite him.

"You're tired," Arnold said.

"Yes, I'm a little tired. I've been on my feet the whole day. It was busy today, thank God."

He sipped at his coffee in silence and then he pushed it away from him.

"You don't like it," she declared.

"I like it fine but I've been stopping on the road every couple of hours, drinking coffee. I guess maybe I've had too much. Now what's the story on Dad?"

She took a deep breath. "What can I tell you? He's had a heart attack. You know what that means. He's got to take it easy. And he's not supposed to fret or worry. That's what the doctor says. How a man in business lying flat on his back while his wife tries to operate the store is not going to worry he doesn't say. When I go to see him, the first thing he asks me is how's things at the store, and each time I tell him we're getting along fine. So who's kidding who?"

"Well, I'm here now, and he can relax. I'll go see him tomorrow and tell him that I'm here for as long as he needs me. I moved out of my apartment and sold my furniture. I brought all my stuff."

"It will help, I'm sure. But——"

"But what?"

Suddenly, the anxiety and the weariness were too much for her. Although she compressed her lips to keep from sobbing, she could not prevent the tears from streaming down her cheeks.

"Aw, Ma. What's the matter?"

She wiped away the tears with her fingertips and then abruptly went to the hallway table where she had left her pocketbook, to get a handkerchief.

186

"What is it, Ma? What's the trouble? Is there something you're holding back from me?"

"I—I know I shouldn't say anything. I should be thankful, but—" Suddenly her vexation overcame her weakness. "Look at you," she cried out. "You'll go to your father and tell him that you'll take charge. And he'll see you with the hair and the beard and the patched clothes, where he is so neat and clean. You'll tell him he can relax now, like the doctor tells him he shouldn't worry. That's all he'll need to relax is your telling him."

"Look here, my beard and the way I dress, that's my business."

"Sure, I know. The beard you'll tell me is for religion. And the clothes, that's for freedom and independence. And the boots? My grandfather, I got a picture of him from the old country, and he was wearing boots, but it was because of the mud and the snow. And if your father tells you he doesn't want you working in the store dressed like that and with a beard, you'll come home maybe and tell me that you gave him a chance and that he didn't take it and that you're going back to Philadelphia. Or maybe he'll think of how hard I'm working and won't say anything but just lie there and worry about it."

"All right, all right," he shouted. "I'll go to the barber tomorrow and tell him to cut my hair like a bank clerk. I've got regular clothes; I'll put them on. Even a white shirt. I'll go there in a tuxedo if you like."

"Oh, Arnold. It'll be like medicine to him."

36

In response to his ring, Leah opened the door the width of the chain and stared at him. Then she recognized him. "Akiva!" She closed the door enough to slide the chain off and then, opening it wide, she asked, "Why didn't you call me first?"

"I didn't want to wait. Besides, I was afraid you'd—you'd—"

"Refuse if I had a chance to think about it? Suppose I was having company? Did you think of that?"

"I thought I'd take my chances. I felt lucky."

She led him into the living room, but she was still not mollified. "And they might think I was the kind of woman men could come to see by just ringing the bell. Did you think of that?"

"No, I didn't," Akiva retorted crossly. "I didn't think of anything except that I wanted to see you. Look," he pleaded, "I'm clean-shaven, my hair is cut, I'm all dressed up like a regular square and I wanted you to see me."

"All right, I see you."

"Do you like it?" he asked eagerly.

"It's an improvement. Even if you couldn't spare the time to phone before coming, why didn't you call to say you were going away?"

"I—I left kind of sudden. Something came up. But I'm back now."

"For good?"

"I don't know," he said. "Maybe you heard? My father got sick—"

"Yes, I heard about it. I'm sorry." Leah did not bother to say that she had dropped into the store on the chance that he might be there.

"I'll tell you the truth," he said earnestly. "When I left, I wasn't planning to come back. Then my mother phoned to tell me what happened."

"I see. And you changed your style, you shaved because of what I said about beards?"

He was tempted to lie, to say he had indeed done it for her. But what he had appreciated most about their short acquaintance, what he had thought of on the long ride back to Philadelphia and again the many times he had remembered her during the week that followed was the feeling that he could be completely honest and candid with her. So he said, "No, I did it for my father."

"Oh?"

"He's my father," he said. "I owe it to him, Leah. You just kind of suggested you didn't like it, but with him it would bother him that somebody like me, like I was, was operating his precious store. And it's not good for him to be bothered. I owe him that much."

She was momentarily disappointed and yet strangely reassured. "How is he?"

"I went to see him this morning right after I had my hair cut. I was dressed like this, like I am now. He was lying there just looking up at the ceiling and he seemed tired and sort of washed out. I don't remember ever seeing him that way before. But when he saw me, he perked right up and started to give me instructions—on what to do in the store. And I just listened." He saw that she did not understand. "What I mean is I didn't argue with him, I

189

just listened and agreed. You see, it wasn't anything very important. It never was. Just his special way of billing, or putting up merchandise or typing labels." He grinned. "I felt good about it, too, like I'd done a mitzvah."

"And what would your rebbe have said about it?" she teased.

He considered the question seriously. "Well, most of the chavurah probably would tick me off for shaving—those who don't have beards use a depilatory or an electric razor, which is supposed to be all right for some reason—especially for shaving and having my hair cut on the Sabbath and for working on the Sabbath, but the rebbe himself would approve, I think. He's not like the ordinary chasidic rebbe. He's very modern. I know it's all right because I felt good about it. Sometimes, you feel good about something you do for yourself, like lying in the sun, or when you make it with a girl and it's just right, but when you do something for someone else—not just a favor, but something you've got to give up like a sacrifice—then you feel good in a special way."

She asked how long he planned to stay in town and he said, "I don't know. My mother said it would be three months before my father could go back to work. I'll probably be here at least that long. I gave up my apartment in Philly."

"Was your job there so much better than you can do around here?"

"No. I settled in Philly because I'd gone to school there, so I knew the city. And then again, I wanted to be far enough away from home to feel free."

"And now?"

He grinned. "Well, how free was I if my mother could bring me back here with a phone call?"

Leah pressed him. "So you might stay?"

He shrugged. "I might have to—and I might want to."

Aware that his mother would probably not go to sleep

190

until he got home, he left at eleven. At the door, he said, "I'll probably be working every night except Sundays. By the time I get through, it's too late to go anywhere—to dinner or a movie, but I'd like to see you—"

"I don't go out much because of Jackie. You can stop by when you get through if you like."

He had had enough experience to realize how unusual was her honesty. "Expect me," he said.

37

The phone rang, and Rabbi Small reached for it. "David? Mort Brooks. Can you give me a lift to the temple? I got a flat."

"All right, but don't keep me waiting."

"I'll be out front when you drive up."

Sure enough, the Hebrew school principal was waiting on the curb as the rabbi, with squealing brakes, brought his car to a halt. "When are you going to trade in this junk heap?" Brooks asked derisively as he climbed into the passenger seat.

The rabbi glanced at the sporty convertible parked in the driveway and replied pointedly, "I'm giving you a lift and not you me."

"A flat tire can happen to anybody." Brooks was wearing flared slacks and a houndstooth sport jacket. His collar was open at the throat, which was encircled by a silk neckerchief knotted at one side.

"You going to a garden party?" the rabbi asked sourly.

"Right. After Sunday school. At least, a cookout." He twisted in his seat to catch a glimpse of himself in the rearview mirror and bestowed a self-satisfied smirk at his reflection. "Sundays I think of as my day of rest and I like to dress for it."

"Not Saturdays?"

"Saturdays, too. With modern tensions and pressures, you need two days a week."

"What tensions are you under?" the rabbi asked.

"Are you kidding? With a schoolful of spoiled brats and their doting mothers and fathers to contend with?" He shuddered delicately. "When I get home, I'm a positive wreck. Caroline is after me to give it up."

"And go back to the theater?"

"Right," Brooks said. "But you know how things are on Broadway these days. Women are so impractical." He slewed around to face the rabbi. "And they're not the only ones, David. I have it from the grapevine that you're planning to challenge the board on their vote last week to sell the Goralsky Block. That's not very practical, not practical at all."

"This grapevine of yours—"

"You mean it isn't true?"

"Oh, it's true enough," the rabbi said. "I just wonder how this grapevine works."

Brooks smiled. "You told Kaplan and he told various members of the board, which includes my neighbor Cy Feinstone. It was a unanimous vote, so do you think you're going to change it?"

"It was unanimous," said the rabbi, "because Kaplan railroaded it through. It doesn't mean there was no opposition. I know how these things work. A vote is taken and then someone says, 'Let's make it unanimous,' so they vote again and it comes out unanimous."

"Don't kid yourself, David. Cy normally doesn't vote with Kaplan, but he voted for this. Why? Because it's a natural. What does the temple want with a block of stores? It's just a lot of trouble. And here someone comes along and offers them a terrific price. Naturally, they're going to take it."

"But they also voted to buy the New Hampshire property," the rabbi objected.

"Well, why not? What are they going to do with all that money around? Raise salaries? Lower dues? The mortgage is paid off. The buildings are in good shape. Some temples, I understand, set up reserve funds to draw on in case of necessity, but people feel that's just an invitation to the rabbi and the cantor and the teachers in the school to ask for more money. Besides, Kaplan very cleverly tied the two motions together in one package. The only way you could have stopped it was with plenty of political muscle. And it's even going to be harder to reverse it."

"Oh, I don't know."

"Be practical, David. Who've you got on your side? On the board, nobody except a couple of past presidents, and most of the time they don't attend meetings."

"Well, maybe not on the board, but in the congregation—"

Brooks shook his head and said pityingly, "Most of them don't even know you."

"Oh, come now."

"I mean it, David. Of course, they know who you are, but that's it. They see you only on the High Holy Days, so that's a couple of days a year. Maybe those who come to the Friday evening services regularly know you, but you never draw more than seventy-five—a hundred tops. And you've got to consider that knowing you doesn't

193

mean liking you, David. It's a fifty-fifty proposition at best, because you're not an easy man to like. You know what you really got going for you? Inertia. That's your ace in the hole. Firing a rabbi is trouble, it means taking positive action. And people are mentally and emotionally lazy. They won't fire you, but that doesn't mean they'll back you in a fight with the board. And this year, remember, it's even worse than other years."

"Why is it worse this year, Morton?"

"Because other years you could count on the Orthodox element, but that's Kaplan and his crew, and it's him you're fighting."

The rabbi smiled. "So what do you advise?"

"Don't fight them. Let it go, David. They've beaten you, so take it like a good sport. You know, let go of the rope."

"Why are you so concerned, Morton? How are you affected?"

Brooks stared at him in amazement. "I'm your friend."

"Oh."

"Besides, over the years we've adjusted to each other. How do I know what another rabbi would be like?"

As the secretary read the minutes, the rabbi counted twenty around the table in addition to himself. It was five or six more than normally attended board meetings, suggesting to him that Kaplan had been actively politicking. Even in the early days, when the board had consisted of forty-five, anyone who was interested or might be induced to become interested was elected to the board. Rarely, however, did more than fifteen attend any one meeting. Now that the board consisted of eighteen elected members, *chai,* as well as the officers and all past presidents, fifteen was still the most they could muster at a meeting, with the advantage, however, that it constituted an undisputed quorum.

Of those present, the rabbi recognized half as close associates of the president. They were on the slate that Kaplan had presented when he ran for the presidency; they attended the minyan; in all likelihood they accompanied him on the retreats in New Hampshire. He recognized several others, like Dr. Muntz and Paul Goodman, as Kaplan's personal friends even though they did not necessarily share his religious views. He did not know about the others, but he was sure that the very fact that they were unexpectedly there meant that they would certainly side with Kaplan.

"*. . . chairman of the House Committee reported that three reputable heating contractors had been contacted and invited to submit bids on . . .*"

The rabbi reflected sadly that if he were more practical, he would have called some of the members of the board, some of the past presidents like Jacob Wasserman or Al Becker or even Ben Gorfinkle to urge them to be present. Not that there was any certainty that they would side with him, but they would at least give him a sympathetic hearing.

"*. . . ruled by the chairman to be Old Business. After considerable discussion, it was voted to lay the matter on the table until the meeting prior to the Chanukah festival,*

195

at which time the board would be better able to deter-mine . . ."

He wondered if he had been wise in hinting to Marcus Aptaker at their last meeting that reconsideration of the sale was possible. Would the disappointment be all the greater for having his hopes raised? It occurred to him that since Aptaker was not a member, some of the board might consider it disloyal on his part to champion his cause against the temple. But he put the thought aside immediately. As the only rabbi in town, he was the rabbi for the entire Jewish community and not merely for that segment of it that paid his salary.

". . . Motion made and seconded that the temple purchase the Petersville property in New Hampshire, the money to be raised through the sale of the Goralsky Block to William Safferstein for the offered price of $100,000.00. The motion was voted on and passed unanimously, and the president, Chester Kaplan, was empowered to insti-tute the necessary negotiations. The meeting was ad-journed at 10:32 A.M. Respectfully submitted, Joseph Schneider, Secretary."

Chester Kaplan looked around at the board. "Correc-tions or additions?" he asked. "None? Then the report is accepted as read. Do we have any committee reports?" He looked from one to another of the committee chairmen, each of whom responded with a shake of the head.

"Nothing today, Chet. Nothing happened. We didn't hold a meeting."

"Uh-uh."

"Nothing new on the insurance situation, Paul?" he asked.

"Well, Chet, I'm waiting to hear from this guy. I'd rather wait until next week and make a full report."

"Okay. Then we move on to Old Business. Rabbi?" as he saw the hand raised.

196

"I move for reconsideration of the motion to buy the Petersville property," he said.

"Do I hear a second?"

Silence.

Kaplan's lips twitched as he strove to suppress a smile. "Since there's no second on the rabbi's motion—"

"Just a minute." The rabbi was nettled. In preparing his case, it had not occurred to him that he might not have a chance to present it. "I'd like to explain the reason for my motion to reconsider."

"That comes during discussion on the motion," the chairman pointed out, "and we can't discuss it if it hasn't been seconded."

The rabbi bit his lip in vexation. He rose. "Point of privilege then. This is a matter on which the rabbi of the congregation has a right—"

Paul Goodman, a former president, called out, "Point of order, Mr. Chairman."

"Go on, Paul."

"I should like to say, and with all due respect, that the rabbi is not an official member of this body. He attends board meetings only on the invitation of the chairman—"

"No, Paul," said Kaplan. "It's true that the rabbi attends these meetings by invitation, but when I extended the invitation at the beginning of the year, I made it plain that the rabbi is to be considered a full member during my term in office. That means he's to have all rights and privileges. But, of course," he added, "I intend to follow parliamentary law in conducting these meetings. Go on, Rabbi, I think you've got the floor."

"I was about to say that there are certain matters on which the rabbi of the congregation has rights inherent in his position. The Petersville property is for the purpose of establishing a permanent retreat. This is an extension

197

of the religious function of the temple, and that concerns the rabbi of the congregation even more than it concerns the board of directors."

"There's nothing in the motion to indicate it," said Goodman. "The motion doesn't say that the property is to be used as a retreat. Speaking for myself, I voted for it because I thought it was a good deal for the temple, but I was thinking of it more as a summer camp for the kids." He could see that the rabbi was angry, and remembering occasions in the past when he had wrangled with him, he was only too happy to add to his vexation.

The rabbi tried hard to recover his aplomb. He sat down and even managed a smile. "All right," he said, "then I move for a reconsideration of the motion to sell the Goralsky Block."

"It's the same motion," said the secretary.

The board of members grinned as they realized the cleverness of their chairman in wording the motion in such a way as to include both the purchase of the Petersville property and the sale of the Goralsky Block.

"These are two separate actions," the rabbi said. "You can't tie them together just by putting them into a single motion."

"Why not; Congress does it all the time," Goodman said. "If that's the way the motion reads, then that's the motion."

And in a whisper to a neighbor, "It looks as though the rabbi is up a tree."

Kaplan considered. "I can see a certain justice in your contention, Rabbi. I'll permit it. Do I hear a second?"

"What are we considering now?" the secretary asked. "I've lost track."

"The rabbi has moved that we reconsider the motion to sell the Goralsky Block, and in spite of the valid objection of the secretary that it is part of the motion to buy the Petersville property, I'm allowing it. Now do I hear a second?"

Again silence.

Kaplan smiled. Several grinned and winked at each other in self-approval. Paul Goodman laughed out loud.

"It looks as though the members are convinced they were right the first time, Rabbi," said Kaplan.

"Or were well drilled," the rabbi retorted. "You leave me no choice but to call for a Din Torah."

"What did he say? A Din Torah? What's a Din Torah?"

"It's like a trial. He's summonsing us like to a trial."

"How can he do that?"

"Just a minute, Rabbi," Kaplan said, his placidity somewhat dented. "Who are you calling to a Din Torah?"

"All of you, individually and collectively."

"Let me get this straight," Kaplan said. "You're planning to hold a trial or a special hearing and you're going to call us to—"

"I have no choice," said the rabbi demurely. "There has been a serious breach of *halacha*—"

"What's he talking about?"

"What's *halacha?*"

"He says we broke the law."

"What law? Is he accusing us—"

"Order, order. Let's have order, gentlemen." Kaplan banged his gavel. Taking advantage of the momentary silence, he said, "Let me get this straight, Rabbi. I know you're opposed to this. You told me so. Are you now planning to set up some kind of trial with yourself as judge and jury as well as plaintiff?"

"That is a valid objection, Mr. Chairman," the rabbi admitted. "I'm not neutral in this matter. So I plan to present the matter to the Greater Boston Rabbinic Council. I presume if they find merit in my plea, they will appoint someone, a rabbi who has standing as a Talmudist, someone like Rabbi Jacobs of Boston, perhaps, and two *dayanim* who will ask both sides to appear before them and present their views."

"Can he do that?"

"What if we don't go?"

"Then they'd notify the press and make a stink," came a whispered reply.

Kaplan looked about him and made a rapid count. Of the twenty who were present, a good dozen were his close associates who came to his Wednesday At Homes regularly and joined him in the retreats at Petersville. Of the others, some had no interest in the retreat, but considered it a good buy for the temple. As for the rest, while they had no strong convictions about the need for a retreat, they were, like Paul Goodman, solidly against the rabbi. So what did he have to fear? He faced the rabbi. "What is it that you want, Rabbi?" he asked.

"I want to be heard on this motion."

"All right, then I second the motion to reconsider," said Kaplan.

"Hey, Chet—we agreed—"

"You can't do that, Chet. You're the chairman."

"So I vacate the chair. Aaron, will you take the chair, please?" he asked of the vice-president.

"Sure, Chet."

"Mr. Chairman."

"Mr. Kaplan."

"I rise to second the rabbi's motion to reconsider," said Kaplan.

"A motion has been made and seconded to reconsider the motion to sell the Goralsky Block and buy the Petersville property," said the vice-president. "Discussion. Yes, Rabbi."

"The reason for my insistence on being heard," the rabbi began easily, "is that I feel that you are all decent, fair-minded men and will do what's right if you have all the facts. Now I think you'll all agree that if anyone

200

should respect the wishes of the testator of a will, it should be the beneficiaries, those who profit from his benevolence. Well, the temple received a valuable property from Mr. Goralsky, and I feel that the least we can do to show our appreciation is to abide by his wishes concerning it."

"If you're referring to the clause that says we should use it for a school or for a permanent residence for the rabbi—"

"No, Mr. Kaplan, I'm not concerned with that clause. I recognize that Mr. Goralsky probably would not have wanted the use of the property to be restricted that way. But to make sure, I took the trouble to see his son, Ben. He confirmed my opinion. There's no problem on that score. I'm referring to Mr. Goralsky's wishes with respect to Aptaker and the store he occupies."

"Aptaker? Who's he?" asked Goodman.

"He's the guy that runs the drugstore in the block."

"That's right, Mr. Reinhardt," said the rabbi. "He got a heart attack the same day that he received a letter from Mr. Kaplan telling him that the block was being sold and that he should apply to the new owner for the renewal of the lease he had requested. His wife thinks that's what triggered the attack."

"Oh, but you can't blame the temple for that." Paul Goodman was shocked.

"That's right," said Dr. Muntz. "You can't tell how a man is going to react to bad news—or good news either. I had a patient who had a heart attack when he heard he'd won the state lottery."

"I'm not blaming you for Mr. Aptaker's heart attack," the rabbi replied. "I'm blaming you for disregarding Mr. Goralsky's wishes and not renewing Aptaker's lease."

"When that property came into our hands, it became our property," said Kaplan, "and we were free to manage and develop it as we saw fit. Since we were going to sell it, naturally I wouldn't renew Aptaker's lease, because that could kill the sale. When the board voted to sell, I wrote to Aptaker, told him that there was a new owner, or that there would be as soon as papers were passed and suggested he apply to him for renewal on his lease. I can't be responsible for what Safferstein does once he takes over. It's a straight business deal."

"Yes, I suppose it is," the rabbi said sadly. "The temple sells the property because it is good business. And a small man like Aptaker who spent his life building up a business is tossed out on the street, and it's all right because it's business."

"It happens all the time, Rabbi," Kaplan pointed out. "You can't stand in the way of progress."

"Progress!"

Kaplan grinned. "All right, then change. You can't stand in the way of change, either."

The rabbi nodded. "Yes, in the face of change, the individual sometimes gets run over. It's all a matter of business, as you say. But is this the sort of business the temple should be engaged in? Ours is an ethical religion. Is this what an institution dedicated to that religion should do?"

"Well, speaking as a lawyer," Goodman said, "I say if it's legal, it's ethical."

"All right, Mr. Goodman, so let's consider if it's legal." The rabbi stopped and picked up a briefcase from the floor and set it on the table in front of him. "I have here the correspondence of Mr. Aptaker on the matter of the renewal of his lease, first with Mr. Goralsky and then with Mr. Kaplan. I'll pass it around later if you like, but I can summarize it for you." He drew a sheaf of papers from the case. "Here is Mr. Aptaker's request for a renewal of his lease which is due to expire in a few months. And here is Mr. Goralsky's reply." He read the letter to them. "Notice the wording; not the usual business style, is it? I asked his secretary about it. She remembered it very well because she had had to do the letter twice. The first time, she edited his dictation as she usually did to conform to normal business usage. But this time Mr. Goralsky was annoyed with her for it and insisted she should write it the way he dictated it because he wanted to show Aptaker that he appreciated the way he had dealt with him over the years. So she rewrote the letter and, perhaps a little spitefully, worded it pretty much as he gave it to her. That letter he signed, and the lawyers were notified accordingly and prepared the leases."

"Yeah, but then Aptaker got greedy," Kaplan said. "He wanted to have one of the clauses struck out, as I recall."

"That's right," the rabbi agreed. "He wrote back to say that the clause calling for him to insure his plate glass had been crossed out in the previous lease and that he'd like to have it left out of this one as well."

"And what did Goralsky say to that?" demanded Goodman.

"He didn't. He died."

"Well, I guess that was Aptaker's tough luck then," said Goodman.

"The letter to Aptaker was written after Mr. Goralsky took to his bed in the illness that finally carried him off. That's when he wrote his will, too," the rabbi pointed out.

Goodman shrugged. "So what? No mention was made of it in the will and it's what's in the will that counts."

"Not in Jewish law," said the rabbi.

"What's that?"

"What do you mean?" Kaplan demanded. "Who says so?"

"The Talmudic tractate *Gittin* says so, as well as the *Shulchan Aruch*. In Jewish law, that is to say in Talmudic law, a distinction is made in the matter of wills on the basis of the physical condition of the testator. If the testator is *bari,* that is, healthy, then the law is as the secular law: only what is in the will counts. But if the testator is *shechiv me-ra,* that is, seriously sick and confined to his bed, and even more if it is a terminal illness as in Mr. Goralsky's case, then the law requires that his wishes are to be carried out even if not stated in the will. The reason for this special exception to the law is that it serves to give the dying man peace of mind in his last days. Now, it was clearly Mr. Goralsky's wish that Aptaker be permitted to renew his lease, so according to Jewish law, it has the same force as though it were so stated in the will."

"Yeah, but how were we expected to know that?" Goodman asked.

"You are not, which is why you are expected to consult with the rabbi of the congregation," said the rabbi sweetly.

"No, I mean what Goralsky intended for Aptaker."

"Ah, because Aptaker mentioned it in his letter to the temple. Let me read it." He selected a paper from the folder and then pushed his eyeglasses up on his forehead to see more clearly. "Here it is. 'Shortly before his death Mr. Goralsky agreed to renew my lease on the same terms and was kind enough to say that he was glad to do it because he considered me a good tenant as per enclosed letter.' And that's a copy of the letter I just read you."

The board members stirred uneasily in their seats, casting glances at Kaplan as though looking to him for direction. Dr. Muntz spoke for the first time. "Then are you saying, Rabbi, that the temple is bound by Talmudic law to honor Aptaker's request for renewal because that's what Mr. Goralsky wanted?"

"That's exactly what I'm saying, Doctor." The rabbi looked about him triumphantly.

Kaplan bestirred himself. "Just a minute, Rabbi. I'm

no Talmudist, but my father-in-law was, and Edie and I lived with him for a few years when we were first married and I was going to law school. We had a lot of discussions about law in general, and as I recall, he said that where there was a difference between Talmudic law and the law of the country, it was the country law that applied."

The rabbi nodded. *"Dina de-malchuta, dina.* The law of the land is the law."

"Well then . . ." Kaplan sat back in his chair, a smirk of satisfaction on his face.

"But the principle is severely restricted," said the rabbi with a smile. "Some rabbis hold that it should be applied only in those matters where the administration of the country alone is concerned, as in taxation. Obviously, it could not have complete application or the Talmud, the Oral Law, which like the Written Law, the Torah, we believe to be the word of God, would be completely invalidated. No, no, it's only where our law runs counter to the secular law, where it is in actual disagreement with it, where something we consider legal is actually illegal according to secular law, that the principle applies, and that for obviously purely practical purposes."

"Give us a for-instance, Rabbi," Dr. Muntz suggested.

"All right. Since we're talking about wills, I'll give you an example from the laws of inheritance. If a man dies intestate, then according to secular law in our country, his estate is divided between his surviving wife and his children, male and female, who share equally. In Jewish law, however, the estate is shared only by the male children, with the firstborn taking a double portion. The maintenance of the unmarried daughters and their dowries are charges on the estate, however, and take precedence over the inheritance of the sons. Obviously, in a matter of this sort, it would be the secular law that would apply. On the other hand, consider the case of

205

a woman getting a divorce from the secular courts. By secular law, she is free to remarry. But not in Jewish law until she has obtained a Jewish divorce, a *get*. Here, the Jewish law is not contrary to the secular law; it is additional to it. Similarly, in the present instance, both the Jewish law and the secular law are interested in having the wishes of the testator carried out. For administrative reasons, obviously, and to prevent interminable litigation, the secular law requires that his wishes be expressed in a will, and that what is not stated in the will is not binding on the heirs. The Jewish law is in agreement, except in the case of the *schechiv me-ra,* the sick, dying man. Here, we say, for the sake of his peace of mind in his last days, we will consider his wishes binding even if he does not get around to having them spelled out in the will."

"But that's just your interpretation, Rabbi," Kaplan said doggedly. "As I see it, we have a right to follow the secular law, especially where the money from the sale of the property is going to be used for a truly religious purpose, for the revival of religion—"

"Religion!" The rabbi was scornful. "Religion with us is ethical conduct. You are an observant Jew, Mr. Kaplan. You pray daily with the phylacteries. You kiss the mezzuzah that is affixed to the lintel of your door when you pass it. But what are these if not reminders to walk in the way of the Lord? If they are not that, then your piety, your meticulous observance of the ceremonials is just so much mumbo jumbo. 'What to me are your sacrifices?' the prophet said. 'Your Sabbaths and New Moons, my soul hateth. . . . Rather, cease to do evil . . . seek justice, relieve the oppressed.' " Warmed by his own rhetoric, he went on, his voice rising, "You may be reviving religion up there in your retreat in the woods, but it's not the Jewish religion. And if this is the direction in which our temple is turning, I want no part of it."

As if to punctuate the rabbi's exhortation, a bell rang

throughout the building, startling the men in the room. It was the bell signaling the end of the Sunday-school session.

The secretary looked at his watch in disbelief. "Jeez, it's twelve o'clock. Look, I've got to take my kid home. The wife raises hell if we're late." He slapped his notebook closed and rose from his chair.

"Yeah, me too."

Kaplan raised his hands to stop what threatened to become a general exodus. "Look, men, we can't leave it like this. We've got to—"

"Lay it on the table until next week."

"Just a minute, just one minute. You're acting like a bunch of kids. Let's do this in an orderly fashion. Somebody make a motion."

"All right. I make a motion that we lay the rabbi's motion for reconsideration on the table."

"Second."

"Rabbi? All right with you?"

"Well, I feel there should be more discussion—"

"Look, Chet, on an important matter we always hold it over for a week at least."

"You didn't on the original motion that I'm asking you to reconsider," the rabbi observed.

"Can I say something?" Dr. Muntz called out. "The way I see it, the rabbi thinks Aptaker ought to get his lease renewed. All right, how do we know Bill Safferstein won't renew it? If he renewed it, then everything is okay, *halacha*-wise, isn't it, Rabbi?"

"He won't," said Kaplan. "I know he won't."

"It won't do any harm to ask him, will it?"

"All right, so I'll ask him, but I know he will not agree."

"Then I make a motion that we lay this matter on the table until our chairman has a chance to speak to Safferstein about Aptaker's lease."

"Second the motion."

"All in favor, say aye. Oppose, nay. The ayes have it. Now I'll have a motion to adjourn. Paul?"

"I'm not making a motion to adjourn, Chet," Goodman said. "I will if you want me to, of course. I asked for the floor because I think the rabbi ought not to be present next week when we discuss this matter. I don't think it should be a motion—"

"Why shouldn't the rabbi be here?" Muntz asked. "Seems to me since he brought it up—"

"Because he's practically accused all of us of having broken the Jewish law on this matter and said he was going to call all of us—'individually and collectively,' he said—to a Din whatyamacallit. Okay, so he's on one side, and we're on the other. He's the accuser, and we're like the defense. Well, common sense would dictate that you don't have the accuser present at a meeting of the defense."

"Now, Paul—"

"I think there's some merit in what Mr. Goodman says," said the rabbi. "I think I should absent myself from the meeting. I have made my position clear, and it is up to you to decide what you're going to do about it. I don't mind waiting a week."

"Just a minute. There's no meeting next week," said Goodman.

"Why not?"

"The Sisterhood Fair."

"Oh yeah. So it will be the week after. All right with you, Rabbi?"

"If I can wait a week, I guess I can wait two," said the rabbi.

39

Edie Kaplan could never understand what her friends found to marvel at in her housekeeping. She kept a kosher kitchen with two sets of dishes, one for meat and the other for dairy products, because for her it was the normal way. Her father had been a sexton in a large synagogue in Boston, and a sexton is expected to be a pious man, strictly observant of the regulations. He not only had to supervise the maintenance of the building, but he also had to make the necessary arrangements for each of the services, lead the daily prayers, read the Scroll and even spell the cantor on occasion.

Edie was raised in a household where the idea of eating meat and dairy products from the same set of dishes was as unthinkable as eating from the floor. As for eating both at the same meal, she found the thought positively repulsive. Just reading a recipe which called for the use of butter or milk in preparing a meat dish gave her a queasy feeling in the pit of her stomach.

She knew, of course, that other people ate things like pork and lobster, but for her they were as alien and outlandish as snails or snakemeat or fried termites, which some people also ate. Nor did she think her eating habits constituted a sacrifice that she was making for religious reasons, as Catholics eat fish on Friday. Intellectually, she knew that the foods she ate were permitted and the foods she did not eat were considered taboo according to her religion, but in point of fact, hers was a pure gut reaction. She could not have swallowed one of the forbidden foods, and if forced to, she would have retched. When the Kaplans dined out with friends, she always ordered fish, and if one of the company ordered meat and then more particularly buttered a roll to eat it with, she would tend to wince and look away.

"But isn't it awfully complicated, Edie, having two sets of everything? Don't you get them mixed up?"

She would shrug and say, "When we were in Israel we saw the Bedouins sitting on the ground, all of them eating from a common dish, and just with their hands. Eating at a table, each person using a separate dish and a knife and fork must have seemed complicated to them."

Edie had married Chester while he was still a student at law school, and for several years they had lived with her folks. It was not uncongenial, but her husband chafed at the necessity. After passing the bar, some of his friends had taken jobs with the city as assistant district attorneys, with insurance companies, with large law firms. Instead, Chester had elected to go into private practice, but clients were not forthcoming.

Edie had faith in him, however, and so did his father-in-law, who would say, "Don't worry, Chester. Have faith in God, and everything will be all right."

"You mean He'll send me clients?" Kaplan gibed.

"I'm sure ambulances He won't chase for you, Chester," his father-in-law said, "and crimes He won't arrange so you can defend the criminals. But if you pray, you'll be satisfied. When I was a young man, I wanted to be a rabbi and I studied for it, but one thing or another prevented. But I didn't lose faith so I got what I really wanted."

"But you became a sexton, not a rabbi."

"True. But what did I really want? At first, I wanted to be a rabbi because of the honor. Later, when I was older and more mature, I wanted to be a rabbi because I thought I would like the life; to study, to advise and influence people in the right way, to teach. So this is just exactly what I do now. I have time to study, I teach a group of men Talmud and most of the time I'm the voice of the congregation when I lead the prayers in the daily services. And I've outlasted three rabbis at the synagogue. Every one of them was so busy with meetings and committees and preparing little speeches that he never had time for study or even to always come to the daily minyan. In the old country, of course, it was different—different for the rabbi and different for the sexton. But we are not in the old country. We are here. And here I am doing what I really wanted to do."

"So why doesn't it happen to me? I go with you to the minyan every morning and every evening and—"

"But one must pray," his father-in-law said.

"So what do I do? Read the newspapers?" Chester asked.

"Like most people, you say the words. It must be in your mind."

In the course of time, things began to improve for Edie's husband. Clients came, in part from contacts he had made in the synagogue, and Edie and Chester were finally able to move into their own apartment. Secretly, he was convinced that it was his faith that was responsible for his success. He did not publicize it, however, because faith was out of fashion, and his contemporaries would have regarded him as odd. As it was, they tended to explain his regular attendance at the synagogue as a mild eccentricity, or as something he did to please his father-in-law or even because it was a good way of getting clients.

When Leah was born, they decided that a city apartment was no place to bring up children and moved to Barnard's Crossing. Chester became a member of an Orthodox synagogue in nearby Lynn and attended the daily minyan regularly. The Sabbath, however, presented something of a problem. The synagogue was a good five miles from his house, too far to walk, and riding was taboo. He discussed the problem with Edie. "I could go to a hotel Friday afternoon and—"

She shook her head. "Then you'd miss the Sabbath meal at home. According to my father, that's more important than going to *shul*. You have to use common sense. Like once, the electricity went off in the synagogue just before the Friday evening services. For some reason the janitor wasn't around. My father knew what to do. It was a fuse that had blown. But to change it meant working on the Sabbath. He thought of going into the street in the hope of seeing a passing Gentile and asking him to fix it, but then he worried that something might happen. He's always been a little afraid of electricity. On the other hand, what would happen when the people arrived and found the synagogue in darkness? So even though it was work and forbidden on the Sabbath, he changed the fuse himself."

"But I can't just ride up to the synagogue on Saturday."

"So park a block away and walk from there," Edie advised.

When Jacob Wasserman started an organization for building a temple in Barnard's Crossing, Chester Kaplan joined as a matter of course, but manifested little interest since it was going to be a Conservative synagogue. However, when their daughter Leah was old enough to attend the religious school, he decided to send her to the one attached to the Barnard's Crossing temple rather than make elaborate arrangements to drive her to the school connected with the Lynn synagogue. As a result, he became more involved with the local temple and correspondingly less with the synagogue in Lynn. While there were things that he missed, there were also compensations. As a highly observant and religiously knowledgeable Jew, Chester belonged to a small elite group in the local temple while in the Lynn synagogue he was only one of many. As a result, he was accorded a special respect.

Shortly after Leah was divorced, her father began the Wednesday At Homes and the retreats in New Hampshire. Edie was not enthusiastic about either, but she did not push her views, vaguely sensing that Chester's new interest had something to do with the divorce, that it was a reaction to the bad luck that had been visited on their daughter, a special religious exercise for having fallen from grace.

Edie was pleased when her husband was elected president of the temple, but only mildly, having grown up in a household where the president of the synagogue was frequently viewed as the enemy or, at the very least, the opposition. When he began to develop plans for a permanent retreat, she showed little interest.

"But how about the effect on the members of the congregation?" Chester said. "It will give them a chance to work at their religion, to make it more meaningful."

"Funny, I never thought of it as work," Edie replied. "There are rules, and everything is spelled out. You always know what to do. So where's the work?"

When she learned that the rabbi was opposed to the retreat, Edie was disturbed, but her husband was so enthusiastic about the project that she did not argue with him. However, when after the meeting she heard him on the phone explaining to Safferstein that there was nothing to worry about, that the rabbi was the only opposition and that he had no doubt that the move to reconsider would be defeated, she could not remain silent.

"It's not good, Chet," she said. "My father had dealings with lots of rabbis over the years. Some he liked and some he didn't like so much. With some he discussed and with some he argued, because he was a learned man and he knew the Talmud as well as any of them did. But when he asked a rabbi a point of law, he accepted his decision. You don't fight with a rabbi, Chet. When you call him in on a decision, you accept his judgment."

"But I didn't call him in on this. He's forcing himself into the issue."

"Same thing, Chet. If you ask him, you accept what he says. And if he feels that it's a matter that pertains to him, you also have to accept his decision. No good will come from this, Chet, believe me."

40

Except for his brief visits to the hospital to see his father, Akiva spent every free minute with Leah. Not only would he drop by at night after closing, but on those mornings when it was McLane's turn to open, he would run over after breakfast to have coffee with her. Occasionally, when his hours at the store permitted, he would pick her up and drive into Boston for lunch at a kosher restaurant. He never phoned in advance but merely arrived at her house. He always assumed she would be there and would want to see him.

"Why don't you phone first?" she asked plaintively. "Suppose somebody is visiting me?"

"Like yesterday morning?"

"You were here yesterday? My mother—"

He grinned. "Sure, I was here. But I saw a car in the driveway and drove on."

"But why couldn't you—"

Akiva put his hands on hers. "Do you mind, Leah? Does it bother you? Because it does something nice for me. It makes me feel that I'm home."

"You mean here in this house?"

"No, I mean where you are, wherever you happen to be."

Rose Aptaker wondered, of course, but after her experience the last time he came home, she was careful not to question him. He might resent it as an invasion of his privacy.

She did question him, however, when she saw him reciting his prayers in the morning. "Don't you go to the minyan in the temple anymore?"

"Well, in the morning I'd rather have the extra sleep and in the evening I'm usually at the store." His real reason was that Leah's father was sure to be there, and he was embarrassed at seeing the father while he was intimate with the daughter.

Akiva did not discuss the future with Leah, what his plans were or her place in them. But after the first week, he said with disarming casualness, "I told my mother about us."

"Oh? And what did she say?"

"She wanted to know if you were a nice girl, what she would call a nice girl."

"And what did you say?"

He grinned. "I told her you were a slut who had got her hooks into me and was pressing me to marry her and that I couldn't see any way out."

"M-hm. Did you tell her about Jackie?" Leah asked.

"I did. She was naturally ecstatic at this proof of your fertility—"

"Seriously," she pleaded.

Akiva sobered immediately. "All right, seriously then. My mother didn't actually throw a fit, probably because she's so involved with my father right now, but she was —er—"

"Upset? Disappointed?"

"All of that and then some," Akiva said.

"Because of Jackie?"

"And your being divorced didn't help any. You've got to understand, Leah, that—"

"Oh, I understand," she said bitterly. "My mother would react the same way if the situation were reversed."

"Well, she'll get over it," Akiva said philosophically.

"Will she?"

"Of course she will. She'll have to."

"Maybe if you had waited," Leah suggested. "It's been such a short time."

"You wait until you're sure. I'm sure now. Aren't you?"

"Yes, but . . . are you going to tell your father?" she asked.

"My mother will probably tell him," he said, smiling faintly. "She was on her way to the hospital when I sprang it on her. Maybe the old man will take it better."

41

It was Marcus Aptaker's first day out of bed. It was demonstrable progress, and he was naturally euphoric.

"Oh, you're sitting up, Marcus," Rose greeted him. "Did the doctor say you could?"

"For meals and a little while afterward," he said with smug satisfaction. "Tomorrow for a little longer, and in a couple of days I'll be allowed to walk around the bed. I could be out of here in a week, but of course I'll be confined to the house for a while."

"That's nice, Marcus."

Her reaction seemed to lack the warmth and enthusiasm he expected. In fact, as he studied her, she appeared unusually subdued. "Is something wrong?" he asked.

"Wrong? Of course not."

"Tell me, Rose. What's happened? Did something happen at the store?"

"That's all you ever think of is the store."

"Then there is something wrong. Arnold?"

She could not contain herself any longer. "Oh Marcus, he's seeing a girl," she announced tragically.

"So?"

"But it's serious. He wants to get married."

"Well, that's normal. He's twenty-eight. It's time he

217

got married. Maybe the responsibility will settle him."

"Oh, it will settle him all right," she said bitterly. "She has a child, a five-year-old boy."

"A widow?" he asked cautiously.

"Worse, Marcus. Divorced!"

"I see. An older woman maybe?"

"No," she admitted. "She must be Arnold's age. She went to high school with him."

"So she's from Barnard's Crossing. Do we know her?" he asked.

She delivered the clincher. "She's Kaplan's daughter."

"Kaplan?"

"The president of the temple who wrote you the letter."

"Then at least we know she's from a good family," he said reasonably. "I don't know him personally, but the chances are they wouldn't make a man president of a synagogue if he weren't a decent person."

"It doesn't bother you? Here you're in the hospital because of him, and it doesn't bother you that your son wants to marry his daughter?"

"You'd like me to be bothered, Rose?" he asked quizzically. "He wrote the letter because the board of directors voted it. I'm sure it was nothing personal. How could it be when he doesn't even know me?"

"And that the girl is divorced and has a son?" she persisted.

He shook his head sadly. "It's not like it used to be, Rose. Nowadays, it doesn't mean anything. Half the marriages end in divorce. Your own sister's daughter got divorced, and she has two kids."

"But she's a nice girl and her husband was impossible."

"So maybe this girl is a nice girl, and maybe her husband was impossible."

"If she were a nice girl, she wouldn't agree to marry him after just a week."

He shrugged his shoulders. "That's the way young

218

people are these days. Once they make up their minds, they go ahead. Who knows? Maybe it's better that way. Your niece went around for over a year before she even announced her engagement. And then after the two kids, she decided he was impossible. So you can make a mistake even if you wait."

"But—"

"When Arnold comes here tonight, I'll talk to him," her husband said. "I'll ask him about the girl, about her child, what his plans are. If I like what I hear, I'll try to help him."

"What do you mean you'll help him?"

"If he's serious, if he wants to settle down, I'll work out some arrangement for him to take over the store."

42

Chief Lanigan's problem of how to meet with Ross McLane was settled by a rookie patrolman, the newest recruit to the force. It was the young officer's first day in uniform, and he was burning with zeal for law and order, when he spotted McLane's car parked outside the drugstore and issued a parking ticket. McLane came rampaging into the police station later that afternoon and shook the ticket under Chief Lanigan's nose. "Now look here, Chief, I always put my car in the parking lot, but some salesman took my usual place, and when he pulled out I was busy in the store and I didn't have a chance to move it."

Lanigan took the ticket, noted the officer's name on the bottom and smiled. "Come on in, and we'll talk about it." He turned and led the way to his office. When they were seated, the chief explained, "It's a new man, and naturally he's conscientious. Actually, we haven't issued a ticket in that area for months. Normally, we don't except during the summer months when traffic is heavy there and cars go scooting by at high speed."

"Well, how about this ticket?" McLane demanded.

"Oh, I guess we can arrange so you won't have to pay the two bucks. Tell me, what do you hear of Marcus? How's he getting along?"

"All right. I was up to see him the other day and he was out of bed and sitting in an armchair. Looked pretty good, too."

"That's fine. How are you managing at the store?"

"Not bad now that Arnold is here," McLane said. "I'm working the same hours I did when Marcus was there. But that first week, when I was all alone, it was murder. I'd get to the store at nine and work till ten at night. Of course, Mrs. Aptaker would open, and lots of times it wasn't too busy and I'd go out and take a breather for fifteen, twenty minutes, but—"

"Marcus was lucky he had you there. Lots of men wouldn't have stood it," said Lanigan.

"Well, I tell you, Mark is decent. When I lost my store, he offered me a job right away. There was a lot of talk around that I'd been hitting the bottle, but he had confidence in me, and I appreciated it."

"And were you?"

"Was I what?" asked McLane.

"Were you hitting the bottle?"

"Hell, no. Look, I'd take a drink every now and then

220

same as anybody else. When I lost my—when my wife passed away, I'd stop at the tavern around the corner because—well, because I was going home to an empty house. Maybe that's how the story got started, but all I had was one or at the most, two. And I wasn't hiding it. I didn't take a bottle to bed with me. Just a drink at the local bar."

Lanigan shrugged. "What difference does it make how much you actually drink? If your customers think you're a lush and stop coming in, then you were drinking too much even if you only took a nip once in a blue moon. It lost you your store, didn't it?"

"No such thing. I lost my store because I was pushed to the wall."

"Aw cummon."

"It's the truth, Chief. You know that guy Kestler, the old geezer that died recently. He had a chattel mortgage on my store and he called it. If he'd given me some time, I could've worked it off. But no, he wanted that store because he had a chance to sell it at a good price."

"So Kestler called your mortgage?" Lanigan smiled. "I guess you didn't feel too bad when he passed on then."

"You want to know something funny? He got a prescription filled with us the very night he died. Dr. Cohen, Dan Cohen, he called it in and I took it on the phone. When I heard it was for Kestler, I thought I'd see him in hell before I'd fill out a prescription for *him.* But do you want to know something? When I heard he was dead, I felt sorry for the old bugger."

"But you did fill it out, didn't you?" asked Lanigan easily.

"I did like hell. I gave it to young Aptaker and told him to do it. As a matter of fact, I was working on one that a guy was waiting for, and he'd volunteered to deliver the Kestler prescription, so—"

"Young Aptaker? Marcus?"

"Hell no. He's older than I am. I mean Arnold."

"But I thought Arnold came to work just last week."

"That's right, but he was up here visiting that day. We were busy as hell on account of the storm, and he came in to lend a hand with the prescriptions."

"You mean he worked just that night?" the chief asked.

"Uh-huh, he came in like he owned the place. He goes right to the prescription room in the back and says, 'I'm Arnold Aptaker. I'll give you a hand.' I looked at Marcus, who was out front, but he just smiled kind of proud and didn't say a word. So I started to show him around, you know, how the place was organized. But these young guys, you can't tell them anything. He says, 'I know, I know,' so I let him fumble around and by God first thing I know he knocks over a bottle of cough syrup. And then starts to clean it up with paper towels. That stuff is sticky. Well, anyone else I would've blown my stack, but this was Mark's son. He was so pleased and proud to have him there, I didn't say a word but just got the mop and cleaned up. After that Arnold settled down and was a real help with the pile of prescriptions we had, and we finished a lot earlier than I thought we would. I was hoping he'd stay on, because it's a little heavy for two pharmacists, but the next day Mark said he'd gone to Philadelphia."

"But now he's back for good?"

"I guess he plans to stay until his daddy gets back on his feet. I don't know if he'll stay after that. You know how these young fellows are." He glanced at his watch. "Hey, I got to get back. We start to get busy now. About that ticket—"

"Don't worry," said Lanigan affably. "I'll take care of it."

43

It was her mother Leah told, because her father was not home and she couldn't wait for him or keep it in any longer. "His name is Akiva—"

"Akiva? Spanish?"

"No, Akiva is his first name. You know, after the famous Rabbi Akiva, the one who—"

"Then his folks must be terribly religious," said Edie.

"I haven't met them yet, but I understand they're not. You see, it's his own name. I mean, he chose it for himself." Leah finally got the story told, editing it a little along the way. How she had met Akiva quite accidentally when he brought Jackie across the road from the beach and it turned out she knew him "because he used to come from around here." How he had come back that night because of the terrible storm and his concern for their safety— hers and Jackie's. "He had this long beard and I joked about it and told him I didn't like it." And then how she had not heard from him for days "and I assumed it was one of those things" and then how he had suddenly appeared again and he had shaved his beard off. And how they had been seeing each other every night and how much he liked Jackie and Jackie liked him.

"But what does he do? How does he make a living?" her mother asked.

"Oh, I thought I mentioned it. He's a pharmacist, working for his father."

"You've got to be practical about these things, Leah," said her mother gently. "I mean where he's only a pharmacist working in a drugstore—"

"But that's what's so wonderful about it. When he told his folks about us, his father offered him the store as a kind of wedding present. You see, he had this heart attack—his father did, I mean—and he's supposed to take it easy. So he'll work for Akiva—"

"Where is this store?" asked Mrs. Kaplan, her voice suddenly very quiet.

"Why, it's right here in town, over by the Salem line. I'm sure you know it. It's one of the oldest stores in the area."

"Town-Line Drugs? Marcus Aptaker's store?"

"That's right, and Akiva is Arnold Aptaker."

Chester Kaplan arrived home shortly after Leah had left. He was overjoyed at the news.

"So what do you intend to do?" asked Mrs. Kaplan.

He rubbed his hands gleefully. "Do? What's to do? We'll invite the young man to dinner, and a week or so later, we'll invite his folks. Then I suppose they'll invite us—"

"You forget his father is in the hospital."

"That's right," he said. "So we'll invite Mrs. Aptaker, and maybe we can go visit him in the hospital."

"And what if she should refuse to come?" Edie asked.

"Why should she refuse? We're not good enough for her?"

"Because if it was me, I'd refuse," his wife replied. "I'd feel that where you were pushing my husband out of business and maybe gave him a heart attack on account

224

of it, I wouldn't want to eat at your house. I'd feel the food would choke me."

"*I* gave him a heart attack? Because we sold the block and I told him to apply to the new owner for a renewal of his lease? And when I file suit against somebody and he gets a heart attack, it's my fault?"

"That you have to do because it's your profession. This you didn't have to do. And Aptaker asked you for the renewal before Safferstein made an offer for the property."

"Sure but Safferstein told me he was interested in the property as soon as the terms of the will were made public. So naturally, where I've got a possible buyer, am I going to spoil it by giving leases?"

"And the rabbi is against it."

"It's a matter of interpretation of the law," he said loftily. "You wouldn't understand about that."

"But how the Aptakers will feel toward you, that I can understand. I'd be surprised if they even came to the wedding."

"So show me where it's written that the parents of the bride have to be friendly with the parents of the groom," her husband said. "The Schneursons and the Feldmans don't even talk to each other. The Blackmans were in Florida all winter last year and Sidney Blackman told me that not once did his son's in-laws invite them for even a cup of tea."

"And if the boy feels the same way toward you?" Edie asked.

"Then we won't be friends," he said philosophically. "As long as he makes Leah a good husband, I can stand it, believe me."

"But now that the rabbi has moved for reconsideration," she pointed out, "you have a chance to make everything right."

Her husband was shocked. "What are you saying?

225

You want me to turn against my friends, the people who backed me, for my own personal interests? No, sir! I'll fight the rabbi, and I'm going to beat him."

44

Mrs. Aptaker did not raise her voice. She was calm and controlled. But she was adamant. "I will not invite the Kaplans here and if they invite me to their house, I won't go."

Her son was anything but calm. He did not shout, but his voice shook with despair and frustration. "But, Ma, will you think of me? Will you please for one lousy second think where your refusal puts me? Mrs. Kaplan tells me she'd like you to come to dinner Sunday night. So what am I going to tell her? That my mother thinks she's too good to eat with them?"

"I didn't say I was too good. I just said I wouldn't go. That's all."

"Yeah, but what am I supposed to tell her?"

"Why did she ask you in the first place, Arnold?"

"What do you mean?"

"If she wants to invite me to dinner," his mother said, "why does she have to ask you by way of a third party? This is the way she always invites people? She sends around messengers?"

"I was there, so she mentioned it. That's all."

"No, Arnold. You know better than that. She asked you to ask me instead of calling me on the phone because she knew if she called, I wouldn't accept. By going through you, she thinks maybe you could persuade me."

He tried a new tack. "All right, let's say you're right. Let's say Mrs. Kaplan is aware that you have a grievance against her or her husband. But I'm marrying her daughter. Doesn't she have a right to meet her future son-in-law's folks? And I should think you'd want to meet the parents of your future daughter-in-law."

"I've met them," said Mrs. Aptaker. "I know who they are. When you carry on a retail business in a small town like Barnard's Crossing for almost forty years, there's not many people in town you haven't met. And don't worry, she knows who I am and she knows what your pa looks like, too."

"Look, Pa offered me the store, didn't he? So the store is like mine, isn't it? So shouldn't I have some say about the lease? I mean, if the store is mine, shouldn't I feel sore if there's been a dirty trick played on us on the lease?"

"But you it didn't give a heart attack."

"Well, I don't think it gave Pa one, either," Arnold replied. "He told me that he'd had several other attacks that he thought were only indigestion. What happened on the lease is one of those things that happens in business. As far as Mr. Kaplan is concerned, he's a nice man. He's religious—"

"Oh, religious!"

"Yes, religious. And the letter he wrote to Pa was just what he had to write as president of the temple. The board voted on it and he naturally wrote to tell us the result. That's all there was to it."

"That's all?" she challenged. "According to Kaplan's letter, it was a unanimous vote. And the rabbi, who is a

227

board member too, said he didn't even know about it. You think the rabbi was telling a lie?"

"Look, Ma, the rabbi wasn't there. The unanimous vote came from those who were there. As for the lease, I don't give a damn. If it expires and Safferstein wants the store, that doesn't mean we have to move out the next day. It can drag on for months. And we can get another store. I'm not crazy about the location anyway. What's more, I don't see why you're so—so stubborn about it when Pa isn't."

"Oh, your father, he thinks the rabbi can do something for him," she said scornfully.

"Maybe he can."

"So when he does, I'll accept Mrs. Kaplan's invitation."

45

"There's the accident and there's the fire policies on the Kimberly Place property. And here's a statement for the premiums," said the insurance agent with a sheepish smile. "Saves a stamp."

"Would you like me to pay you now, Murray?" asked Safferstein.

"Well . . ."

Safferstein reached for his checkbook.

"I can always use the money," said Murray Isaacs. That

228

was what was so nice in dealing with Bill Safferstein. Anybody else would at least make him wait until the first of the month.

Safferstein passed the check across the desk. "You going to the board meeting Sunday?"

"You bet," Isaacs assured him. "I'll be there. The missus wanted us to run down to New York for the weekend to see my daughter. But I told her nothing doing, I had to be at the board meeting."

Safferstein clasped his hands behind his head and leaned back in his chair. "Something special expected at the meeting?"

Isaacs stared at him. "We're voting on the rabbi's motion to reconsider the sale of the Goralsky Block. Didn't you know?"

"Oh sure, but is there any question on it?"

"Well, you can never be too safe, I say, and every vote helps."

"But it was carried unanimous—"

"Yeah, but that was before the rabbi made his spiel."

"And you mean that could change some votes? I didn't think he was that convincing," said Safferstein easily.

"It's sort of funny about the rabbi. He's such a low-keyed kind of guy, you know, never raises his voice. Even in his sermons, it's like a professor lecturing to a class. So when he does get excited, it makes a special impression, like this is something that means a lot to him."

"Yes, but—"

"And remember, Billy, not all the guys that voted for that motion were sold on the idea. I mean, everybody was anxious to sell the Goralsky Block, but not everybody was keen on using the money to buy the property up in Petersville. But where the two are tied together in one motion, they went along."

"So you could always split it into two different motions, couldn't you?"

229

"Well, of course, but some of the guys have been saying that maybe the board acted hastily, that if it's against
the Jewish law like the rabbi says—well, you know. And
then there are the guys who weren't at the meeting, and
the past presidents. If the rabbi was to contact them . . .
see what I mean?"

"How does it look to you right now, Murray?"

"Oh, we'll win. There's no question about that."

But Safferstein detected doubt underneath the brave
assurance, and for some minutes after the insurance agent
left he sat staring gloomily out the window at the gray
afternoon sky. Then he reached for the phone and called
Kaplan.

"Murray Isaacs is an idiot," declared Chester Kaplan
flatly. "Sure some guys will switch their votes, but I'm not
worried."

"He said the rabbi made a big impression with his
speech at the meeting."

Kaplan laughed. "Yeah, he really had them going for
a minute or two. But then do you know what happened?
The school bell rang, and it just petered out. Look, the
rabbi is a rabbi. It's his job to point out any little corner-
cutting ethicswise. But the people on the board are practical men, and they've had a chance to think about it. I'm
sure they'll vote the right way Sunday."

"Have you done anything about it, though?" asked
Safferstein.

"How do you mean?"

"Have you spoken to each member of the board? Have
you done any campaigning?"

"Oh sure, Bill, that goes on all the time. I'm always in
touch with the membership. But I'll tell you something
that would really clinch it, make it a unanimous vote, in
fact."

"What's that?"

"Well, the big thing appears to be Aptaker's lease," said

230

Kaplan. "That's what got the rabbi worked up in the first place. Now if you could give Aptaker a renewal—"

"No."

"No?"

"No, I've got special plans for that store. Look, Chet, what you've got to do is call each and every member and make a real strong pitch."

"There's no time, Billy."

"What do you mean, there's no time. You've got tonight and tomorrow—"

"It's the Sabbath. I don't do business on the Sabbath," said Kaplan stiffly. "I could make a couple of calls now and a few Saturday night—"

"If you pick the right ones that could help a lot."

"All right, Billy, I'll do what I can. And don't worry. I'm sure we'll win."

Brave words, but the more Safferstein thought about it, the more it seemed that Kaplan was anything but certain of the outcome. He got up and paced the floor, trying to assess the situation. He felt hemmed in. He opened the door and, taking his hat from the rack, he announced to the receptionist that he was going home.

She glanced at the clock. "You all right, Mr. Safferstein?"

"Yeah, I'm all right. Just a little headachy."

"Hadn't you better take your raincoat? It's hanging in the closet. You could be coming down with something."

"No, I'm okay." But Safferstein went back into his office and shrugged into his raincoat. Automatically, he thrust his hands into the pockets and felt something unfamiliar in one of them. He drew out a bulky manila envelope and stared at it for a moment. And then he remembered: it was the envelope of pills, the original one that he had got for Mona. Curious, he went to the desk and opened the bottle and shook a couple of pills out on the desktop. Then he reached for the phone and called Dr. Muntz.

"Bill Safferstein. You remember about somebody swapping coats with me at Chet Kaplan's the other night, the night of the big storm? Well, the next day I got a refill on that prescription you wrote—"

"From Town-Line Drugs?"

"Sure from Town-Line. They had the prescription. Well, I just came across the original pills. See, I got the coat back from Chet and the pills were still in the pocket. What I'm calling about is that they're different from the ones I gave Mona. I mean they're different from the refill. They're the same size and shape, I guess, but these are a different color. So I wonder could it be because they were in my pocket and maybe got wet, or—"

"I'd have to take a look at them, Billy," said Dr. Muntz. "I'm going to be tied up here for another half hour or so. Where are you calling from?"

"From the office, but I'm on my way home right now."

"Suppose I stop off at your house when I get through here. I'd like to see them."

As soon as he hung up, Dr. Muntz smiled broadly and strode into the office of his colleague, Dr. Kantrovitz. "I think I have the solution to the problem of our young friend, Dan Cohen," he said, rubbing his hands. He then described the phone call he had just received from Safferstein.

"I don't get it, Al. How does that help Dan?"

"Don't you see?" said Dr. Muntz. "This is another mistake that Town-Line made on a prescription. But I can do something about this one because it's my patient, Mona Safferstein, who was affected."

"What are you going to do?" asked Kantrovitz.

"I'm not sure yet how I'll handle it. The important thing is that now I can do something. Marcus Aptaker is a nice guy and I wouldn't want to hurt him. But if it's a choice between him getting hurt and Dan Cohen getting hurt, naturally my loyalties have to be with Dan."

232

46

The board meeting began shortly after the morning weekday services, which on Sundays were held at nine o'clock instead of at the customary hour of seven. In the few minutes between the end of the service and the beginning of the meeting, the members stood around in the corridor gossiping, joking and arguing, then gradually drifted toward the boardroom. Today, all the conversations were related to the principal business of the meeting.

"If Bill Safferstein would just agree to extend Aptaker's lease, there'd be no problem. Do you realize that? I don't understand why he doesn't. He's a good tenant." Oscar Levy had a high-pitched whining voice that made everything he said seem like a complaint.

"How do you know he won't? Chet was supposed to ask him."

"I know," Levy replied. "At least I'm pretty sure from something Chet said the other night."

"He won't," said Manny Levine flatly. Manny was never in doubt about anything. "He won't give him a lease, because he's sore at him. It's as simple as that."

"How do you know?"

"Remember a few years back, we had this membership drive," Manny said. "Well, Billy drew Aptaker's

233

name. It was one of the names on his list, and he went to see him. Now Aptaker not only turned him down flat, but gave him a lot of lip. I remember Billy being sore about it."

"Nah, Billy Safferstein is not that kind of guy," said Marvin Kalbfuss. "He's not one to bear a grudge, especially where it's a matter of business that's involved. What I think is that he's planning to clear out the whole block and make one big store by knocking down the separating walls. It'll be one of these big liquor stores; you know, a package store—"

"Where'd you get that idea?"

"Well," Kalbfuss said, "there was an item in the paper about Lenox Corporation planning a unit on the North Shore. If Billy was planning to operate it as a regular block of stores, why would he pay so much more than the income warrants? And it would be to his advantage to keep the drugstore, wouldn't it? A drugstore snazzies up a block. All right, so he might want to raise the rent, but I don't think Aptaker would make a stink about that. So it stands to reason Billy has something else in mind. And it can't be just some other store, because then he'd kick out one of the other tenants, none of whom, by the way, have leases. And remember, there's a vacant store. So it must be something that involves the block as a whole. Right? Now, you ask yourself—"

"Hey, look who's just come in. Al Becker."

"What do you suppose it means? He hasn't been to a meeting in years."

"Will you please come to order." Kaplan banged his gavel on the table. "Come on, guys, let's get the show on the road. Come to order."

There were twenty-one members present, the same number as at the last meeting, but they were not the same twenty-one. The rabbi was not there, of course. And two of Kaplan's close associates were also absent. One had gone out of town on business; the other was home, nursing a bad cold. His wife had threatened to leave him if he set foot out of doors "just to go to a board meeting." The secretary had a note from each of them to be polled against the motion to reconsider. It had been at Kaplan's suggestion that the notes had been sent, and he planned to make use of these proxies if it looked as though the vote would be close.

Of the three who had not been present at the last meeting, one was a regular who had promised Kaplan his support. The other two were past presidents: Ben Gorfinkle of a few years back, who occasionally attended meetings, and Al Becker, who had succeeded Jacob Wasserman, the founder of the temple, in the presidency and who had not come to a meeting in years. Chester Kaplan welcomed him warmly, although he was puzzled by his appearance—and a little disturbed.

Kaplan rapped smartly on the table and announced, "We will now take up the rabbi's motion to reconsider the sale of the Goralsky Block. Discussion. Mitch?"

Mitch Danziger lumbered on his feet. He was a big man, with a surprisingly gentle voice. In calling him first, the chairman felt that he was demonstrating his fairness, since Mitch was not one of his active supporters. "I'd like to make my position clear. I'm in favor of selling the block to Safferstein. In fact, I can't imagine how anyone could be against it, because it's a good deal. I mean if a stock is selling for sixty and a broker comes along and offers you a hundred, wouldn't you take it? But I'm not convinced that buying land in New Hampshire is such a good deal—"

"Have you seen it?"

"No, I haven't, but—"

"And that's not the basis for the rabbi's motion that's on the floor—"

"Oh, yes it is. You remember the rabbi said—"

"But Paul Goodman it was, I think, who pointed out that—"

"But he said—"

"No, what he said was—"

"Order, order." Kaplan rapped on the table. "Look, fellows, everyone will get a chance to speak his piece, but let's address our remarks to the chair. Now before this whole discussion gets out of hand, let me try to narrow it down so that we can all talk on the same point. I think everyone agrees with Mitch that selling the stores is a good deal for the temple. And I'm willing to admit that some who voted for it weren't so keen on buying the New Hampshire land. If you want, if you think that there are enough to make that a contest, then I'm willing to split the two ideas into separate motions and vote on each of them. But right now, we're not actually concerned with either one. It's not a question of whether we should sell the Goralsky property so much as whether we have a right to. The rabbi claims we haven't, according to Jewish law, or at least that we have to give Aptaker his lease before we do. But I can tell you definitely that if we did, it would kill the sale. Now, there's the other regulation in Jewish law that I brought up, namely that where there is a conflict between Jewish law and the law of the land, it is the latter that applies. The rabbi claims that it doesn't apply in this case. All right, so where do we stand? To me, it's a question of priorities. I'm inclined to think that if we asked another rabbi, he might rule that in this case, the rule I mentioned does apply—"

"So why don't we ask another rabbi?" asked Paul Goodman.

"Because," Kaplan replied, "it isn't like appealing to a higher court, as in our system, where the ruling of the higher court automatically supercedes the ruling of the lower court. With us, all rabbis are the same. Some have bigger reputations than others, but their authority is no greater. So we could go from one rabbi to another, and one would say yes and the other no and the third yes and so on. It could go on forever. As I see it, it's for us to decide whether the rule I suggested is completely without relevance and that the law the rabbi mentioned is binding on us because this is a synagogue. In which case, we notify Safferstein that we have to renege on our promise to sell. Of course, he could turn around and sue us for breach of contract, although I don't think he would. Or we can decide that the rule I mentioned gives us an out, even though it's a squeaker, and turn down the motion for reconsideration. Now that's what I'd like you to address yourself to. Paul?"

Paul Goodman got up. "I'd like to start by saying that our president has just done a masterly job in shearing away the superficial aspects of this situation and focusing our attention on the kernel of the problem. Now one of the hardest aspects of practicing law, and I'm sure Chet will bear me out, is explaining to your client that the law is not a yes-or-no thing. He always wants to know if something is legal or not, and you have to explain that one set of precedents say it is and that other precedents suggest that it might not be, that in the final analysis the law is what the judge and jury—that's us in this case—say it is. And what's apt to determine their finding is the hard practicality of the situation as much as anything else. I'd like to point out, and the rabbi himself admitted it, that the rule that Chet brought up was originally adopted by the rabbis only because it was the practical thing to do under the circumstances. Oh yeah, and one other thing, as I understood it, this Din Torah thing the rabbi mentioned calls for some big-shot rabbi and two assistants. Well, I don't know how it works, since I've never seen one in operation, but I would imagine that they sit as a board of three and decide on the basis of the majority. Well, why would you need three judges if it were an open-and-shut case?"

Henry Vogel got the floor. "As far as I'm concerned, I don't see that Aptaker deserves all the consideration we're showing him. I happen to know him on account the market next door is one of my clients. So when I'm in the neighborhood servicing my client, I might drop in to the Town-Line. So one day, we get to talking, and I tell him I'm a CPA. I wasn't soliciting his business, you understand. I just happened to mention it, and he says, as if I asked him or was even interested, that he has his work done by Kavanaugh and Otis, which is a Gentile firm to begin with and this Otis is an A-number-one anti-Semite. Now here's the point I'm trying to make. Aptaker is one of the first Jews in town. But is he a member of the temple? No, sir. He's been approached every time we've had a membership drive, and each time he wasn't interested. As a member of the Membership Committee, I know what I'm talking about. He probably figures that up there on the Salem Road where there's no Jewish residents to speak of, where it's practically a hundred percent Gentile, he don't have to belong. But I'll tell you something else. He didn't have his kid Bar Mitzvahed, not in our temple or anyplace else. Now, I know that for a fact. So if he's not interested in anything Jewish, why should we go out of our way to give him the benefit of a special Jewish law?"

Murray Isaacs raised the question of Aptaker's physical condition. "We could end up with egg all over our face. Here's a guy that's just had a heart attack. No insurance company would issue a policy to him, and we're planning to underwrite him for ten years. Suppose we go along with the rabbi, give him his lease and stop the sale, and then after a couple of months he decides he can't carry on and closes his store. What are we left with? I'll tell you—a second vacant store."

Several hands were raised, but out of courtesy to a

past president, Kaplan nodded to Ben Gorfinkle. "I wasn't here at your last meeting," said Gorfinkle, "but I got the impression from what I heard that the rabbi felt strongly enough about this matter to make it a test of whether he stays on. If that is so, then it puts the whole business in a different perspective. Because if he feels that strongly about it, then it must be a lot more basic to Judaism than some of the previous speakers seem to suggest."

"I think you were misinformed, Ben," said the chairman. "The rabbi said nothing about resigning if the vote went against reconsideration. It was some idea he had about our retreats in New Hampshire. He thought the kind of services we had might not be in keeping with traditional Judaism and that if the temple went that way, he wanted no part of it. But then, neither would most of us."

"I'd like to say something," said Paul Goodman, and without waiting for permission from the chairman, he went on, "I don't think the consideration of how the rabbi might react should have any effect on our deliberations here. Certainly not on the present matter. It's up to us to decide, because we are the elected directors of the temple. If we stop to think each time we decide something whether the rabbi is going to like it or not, then we stop being the directors and he becomes the one running the temple. And if that's what the congregation wanted, then they would have appointed him temple manager. I think we all know our minds and I move the previous question."

Several members applauded and a few others approvingly patted the table top in front of them. The chairman chose to disregard Goodman's remarks but responded to the motion. "Paul has moved the previous question—"

"Yeah, let's vote."

"Second."

"Just a minute, Mr. Chairman." It was the loud harsh

voice of Al Becker. "I don't get down here often, but I'd like to say a few words right now, if I may."

"Of course, Mr. Becker."

Becker rose and leaned forward, supporting his heavy torso by placing his two clenched fists on the table. "I came down today because Jake Wasserman asked me to. He would have come himself, but he doesn't go out too much these days. He heard that this was going to be a meeting where the rabbi was asked not to be present and he thought somebody should be here to watch out for his interests. Now, I don't know too much about the issue you're discussing, but I know quite a bit about our rabbi. In the early days of the temple when Jake Wasserman was president and when I was president and for the years when I took an active part in temple activities, I never knew the rabbi to get involved in politics. He'd come to the meetings, but he took no part in the discussion unless it concerned him directly. But every now and then a matter would come up which he thought *was* his business and he'd take a stand and he'd stick to it come hell or high water. Jake Wasserman says he's got a kind of built-in radar that warns him if the congregation is drifting away from our tradition, and that's when he takes a stand. And it's been my experience that he's usually proved right. Now without knowing all the ins and outs of this business, I feel that if he's taken a stand on it, then it's because his radar tells him we're drifting. I'd like you to think about that when you vote."

"Thank you, Mr. Becker," said Kaplan. "I think we're ready to vote now."

The secretary cleared his throat to attract the president's attention as he nodded at the proxies lying on the table in front of him. Kaplan responded with a barely perceptible shake of the head. He felt quite confident. "We'll vote by a show of hands. All in favor of reconsideration.

240

All opposed." Kaplan beamed. The vote was fifteen to five against reconsideration.

Later, as they made their way to their cars, Dr. Muntz asked, "Are you going to stop by to tell the rabbi how the vote went?"

Kaplan halted suddenly. "Do you think I should?"

"Would you rather have him hear some garbled report through the grapevine, maybe from his wife who over-hears a couple of women talking in the supermarket?"

"You're right. But it's not a job I relish particularly. It'll be pretty embarrassing."

"Would you like me to tell him, Chet?"

"Would you? Then I appoint you a committee of one. You going right now?"

"No," said Dr. Muntz. "Why spoil his dinner? I'll drop in on him sometime this afternoon."

47

Lieutenant Jennings finished the typescript of the McLane conversation tape recording and tossed the folder on the desk. "Are you buying it, Hugh?"

"I've got to check it out," said Lanigan mildly.

"He could be lying—"

"Of course."

"I mean about giving the prescription to young Aptaker to make up," Jennings said. "And since it happened a couple of weeks ago, Aptaker wouldn't remember and couldn't deny it."

Lanigan nodded. "On the other hand, you'd expect that the name Kestler on the prescription would ring a bell. But there are other things that incline me to believe McLane's story. Begin with the fact that he voluntarily told us about the prescription. If he were guilty of having deliberately given Kestler the wrong drug, he'd keep quiet about it."

"Unless he's smarter than you think."

"All right," said Lanigan. "Then consider this: McLane gets the prescription from Cohen over the phone, so there was nothing to prevent him from changing it to penicillin. He could insist that was what he had been told over the phone, and there'd be no way for Dr. Cohen to disprove it."

"But then he'd have to write penicillin on the label, and the chances are that Kestler would know his father couldn't take penicillin."

"No," said Lanigan, "he'd use the manufacturer's name for the drug, Vespids. Kestler wouldn't recognize that as penicillin. But then the more you think about it, the stranger young Aptaker's behavior appears. He comes here all the way from Philadelphia to see his folks. If he drove up, it's a long drive. And if he flew up, it's costly. If he was on vacation, you'd think he'd at least have a week. You'd expect he'd come up Sunday or Monday and stay through to the following Sunday."

"How do you know he didn't?" Jennings asked.

"Well, Eban, if we're to believe McLane, he left the next day. And on that, we've got to believe McLane, because it's something that we can check out easily enough with Marcus Aptaker or with Mrs. Aptaker. But you'd think that if young Aptaker had arrived Monday, he would have gone to the store and his father would have introduced him to McLane. But no, he waits until Wednesday evening before coming in. And then the next day, he's gone."

"So what?"

"So it's strange," said Lanigan. "It's a long way to go for a one-day visit. On the other hand, if he did something criminal that Wednesday night because the opportunity happened to come up, then I could understand his running off the next day."

"Yeah, but he came back," Jennings objected.

"Sure, because it looks safe. Two weeks have gone by and there's been no mention of any police investigation in the papers—"

"Oh hell, how would he know if it was in the papers? He's in Philadelphia. Even if it made the Boston papers, it still wouldn't make the papers in Philly."

Lanigan dismissed the objection with a shake of the hand. "There are hometown newsstands in all large cities. There's the public library—"

"They wouldn't carry the Lynn *Examiner,* much less the Barnard's Crossing *Courier,*" Jennings objected.

"He could have heard from his mother when they talked on the phone. That doesn't bother me any."

"Seems to me you've got your mind made up," said Jennings. "Are you going to charge Arnold?"

"I don't have enough yet, but I sure would like to talk to him."

"Want me to bring him in?"

"Right now, I don't feel that I have enough even for that."

"So you're going to wait until he gets a parking ticket?" asked Jennings.

Lanigan ignored the sarcasm. "What time does the drugstore close on Sundays?"

"Six o'clock. But you know how it is, sometimes he

stays later. He wouldn't turn anyone away because it was closing time."

"Only one man on duty?" asked Lanigan.

"Yeah, young Aptaker. It's slow on Sundays, I guess."

"Good. So here's what I'd like you to do. Go down there a few minutes before six and sit in your car until you see him closing up. Then you ask him to come here. Say that I want to talk to him."

"I don't arrest him?"

Lanigan shook his head. "No, just that I want to talk to him. That's if he's alone. If there's someone else there, let it ride."

48

"What's it all about?" asked Arnold. He locked the door and then tried it by jiggling the knob.

"The chief wants to talk to you. That's all I know," said Jennings easily.

Arnold singled out the ignition key from the bunch on his ring and headed for his car, Jennings falling in step beside him. "If you're too busy to see him now, he can drop by your house tomorrow morning," said the lieutenant.

"No, that's all right. I have a date right now, but it's

not—I mean, I can cancel it. Look here, if it's about the parking situation in front of the stores—"

"My car is right here," said Jennings. "I'll follow you down."

"The chief's at the stationhouse?"

"Right."

When they arrived, Arnold used the pay telephone to call Leah. "Look, Leah, something's come up and I might be tied up for a while."

"Oh, that's all right. I'm kind of glad. I've been headachy all day. I might be coming down with something. I thought I'd get undressed and get into bed."

"Was that a lawyer you called?" asked Lanigan pleasantly.

"No, it was my date. Why should I call a lawyer? Say, what is all this anyway?"

"Come in and sit down." Lanigan led the way into his office and waited for the young man to be seated. "It's just that some people feel they need a lawyer when they come down to the stationhouse," said Lanigan genially. "You were here in town before, weren't you?"

"Sure, I was born here. You know that."

"I mean recently," said Lanigan. "You were here a couple of weeks ago. That right?"

"Yeah, I had a week's vacation and I came home. What about it?"

"And while you were here, you worked in the store, didn't you?"

"That's right. One night. They were busy, and I came in to give them a hand."

"That was the night of the big storm?"

"Uh-huh."

"You worked in the prescription room, filling prescriptions?"

"That's right."

"All the time you were there?"

"Right. My father was out front and Ross McLane, the other pharmacist, had a bunch of prescriptions he had to get out, so I helped him. Say, what is this? If you're worried about my Massachusetts license—"

"All in good time, Arnold. Now, did anything unusual happen while you were working on prescriptions?"

"Unusual? What do you mean? Unusual in what way?"

"In any way," said Lanigan blandly. "Unusual in any way at all. Anything out of the ordinary. An unusual prescription maybe, or an unusual problem filling it."

Light dawned. "Oh, you mean when I knocked over the cough medicine? How'd you hear about that?"

"Never mind how I heard about it. Just tell me about it."

"Well, this customer came in with a prescription for cough syrup, and Ross started to fill it. We get it in these gallon jugs, see? But there wasn't enough in the jug. So that meant he had to go to the storeroom to get another jug. But it was exactly the same formula that's put up for us in four-ounce bottles under our own label by this drug house. So he had the idea of just getting one of these small bottles and using that instead of hassling the gallon jug out of the storeroom."

"Why didn't you just give the customer one of those four-ounce bottles the drug house puts up for you?" Lanigan asked, interested.

"Oh, you can't do that," said Arnold quickly.

"Why not?" the chief asked. "Because it's cheaper, and you won't make as much money on it?"

"Well, sure, but when a customer comes in with a prescription, you can't give him a patent medicine. The customer would feel, well, he'd feel that the doctor was cheating him. And the doctor wouldn't stand for it. He'd raise Cain. And maybe it wouldn't do the patient as much good as getting it in a prescription. Know what I mean?"

"I guess so. And then what happened?"

246

"This guy came in for a prescription and he was like in a hurry," Arnold continued. "And I guess he's some sort of big shot. So McLane left the half-full bottle standing there and started to work on this guy's prescription—"

"Because he was a big shot?"

"No-o, but the cough-syrup guy was busy buying things and was in no particular hurry, and Ross had to get a bottle of the patent medicine anyway—"

"Okay. I get it."

"So the bottle that was half full was standing there uncapped, and I happened to knock it over. Naturally, Ross blew his stack, because it dripped on the floor and that stuff if you step in it is—"

"Sticky."

"Yeah. Well, Ross cleaned it up. I mean, I didn't know where they kept the mop—"

"Where do they?"

"In the toilet right off the prescription room. I offered to do it, but Ross went right ahead and did it."

"And that was the only unusual thing that happened that night?" asked Lanigan.

"I guess so. It's the only thing I can think of."

"Nothing funny about any of the prescriptions you had to fill."

Aptaker shook his head, mystified.

Lanigan looked up at the ceiling. "Remember one for a J. Kestler?"

"How could I remember a prescription I filled a couple of weeks ago?"

Lanigan leveled shrewd, appraising eyes at the young man. "Oh, come now, Arnold, you knew a man named Kestler, didn't you?"

"Yeah, I knew a man named Kestler. What of it?"

"You don't remember filling a prescription for him?"

"No."

"The name didn't ring a bell?"

"Uh-uh."

"You got no reaction when you saw the name on the prescription?" Lanigan coaxed.

Aptaker shook his head.

"All right, let it go. Now that was the only time you came into the store to work?"

"That's right."

"Why?"

"What do you mean, why?"

"Why didn't you come in to help the next day?" the chief asked. "Was it because of this fight you had with McLane?"

"I didn't have any fight with McLane."

"Oh, I thought you said he blew his stack."

"That was just for a minute. I didn't come in again because—because I went home the next day."

"To Philadelphia?"

"That's right."

"How'd you come to Barnard's Crossing?"

"I drove."

"When?"

"Tuesday."

"And Thursday you went home?" said Lanigan. "That's a long drive for a one-day visit. Why?"

Arnold squirmed in his chair. He did not like the line that the questioning was taking. For that matter, he did not like it that he was being questioned at all. He had never had dealings with the police before, but during his two years of wandering across the country, he had associated frequently with those who had, and their tactical wisdom had been succinctly summarized by one of them: "If you're busted, you button up, you don't go spilling your guts to the fuzz." He wondered uneasily if he had not already said too much.

Young Aptaker came to a decision. He sat back in his

248

chair and folded his arms across his chest. "I'm not saying another word until you tell me what you're driving at."

Lanigan nodded. "That's smart. Maybe you'd like to call your lawyer."

"I don't need any lawyer."

"Well, maybe if you call your mother, she—"

"I'm not calling my mother, either. I'm no kid. I'm of age— Look here, am I under arrest or something?"

Lanigan shook his head.

"You mean I'm free to go? I can walk right out of here?"

"Sure."

"Then—then what? What are you planning to do?"

"Oh, if you walk out, we'll have to ask around. I thought you might level with us, cooperate. I thought we could have an informal talk."

Arnold sensed a trap, and his mind cast about wildly for a means of eluding it. If he were in Philadelphia, he would call Reb Mendel. He'd know what to do. Maybe he could phone him long distance. . . Then he had another thought. "All right," he said. "I've got somebody I want to call."

Lanigan pushed the phone toward him. "Go ahead."

"I need the phone book."

Lanigan reached into the bottom drawer and gave him the directory. "Who are you calling?"

"I'm calling Rabbi Small."

49

Lounging in the doorway of the kitchen watching Miriam putter, the rabbi said, "How would you like to take a long drive in the country to look at the foliage?"

"With the children? Hepsibah gets carsick."

"Not with the children. Just the two of us. Can you get Sandy to baby-sit for the afternoon?"

"She's coming tonight, David. We're due at the Bernsteins. Remember?"

"Oh yes. Well, maybe she'd be willing to come for the whole day. Why don't you call her?"

Sandy was willing. So, with a plastic bag of sandwiches, fruit and a thermos of coffee, the rabbi and Miriam started out.

"The foliage is probably as good around here as it is up-country right now," Miriam remarked.

"Sure, but I'd rather be up-country. We'll drive along the back roads and stop whenever we feel like it. Then when we get hungry, we'll eat and then—"

"Are we going anyplace in particular, David?"

"No, just away."

"Any reason for running away?"

"I'm not running away. I just want to *be* away. I don't care to sit around chewing my nails waiting for the phone to ring or for a visit of a delegation from the board to tell me that they decided not to reconsider the vote to sell the Goralsky property."

"You think they'll vote against you?"

"I'm pretty sure of it."

"And what are you planning to do?" she asked anxiously.

He grinned. "I'm doing it right now. I'm not thinking about it. And we're not going to talk about it. Look at that maple."

It was a lovely sunny day with a blue sky and picture-book clouds. And because they kept to the back roads, they encountered little traffic. Once, they stopped and watched the elaborate procedure of pulling a large boat out of the water for winter storage. At another place, they stopped in a small town to watch a football game, munching on their sandwiches as they sat in their car. For the most part, they rode, pointing out to each other things of interest, a view of the lake nestled in the hills, a majestic tree in spectacular red and gold, a herd of cows grazing on a grassy slope. When they saw a road that looked interesting, they turned into it and when they became bored with it, they branched off at the next turn.

"Do you have any idea where we are, David?" Miriam asked at one point.

"No, but we're traveling north—in a general sort of way."

"How do you know?"

"By the sun, of course," he replied scornfully. "When you're used to facing east to recite your prayers, you develop a sense of direction."

"What if it's night time?"

"Then you can tell by the North Star."

"And if it's cloudy?"

"Oh, there are ways," he said airily. "You've no doubt heard of the chasidic rebbe of Chelm, the village of simpletons. It was easy for him, since he could perform miracles. Whichever way he faced when he recited his prayers automatically became east."

They stopped for gas and found out where they were. "It's time to turn around," he said, "if we want to get home before dark."

"Do you know what road to take?"

"No, but we'll just travel south now. We should get home around six."

To Miriam's surprise it was just six o'clock when they came in sight of the tower of Barnard's Crossing's Town Hall. The children, on their bellies on the living room rug, engrossed in the television screen, greeted them—as expected—perfunctorily. Miriam asked the usual questions of the baby-sitter. Did they behave? Did they eat well?

"They ate fine and they napped," Sandy assured her. "At least Hepsibah did, and Jonathan a little. And they've had their supper. There were quite a few phone calls, Rabbi. Here's the list. Some wanted to know what time you'd be back."

"And what did you tell them?"

"I said I didn't know," said Sandy, "but sometime before eight, because I know you're going out for the evening."

"Good girl."

They had a snack, and then while Miriam readied the children for bed, the rabbi went to his study to recite the evening prayers. He had no sooner returned to the living room when the doorbell rang. It was Dr. Muntz.

"I phoned earlier and you weren't in," he explained, "but going by I saw your car."

"Come in, Doctor."

"Since you weren't at the meeting"—he chuckled—"by invitation, Chester Kaplan thought you ought to be notified."

252

"And he found it embarrassing to come in person because he had won and I had lost, so he sent you?"

Muntz laughed again. "Just about. Chet is a very sensitive guy. The vote was fifteen to five."

The rabbi nodded. "That's better than I expected."

"With some, maybe most, it was because they felt the sale was a good deal for the temple and they didn't want to lose it."

"A vote to reconsider didn't necessarily mean that the property could not then be sold, only that Aptaker would have been considered."

"Well," Al Muntz said, "there were others who felt that there was no consideration due him since he wasn't a member of the temple and hardly had any connection with the Jewish community. He doesn't care anything about us, so why should we go to any trouble about him. That was the attitude of some of the members. Even from your point of view, Rabbi, I don't think you should worry too much about Aptaker. The chances are he'd have to give up his store sooner or later anyway. He was getting mighty careless in filling out prescriptions. He balled one up for a patient of mine only a couple of days ago. Luckily, no harm was done, but there have been other cases. Now, how long before that gets around? Then who'll come to him to have a prescription filled, even if his license isn't revoked?"

"How could he have made a mistake in the last couple of days when he's been in the hospital for the last couple of weeks?" the rabbi protested.

"I mean I heard of it a couple of days ago," said the doctor. "It actually happened when Marcus Aptaker was still in his store." He recounted the events on the night of the big storm.

"And there was something the matter with those pills?"

"No, no, the pills Safferstein obtained the next day to replace the ones that had been in his coat pocket were all

253

right, and his wife got better. But a couple of days ago he found the original bottle of pills, and he noticed they didn't look the same as the others. They were a different color from the refill pills. So naturally he was a little concerned. Which were the right ones? If his wife took the wrong pills was there danger of some aftereffect? You know how your mind runs on. So he called me, and I stopped off on my way home to look at them." Dr. Muntz paused to give dramatic effect to his words. "Rabbi, they were the wrong pills. They weren't what I'd ordered at all. The label was right, but the pills were wrong."

"And if Mrs. Safferstein had taken those pills?"

"Well, it so happens that nothing would have happened. But that's not the point. The point is that they were the wrong pills. Now, how many times can a druggist pull a stunt like that and continue to stay in business?"

"You told this to the board?" the rabbi asked.

"Oh no. If I told them, it would be all over town by the next day. I'm telling you because—well, because I know you won't spread it around, for one thing, and because you were so upset at the raw deal Aptaker got and kind of hinted you might resign. I thought you ought to have all the facts before you made up your mind, about resigning, I mean."

The rabbi looked at him in surprise. "Are you concerned whether I—"

"I wouldn't want you to resign."

"Strange," the rabbi mused. "I wouldn't have thought of you as—"

"As being on your side?" Muntz chuckled. "It's like this, Rabbi. Chet Kaplan is a good friend of mine, but on certain matters, he's a damn fool. He's so caught up with the retreat and religion that he can't think straight. Well, I think the congregation needs you to counterbalance him."

"I see." The rabbi smiled. "You'd like me to continue

as rabbi here because you're afraid I'd be replaced by a religious rabbi."

The doctor laughed. "It sounds funny put that way, but I think you know what I mean."

"Yes, I do. I just wonder if you do."

"I don't understand," said Muntz.

"Well, most Jews, like people generally nowadays, have given very little thought to their religion. Nevertheless, they have a subconscious feeling for it. And sometimes, when they go at it with great enthusiasm, it is with little discrimination, and they're apt to get it all wrong, like Mr. Kaplan. So you're likely to find that his Judaism doesn't square with what you feel subconsciously. You see, Doctor, ours is an ethical religion, a way of life."

"Aren't they all?"

The rabbi pursed his lips. "Why, no. Christianity, for example, is a mystical religion."

"You mean that Christians are not ethical?"

The rabbi made a gesture of impatience. "Of course they are. But it is a secondary thing with them. What is enjoined on them primarily is faith in the Man-God Jesus. And their ethics are derived from the principle that if they believe in Jesus as the Son of God and their Saviour, then they will try to emulate him and hence will behave ethically. There is also the belief, common among the evangelical sects, that if you truly believe, 'if you let Jesus come into your life' is the usual formula, ethical behavior will come automatically. And sometimes it works." He cocked his head to one side and considered. Then he nodded vigorously. "Sure. If you have your thoughts on heaven, you are less likely to covet the things of this world. Your foot may slip occasionally, of course, but not as much as it would if that were all you had to think about. On the other hand, you might get to thinking that any fancy that flits through your mind is the word of God.

"With us, however, faith in the Christian sense is al-

255

most meaningless, since God is by definition unknowable. What does it mean to say I believe in what I don't know and can't know? Theoretically, Christianity has the same view of God, which is why His Son was born on earth and lived as a man. Because being a man, He could be known. But we don't share this belief. Our religion is a code of ethical behavior. The code of Moses, the Torah, is a set of rules and laws governing behavior. The prophets preached ethical behavior. And the rabbis whose discussion and debates form the Talmud were concerned with spelling out in meticulous detail just how the general rules of behavior were to be implemented. I might mention in passing, that's why we have done so little proselytizing over the years. Because we have nothing to sell; no secrets, no magic formula, no ceremonial initiation that will open the gates of heaven. When a Christian comes to me for conversion, as they do now and again, that's what I tell them, because, of course, we have nothing to offer except our ethics and our way of life. And if he says that's what he's interested in, that he'd like to share it, I tell him to go ahead, there's nothing to prevent him, that with us the ethical Gentile stands as high before God as does the High Priest of Israel."

"You mean that's all there is to our religion? Only ethics?"

"That would be all if we were robots with minds programmed by a computer. But since we are human, with all the normal human failings and imperfections, we need rites and symbols and ceremonials to remind us and to combine us into a cohesive group. Also, some of us learn better that way. And because we remember, our history and our traditions take on importance. But it is our ethics that is the basis of our religion."

"But you do convert sometimes, don't you?"

The rabbi nodded. "Yes. Conversion usually is involved with marriage to a Jew. There are practices and ceremonials, tribal customs really, which implement and ingrain our ethical ideas. And conversion is largely adoption into the tribe. The convert takes a new name and it is as though he were born a Jew. But that's quite different from conversion to one of the mystical religions."

"But there have been Jewish mystics, haven't there?" Muntz objected. "I was reading—"

"Oh yes," the rabbi interrupted impatiently. "The Essenes, the Dead Sea community, the Kabbalists, the Sabbatean movement, and I might add, Christianity, all were mystical movements in Judaism. But we sloughed them off, because from the point of view of traditional, central Judaism, they are errors. Only Chasidism has persisted, and that's because their mysticism is in addition to their adherence to traditional ethics and the Jewish customs which reflect and symbolize them. The chasidic legends of wonder-working rebbes are so much superstitious nonsense. But the chasidic rebbe who is most revered is the one whose charitable way of life, whose concern for people, made him a saint."

Rabbi Small leaned forward. "I don't deny the validity of mystical experience. It's just that my bent is not in that direction. Perhaps it is a failing in me. But in the present case, we are breaking a Talmudic law which is clearly ethical, and peculiarly Jewish, I might add, in order to promote not religion but religiosity. You suggest that Mr. Aptaker is not worthy of our concern. But how about Mr. Goralsky?"

The phone rang, and the rabbi picked up the receiver. As he listened his face grew grave. Finally, he said, "All right, I'll be right down." He turned to the doctor. "I'm afraid you'll have to excuse me."

50

When he arrived at the police station, the rabbi found Akiva sitting on a bench in front of the sergeant's desk in the outer room. His eyes were closed, and there was a little smile on his face as though he were having a pleasant dream. The rabbi went over to the sergeant and nodded questioningly at the young man.

"He's been like that for the last ten or fifteen minutes," the sergeant explained in a whisper. "He comes out of the chief's office and he says he's going to wait here for you. He asks me which way is east and he goes into the corner and just stands there like a kid in school. Then he starts swaying and twisting and bending back and forth like he was doing exercises or maybe having a fit. And he's whispering to himself all the time. I couldn't hear him but I could see his lips moving."

"It's his way of praying," the rabbi explained with a smile.

"Is it now? Well, after a while he sits down and just closes his eyes. But I don't think he's sleeping."

When the rabbi sat down beside him, Akiva opened his eyes, and with a broad smile said, "Hello, Rabbi. I sure appreciate your coming."

"The sergeant tells me you were praying."

258

"That's right. I recited the *Shema* over and over again."

"Why the *Shema?*"

"Because it's the only prayer I know by heart," he said simply.

"Why are you here, Akiva?"

The young man shook his head, but he did not appear in the least upset. He even smiled.

"You certainly look a lot different from the way you sounded over the phone," the rabbi remarked.

"When I called, I was really freaked out," Akiva explained. "I just didn't know what was happening. It was like a nightmare, like everything was closing in on me. And then I made contact with my rebbe."

"What do you mean, you made contact with him?"

"I called to him and he appeared. I saw him as clearly as I see you now. He told me to pray and that everything would be all right. So I prayed and I feel fine now."

"Well, that's good. Now suppose you tell me just what they want of you. Over the phone you said—"

Akiva shook his head. "I don't know what they want. The chief had me come down and we just talked."

"Does he think you know something or did something?"

"He don't say. He asked me about my leaving town to go home after the big storm. And he asked me about a man named Kestler. I'm sure he's got me mixed up with somebody else. But don't you worry, Rabbi, everything is going to be all right."

"Because your rebbe said so?" Rabbi Small asked sourly.

"That's right."

They talked for a while. The rabbi was unable to learn anything specific from Akiva, but as he began to understand what had happened, he grew indignant. Finally, he rose and strode into Lanigan's office.

"That's not like you, Chief," he said.

"Sit down, David. Now what is it that isn't like me?"

"This fishing expedition. If you've got something against Arnold Aptaker, tell him and then he can explain. If you think you have evidence of some crime, charge him so that he can set about defending himself. But just asking him to talk on the chance that he might say something that might incriminate him, that's not fair and I don't think it's even legal."

"I haven't arrested him and I'm not holding him. Believe me, David, I'm just trying to help him."

"But he doesn't know what it is you think he did."

"Oh, I believe he knows what he's done all right," said Lanigan confidently. "There's a chance, about one in a hundred, that it was an accident or an understandable mistake. Well, let him level with me and I'll try to see it his way if I can."

"Then why not tell him outright and—"

"And let him start rigging explanations?" the chief said. "No, sir. If he's innocent, if he did it without malice, if—" He broke off suddenly and looked sharply at his visitor from under bushy eyebrows. "You mean to say he has no idea of what I was driving at? No idea at all?"

The rabbi shook his head. "Was it some sort of highway accident the last time he was here? Does it have something to do with Kestler?"

Lanigan stared. "That's what he thinks? That's what he told you?" He smiled broadly. "He's putting you on."

"All right, then suppose you put me off."

"It has to do with Kestler all right, with the old man who died," Lanigan said. "Remember my coming to see you about it because the son, Joe, claimed it was the medicine that killed him? Well, he was right. But it wasn't Dr. Cohen's fault. He prescribed something called Limpidine." He pulled open a drawer and brought forth a bottle. "Here it is. That's what it says on the label, right? But what's in the bottle is not Limpidine. It's a form of penicillin, and the old man was allergic to it, which is why

Cohen prescribed the Limpidine in the first place. So the mistake was made in the drugstore by the pharmacist."

Lanigan sat back and let his visitor digest the information. "All right, mistakes happen," he went on. "But when I inquired around I found that a mistake like that was all but impossible. It's about as unlikely as a housewife making the mistake of using the salt for the sugar in baking a cake. And why couldn't she make a mistake like that? Because for all that the two look alike, they come in different type packages and they're kept in totally different type containers. That's the kind of mistake she wouldn't make even if she were blindfolded. All right, so if it's not a mistake, it must have been done on purpose. Or can you think of a third possibility?"

"Go on."

"So now the question is who would do a thing like that?" Lanigan continued. "Obviously someone with a grievance against one or the other of the Kestlers. I say either Kestler because Dr. Cohen phoned in that prescription and gave the name Kestler as the patient. The pharmacist, Ross McLane, asked him for the initial, and he said J. But J could be either Jacob, the father, or Joseph, the son."

"Ross McLane took the prescription over the phone?" the rabbi asked. "He remembered it?"

Lanigan nodded approvingly. "You're thinking it's strange he should remember a prescription he took days before? Well, he did because the name Kestler meant something special to him. You see, *he* had a grievance against the old man."

"Well then—"

Lanigan held up a finger to halt the interruption. "There were three pharmacists at the Town-Line Drugs that night, and each and every one of them had a grievance against one or the other of the Kestlers. Ross

McLane's was against the father; Marcus and Arnold Aptaker both had grievances against the son."

"What kind of grievance?" asked the rabbi impatiently. "There's a measure and a scale in grievance as in other things. My neighbor's little boy broke one of our cellar windows, so I could be said to have a grievance against him, but not as great as if he'd broken the large picture window in our living room. And in neither case would it be sufficient to make me want to do him an injury, at least not anything more serious than spanking his bottom, which would be an excellent thing for his character, by the way, but which would then give his parents a grievance against me because they don't believe in punishing children, which accounts for his breaking the window in the first place."

"That's the Damon kid?" Lanigan chuckled. "I ought to begin keeping a file on him. In another couple of years, I figure he'll be coming to our official attention. But these grievances against the Kestlers are more than you'd have from a broken cellar window, or even a picture window." He summarized the dealings each of the three pharmacists had had with the Kestlers. "So you see, " he concluded, "each of them had good reason for hating either the old Kestler or the young one."

"And because you think Arnold's was the greatest grievance, you suspect him?"

"Oh no, David. At first I thought it was McLane, especially when I found out that Marcus Aptaker had been out front waiting on trade and that it was McLane who'd been filling prescriptions. At the time I didn't know that Arnold had been in town. I was sure I had the right man. But I didn't want to act hastily, especially where it could affect Aptaker's business, and him being in the hospital and all. So when McLane came in on another matter, I invited him into the office here and we just chatted. We got to talking about how he'd lost his store, and he was completely candid about hating Kestler." He hitched forward in his chair, indicative of the importance of what was coming. "What's more, he didn't hesitate to admit that when he found that the prescription he was taking over the phone was for Kestler—he remembered it all clearly—he said he'd be damned if he'd fill out a prescription for him and handed it to Arnold to do. Now if he'd wanted to do Kestler dirty, he had only to change the prescription and say that was what Cohen gave him over the phone. How could the doctor prove he hadn't?"

The rabbi sat silent, his mind running over the evidence. It suddenly came to him that the story Dr. Muntz had told him related to the same evening, the night of the storm. "Now I'll tell you something," the rabbi said. "I'll give you some information that will knock the pins from under your case. Not an hour ago, Dr. Alfred Muntz was at my house. And he told me in the strictest confidence —but I guess the present situation warrants my telling you —that the prescription he gave Safferstein for his sick wife and that he had filled at the Town-Line Drugs that same night was not at all what he'd ordered. There, too, the label was right but the pills were wrong. Now according to his own statement, McLane made out the Safferstein prescription, so he made the same kind of mistake that you say Arnold made on the Kestler prescription. You said a mistake of that kind was as unlikely as a woman mistaking salt for sugar. But if there are two women working side by side in the same kitchen and one uses salt for suger in baking a cake while the other uses sugar for salt while preparing a stew, then no matter how unlikely it is, you've got to assume that just such a mistake was made, all the more so because two such mistakes are even less likely than one. In the present case, if it was not an accident, then you have to assume it was a conspiracy, that McLane and Arnold held a whispered conference while Safferstein waited, and they both agreed to change the prescriptions that two different doctors had ordered

263

for two different patients, one of whom, Mrs. Safferstein, they had nothing against. And that is nonsense."

Lanigan smiled broadly. "Thank you, David. Your story explains how Arnold managed it. I'll admit I was a mite bothered about it. It seemed as though young Aptaker would be taking an awful chance putting up the wrong pills with McLane just a couple of feet away. Since McLane had taken the prescription over the phone, he'd know what was supposed to go into the bottle Arnold was working on. But I see how he managed it now, thanks to you. They've both typed up the labels and pasted them on their respective bottles. Then Arnold distracts McLane's attention and switches the two bottles. Then each fills the bottle in front of him and Safferstein gets Kestler's medication and Kestler gets Safferstein's."

"But what goes for Arnold goes equally well for McLane," the rabbi objected. "McLane could have distracted Arnold's attention."

"But he didn't. Just a little while ago, Arnold told me he knocked over a bottle of cough syrup and McLane went into the toilet to get a mop to clean it up. I might add that McLane didn't pretend he didn't know who Kestler was. And McLane didn't leave town the next day, either."

"But if it's a case of the two being switched, anyone who had the two bottles could have done it. Safferstein could have—"

"Now that's not like *you*, David," said Lanigan reprovingly.

"What do you mean?"

"Throwing suspicion on one of your people to save another."

"I was merely listing the possibilities," said the rabbi coldly.

"Yeah, but Safferstein is not one of them. Why? Because he didn't even know Kestler, not the son or the

264

father. And Kestler didn't know him. They'd never had any dealings whatsoever. What's more, Bill Safferstein had no way of knowing what would happen if he gave Kestler his wife's medicine."

The rabbi sat silent. Then he asked, "Are you going to charge Arnold Aptaker?"

Lanigan considered. "Not yet. Maybe there *is* some explanation. Look how it was with McLane. I thought I had him, and he wriggled off. Well, maybe young Aptaker can be lucky too. I'll talk to him again. Maybe if you spoke to him first . . ." He looked at the rabbi questioningly. "I'm willing to gamble a little."

"Not to mention that you don't have a case that would stand up in court."

"Why haven't I?"

"Because you don't have proof, real proof, that Kestler died from that pill," the rabbi said. "No autopsy was performed and—"

"With what I have right now, I could get an order for an exhumation without any trouble at all. Believe me, David."

"All right. I'll talk to him."

With Lanigan watching through the open door, the rabbi sat beside Akiva, and in low tones he explained the case against him. At first, the young man registered shocked disbelief, but by the time he had finished, he was confident and placid once again.

"He's all wet," Arnold said. "I didn't hate Kestler. I was sorry for him. I'll admit I was sore when it first happened, and for some time after that. I used to dream of getting revenge. You want to know something? I'd get homesick plenty of times, especially at first. And when I thought of what happened, why I wasn't at home, I'd daydream of getting even in all kinds of ways. But never once did I think of doing it by giving him the wrong medicine on a prescription. It just never entered my

265

mind. It was against my professional instinct, I suppose. Then when I joined Reb Mendel and the chavurah, I realized that any hatred I had for Kestler was like hatred for myself. Because he was me and I was him since we're all part of the same unity. Do you understand?"

"And when you saw J. Kestler on the prescription?"

"Nothing. It could've been Joe Blow. Sure I recognized it. But nothing. No reaction. You know, sometimes you see a prescription for someone you know and you say to yourself, 'Hm, Bill must have a bad cold.' Like that, but that's all." He patted the rabbi's arm. "Look, don't you worry. I didn't do anything wrong, so everything is going to be all right. You'll see."

A policeman came up from the wardroom in the basement. He walked by to go to the chief's office and then stopped and did a double-take, "Hey, Arnold. I didn't recognize you. What are you doing here?"

"Hello, Purvis," said Arnold, smiling.

"You know him?" Lanigan called from his office. He came to the doorway.

"Arnold Aptaker? Sure. We went to high school together. Last time I saw him he had a beard like an old Jewish rabbi—" He blushed. "Sorry about that, Rabbi, it just slipped out."

"That's all right, officer, but nowadays it's the young ones that have the beards."

"And when was that, Purvis?" asked Lanigan.

"Last time I saw him? It was the night of the big storm. I was on duty patrolling the entrance to Route 1A, to slow cars down because of the broken branches on the highway ahead. And this car comes barreling along—"

"You mean he was speeding?"

The policeman colored as it occurred to him that he might be faulted for not having given Aptaker a ticket. "Well, not really speeding. Well, maybe just a little

266

speeding. I mean maybe not enough to hand the guy a ticket, but enough to make him think I might to get him to slow down. So I blow the whistle on him and walk over and it turns out we know each other."

"Where were you going, Arnold?" asked Lanigan.

"He said he was driving down to Philadelphia," the policeman volunteered.

"And what time was this?"

"Oh, around three o'clock in the morning, I'd say."

"Three o'clock Thursday morning and he said he was on his way to Philadelphia? Come in here, Purvis." Lanigan stood aside for the policeman and then shut the door of his office behind him.

"Now, Purvis, this is important. I want you to tell me, as well as you can remember, just what he said."

"Gosh, Chief, that was a couple of weeks ago. I just sort of walked over to where he'd stopped and said the usual—you know, like 'Going to a fire, buddy?' And he said something about how he was trying to make time getting to Philly. Then he recognized me and then I recognized him. Maybe I made some crack about his whiskers, the way anyone would."

"Of course."

"Then I guess we talked about what various people we knew in high were doing now, and he asked me about my brother Caleb, and I told him he was working on the town paper. Then he takes out his billfold and hands me a fiver—"

"He tried to bribe you?"

"Oh no, Chief, nothing like that. You know me. If I thought he was trying to bribe me, I'd've hauled his ass right out of the car and taken him down to the stationhouse."

"Naturally."

"It was for a subscription to the *Courier*. You know about Caleb working on this campaign to get the old-timers that moved down to Florida to keep in touch with the town. I happened to mention it, and that's when he outs with the five-spot."

"I see. He wanted to get news of the town regularly."

"That's right."

Lanigan flung open the door and called out to the sergeant on the desk, "Sergeant, book that man."

"What charge, sir?"

"Willful murder of Jacob Kestler."

While Akiva was being booked in the outer office, Lanigan in his own office was explaining to the rabbi. "Here's a young fellow who hasn't seen his folks in a couple of years, finally gets around to driving up here. He comes up Tuesday night and leaves Thursday. That's a mighty short visit for all that driving. You'd expect him to stay through Saturday, anyway. Well, that made me a little suspicious of him. But now it turns out that he left in the middle of the night. He works at the store Wednesday evening and a few hours later, he's on his way to Philadelphia. The courts always regard flight as evidence of guilt."

"But—"

"Just a minute, there's more," said Lanigan. "Naturally I wondered about his coming back this time. I mean, if he'd done something and was running away, why would he come back? Well, he would if he thought it was safe. If we started to investigate Kestler's death, it wouldn't make the Philadelphia papers. Chances are it wouldn't even make the Boston papers. So how would he know? Why would he take the chance? Well, Officer Purvis just told me that your young friend gave him five dollars to subscribe to the *Courier* for him. What do you think of that?"

In the cell block in the basement, the rabbi tried to

268

talk some sense into Akiva. "You've got to get a lawyer. You're just hurting yourself."

Akiva shook his head. "No lawyer."

"Why not?"

"Because he'd just get in the way and mess things up. He'd tell me what to do or he'd start filing motions or something, and it would just interfere."

"Interfere with what?"

"With the natural course of events."

"But when you're arraigned tomorrow morning, the judge will assign you a lawyer if you don't have one."

"So *he'll* assign him, Rabbi. I can't help that, but it won't be me lacking faith and picking one on my own."

"How about your mother, Akiva? Are you going to call her? Would you like me to go see her?"

"She's visiting my aunt in Boston. She's not due back until sometime tomorrow."

"Do you have the phone number? I'll call her for you if you like."

Again the young man shook his head. "No, she wouldn't be able to sleep all night for worrying. More likely, she'd come a-running. No, she'll find out soon enough."

"How about the store?"

"It's McLane's morning on. He's got a key."

The rabbi tried another tack. "Why did you start out for Philadelphia in the middle of the night?"

"I'd rather not talk about that, Rabbi."

"Then tell me why you subscribed to the *Courier*."

Akiva began to laugh. "I wasn't subscribing to no paper, Rabbi. That was a bribe I was giving Joe Purvis. He was being friendly and all that, but I still thought he might give me a ticket. If I offered him a bribe and he wasn't on the take, I could be in deep trouble. But when he told me about his brother taking these subscriptions I gave him a fiver for one. I figured sure he'd keep it. I was pretty surprised when I actually got the paper delivered."

269

"It would have been better for you if you hadn't," said the rabbi gloomily. "I'm afraid I'll have to leave you now. If there's anything I can do . . ."

"Yeah, there is at that, Rabbi. If you could drop off a *siddur*—"

"You want me to get you a prayerbook?"

"Sure. I'd like to recite some prayer besides the *Shema*."

51

"I thought you'd forgotten we were due at the Bernsteins," said Miriam when her husband returned.

"No, I didn't forget." He told her what had happened.

"Oh, his poor mother!"

"What's that, the women's lib point of view? What about his poor father? What about the poor young man himself?"

"Mrs. Aptaker is the only one of the three I've really ever met. Do you think Akiva did it, David?"

He shook his head gloomily. "There's no question that Lanigan has a good case against him. There's motive—he had reason to hate Kestler. There's the weapon—the medicine. And there's opportunity—he was in the drugstore at the time when the prescription had to be filled, and it looks as though he filled it. At least, the other pharmacist says he did, and Akiva doesn't deny it. Then there's the fact that he left town shortly after, which suggests guilt."

"But then he came back."

"True. But it was a couple of weeks later. And it could be argued that since there was no mention in the press that there was anything suspicious about Kestler's death he felt it was safe to return. Particularly damning is that he took the trouble to subscribe to the town newspaper. That way he could know if the police were investigating the death."

"It looks bad, doesn't it, David?" she asked soberly.

"M-hm."

"And yet you don't feel he's guilty. Is it because he's religious?"

"Religious? His religion wouldn't keep him from killing Kestler. Quite the contrary."

"I don't understand," she said simply.

"The outer forms of a religion aren't important unless they reflect the basic philosophy and ethics that are inherent in it. I got a clue to Akiva's philosophy when he tried to convince me that he had no hatred for Kestler. It was the mystical business of everything and everyone being part of the Eternal One, and you are your enemy and he is you, so why should you hate him or try to injure him? But you can work that in reverse. You can justify hurting someone on the grounds that you are really hurting yourself. And who has a better right? When I saw him, he wasn't the least bit worried, and he should have been, even if he's innocent. Innocent men do get convicted occasionally. And even if they're acquitted, it's a troublesome and expensive business. No, he should be worried, and if he isn't, it's because he's rationalized and tricked his mind into not seeing the facts. If he can do that, he can also arrange his thinking to convince himself that he did not do something that he actually did."

"Then why—?"

"I suppose because I rather like him."

"Look, David, if you'd prefer not to go tonight—"

"No, we might as well. There's nothing more I can do for Arnold tonight—Oh yes, there is. I can bring him the *siddur* he asked for. Go ahead. Get dressed."

"I am ready. I've just got to change." She wriggled into a black sheath and then turned her back to him so that he could zip her up. Then she handed him a string of pearls so that he could clasp them around her throat as she held up the hair at the back of her neck.

He looked at the clasp critically and said, "The string is worn through. There's just a thread."

"Oh, it's all right."

"But it can break, and—"

"No great harm if it does, David. They're not real pearls, you know. It's just costume jewelry, but it's all I've got that will go with black."

The rabbi waited at the front door, the prayerbook he was bringing to young Aptaker in one hand while he jingled his keys impatiently in the other, as Miriam gave last-minute instructions to the baby-sitter. In the car, she reached up and pulled at the shoulder harness and buckled it at her waist. Then she tightened the strap. The rabbi's driving was erratic at best, but when he was moody and abstracted as he was now, he was given to sudden bursts of speed and equally sudden applications of the brake, which she assumed mirrored his flow of thought.

"All right, where to?"

"The Bernsteins, dear, on Harris Lane."

"Where's Harris Lane?"

"Oh, it's in that very nice section where all the big shots live, the Epsteins, the Dreyfusses. It's right around the corner from the Saffersteins."

"I don't know where the Saffersteins live."

"All right," she said. "I'll direct you. Go down to the Salem Road. Then you turn off on Minerva Road—"

"I know where Minerva Road is," the rabbi said petulantly.

"Well, Harris Lane is off the upper part of Minerva."

He drove along the Salem Road and passed the Goralsky Block.

"Minerva Road," she murmured.

He gave her an indignant glance, "I know, I know," and made the turn. After a couple of minutes, he nodded back and remarked, "That's the Kestler house."

"The white one?"

He glanced at the rear-view mirror and said, "No, the brown one before it."

"There were a lot of cars in front. Do you suppose they were having a party?"

"It doesn't seem likely," the rabbi said. "It's probably the people from the white house. Kestler is certainly not observant. Did I tell you about his playing cards with his wife during the mourning week? But I'm sure he wouldn't have a party a couple of weeks after his father died, if only because he'd consider it bad luck. His wife would be even more apt to, I imagine. It certainly wouldn't be observance of the mourning regulations with her, since I'm sure she's not Jewish."

"How did you know? Did she tell you?"

"With the name Christine?" The rabbi laughed. "The first time I came there to see the old man, she bobbed a curtsy to me the way Irish country girls do to priests. I had to explain to her—"

"Stop!" Miriam called out.

He jammed on the brakes, and she was thrown against the harness.

"It's back there, David. You passed it."

"There was no street there, just an alley."

"Well, that's Harris Lane. It opens up into a circle. You'll have to turn around."

"Are you sure?"

"Mrs. Bernstein said it was two houses before the Safferstein house and that's the Safferstein house, so that must be it. O-oh!"

"Now, what is it?" he asked testily.

"Oh, David, my pearls broke."

"I told you—"

"It was when you jammed on the brake," she said accusingly. "I was thrown against the shoulder strap."

She reached up and, gathering the broken strand, she handed it to her husband. "Here, put them in your pocket. Careful! They're falling off the string. There's one on the floor." She squirmed. "Ooh, one went down the back of my neck. It's caught on my bra."

"Well, if you think I'm going to unzip you here on the street . . . Get out and you can jump up and down and maybe dislodge it."

Unfastening her safety belt, Miriam opened the door. As she slid off the seat, another bead rolled off her lap onto the car cushion. "There's another one, David. It's gone down in the crack between the seat and the back cushion." Outside now, she bent forward into the car and with splayed fingers extended groped down into the crack. "No, I can't reach it."

"Get in," he said.

"But David—"

"Get in," he ordered peremptorily.

He set the car in motion. "Harris Lane is back there," she said meekly. "Aren't you going to turn?"

"I want to go to the stationhouse first."

She remembered the prayerbook on the seat between them. "Oh well, coming back, it will be on the right, and there'll be no chance of missing it."

"Don't worry. We'll get to the party in good time."

He drove to the end of Minerva Road and then headed for the center of town, negotiating the narrow crooked streets with reckless speed until he reached the police station. He was out of the car and running up the granite steps of the stationhouse when Miriam noticed that he had forgotten to take the prayerbook with him. Shaking

274

her head at his characteristic absent-mindedness, she picked up the *siddur* and followed him.

Chief Lanigan, coat in hand, came out of his office. "Hello, David." He looked beyond him. "And Miriam, too. What's up?"

"Miriam lost her pearls," the rabbi gasped.

"You mean they were stolen? You've come to report a theft?"

"No, no. She was wearing them."

"They're not real pearls, Chief," Miriam explained, "and the string was frayed."

"Then . . ." Lanigan looked from one to the other. "You better come in." He led the way into his office. "Now what's this all about?"

"The pearls," the rabbi began. "Miriam broke the strand and it gave me an idea about this business. Your theory is that Arnold switched the bottles while McLane was away from his station getting the mop or while he was cleaning up. Now picture it. They each have a pill counter in front of them. It's a kind of plastic tray with a trough on the side. They count out the pills on the tray and then tilt it so the pills slide or roll into the trough. There's a spout on the trough that they insert in the bottle, and the pills slide down. No chance of a pill rolling away."

"I've seen them."

"Now suppose you want to switch the pills after they've been put up in their proper bottles."

"Then you dump them back in the trays again," said Lanigan promptly, "and you switch trays."

"Right," said the rabbi. "And in either case, there would be the right number of pills in each bottle. But suppose you didn't have a tray, not even a table, then how would you make the switch? You'd have to empty one bottle into the palm of your hand. Then you pour the contents of the second bottle into the empty bottle.

275

Then you have to feed the pills you've got in the palm of your hand into the second bottle. And it would be a miracle if one didn't roll away."

"What are you suggesting, David?"

"That it was Safferstein who switched those pills, while he was sitting in his car under the street lamp, before the cruising car came along."

"Just because there was a pill missing?" Lanigan smiled. "You yourself suggested half a dozen ways in which that pill could be missing when I first spoke to you about it."

"True," the rabbi admitted, "but we also have to keep in mind that he had both bottles and time enough to make the switch without fear of being observed."

"But why would he want to hurt the Kestlers? He didn't even know them."

"He didn't?"

"No, and they didn't know him."

The rabbi nodded as he digested this information. "All right, then let's consider all possibilities."

"You going to work some of that whatdoyoucallit—pulpil—on me?" asked Lanigan.

"Pilpul," the rabbi corrected. "Why not? Talmudic pilpul is just logical reasoning that makes use of fine distinctions."

The chief grinned. "Go ahead, I'm in no hurry. It' you folks who seem to be dressed for the evening."

"The Bernsteins *are* expecting us," Miriam reminded him. "They're having a lot of people over."

"Then we won't be missed," the rabbi answered tartly "Besides, no one comes on time." He turned to Lanigan "Let's suppose it *was* Safferstein."

"Why should we?"

"Why shouldn't we? It's only an assumption, something to start on. Besides, there are the reasons I gave, so it isn't a frivolous assumption."

"All right." Lanigan tossed his coat on the desk, and

motioning his visitors to seats, he pulled back his swivel chair. Miriam sat down, but her husband remained standing.

"Let's clear the ground first," the rabbi began.

"How?"

"Oh, by eliminating the obvious," said the rabbi breezily. "I mean, that if we assume that Safferstein switched the pills, then it couldn't have been an accident."

"It was you who urged it was an accident originally," Lanigan pointed out smugly.

"But that was when we thought it happened in the drugstore. There, however unlikely, it's possible. But not sitting alone in the car like a small boy who might play with them and then get them in the wrong bottles."

Lanigan grinned. "I guess I can allow that."

"So it was intentional," the rabbi continued, "whether as a joke, or—"

"I can't see how a grown man could possibly consider it a joke to switch medicines on a couple of sick people, one of them his wife."

"Neither can I," said the rabbi. "So it means he did it to hurt someone. And probably not Kestler, since he didn't know him. But that suggests Mrs. Safferstein as the intended victim."

"Not a very good suggestion," said Lanigan. "If it was his wife he wanted to hurt, he would have gone right home and given her one of the pills. But he didn't go home at all. He went to the Kaplan house instead."

"Why?"

"He said because it was storming so hard and he wanted to get in out of the weather."

The rabbi began pacing the floor, his head back and his eyes fixed on the ceiling as the others watched. He stopped suddenly and turned to Lanigan. "Do you know where Kaplan's house is?"

"Of course."

"And Safferstein, do you know where he lives?"

"Certainly."

"Well, I just found out," said the rabbi. "Safferstein's house is no further from Town-Line Drugs than Kaplan's. So if he were bothered about driving in the storm, he could just as easily have driven home."

Lanigan's brow furrowed, and his head made little motions as he followed the two routes in his mind's eye. Finally, he nodded. "You're right, give or take fifty yards."

"So why did he go to the Kaplan house?"

"You tell me," said Lanigan.

The rabbi smiled. "It's strange, isn't it? His wife is sick, so he runs out to get her medicine. And then doesn't go home to give it to her. It's what started me thinking of him. Because if he had made the switch, there was no point in going home. He couldn't give her the pills he had with him, since they were Kestler's. Nevertheless, I think he would have gone home anyway and made some excuse for not having the medicine, if only for the sake of appearances."

"Then why didn't he?"

"Because he had to go to Kaplan's, of course."

"There was someone there he had to see?" asked Lanigan. "Kaplan?"

The rabbi shook his head. "No, not Kaplan. Since it was the pills he was concerned with, I suppose it was Dr. Muntz, the man who had prescribed them."

"What would he want with Dr. Muntz?"

"To show him the pills, I presume," said the rabbi quietly.

"But he didn't."

"No, he didn't. That's the irony of the situation. He wasn't able to because he was himself the victim of a switch. He had the pills in his coat pocket, and someone took his coat by mistake."

"But if he had shown them," Lanigan insisted, "then

nothing would have happened. The doctor would have spotted the mistake right away. There might even have been time to call the Kestlers. Then no one would have got hurt."

"No one? Let's think about it." Once again, Rabbi Small began to pace the floor, his voice lapsing into the singsong chant traditional in Talmudic argumentation. "We assu-ume he had no intention of hurting the Kestlers because he did not know them and had no reason to. A-and no intention of hurting his wife because he did not go home. Bu-ut we know that his intention was malicious. So-o, we must ask ourselves who would be affected even if neither patient took the pills?" He looked at Lanigan expectantly.

"It doesn't make sense, David. A-and," he continued, mimicking the rabbi, "i-if we accept your assumption that he came to Kaplan's house to show the pills to Dr. Muntz, it makes even less sense because what's the point of going to the trouble of switching the pills and then having the doctor switch them back, so to speak?"

The rabbi grinned. "Not bad. You're getting the hang of it. All right, let's see what would happen. Here's a room full of people. Safferstein makes some excuse for showing Muntz the pills. 'Those aren't the pills I prescribed,' the good doctor exclaims. 'There's been a mistake made.' Then Safferstein tells him about the other bottle of pills, and Dr. Muntz says, 'They must have switched them somehow. I better call the Kestlers and warn them.' But the point is that kind of thing isn't carried on in whispers. And keep in mind that there's a good chance that Dr. Cohen might be there, too. He'd be consulted. Within minutes, everyone in the room would know what had happened, that Town-Line Drugs had made a couple of bad mistakes in filling prescriptions. And no one would be hurt? How about Marcus Aptaker?"

Lanigan nodded slowly. "The druggist down my way

said it could drive a man out of business. But what did Safferstein have against Aptaker?"

"I know only that Safferstein had been trying to buy the drugstore," said the rabbi, "and Aptaker wouldn't sell."

Lanigan's eyes opened wide. "What would a big-shot realtor like Bill Safferstein want with a small local drugstore?"

"Ben Goralsky told me the drugstore had a long-term lease, ten years," said the rabbi. "He thought it meant that Safferstein was planning to tear down the building and put something else in its place. But he wouldn't be able to as long as the lease was in effect. What Safferstein was trying to do was drive Marcus Aptaker out of business."

"Damn!" Lanigan muttered. "Safferstein confided in me that he was planning to build a shopping mall there." He nodded. "It all fits."

Miriam, who had been looking from one man to the other like a spectator at a tennis match, now said, "Since you have a case against Safferstein at least as good as the one you have against Arnold Aptaker, I should think you could let the young man go."

Lanigan stared at her for a moment and then got up. Opening the door, he called out to the desk sergeant, "That young fellow you booked earlier—Arnold Aptaker —release him." He returned to his seat. "Of course, I'll talk to Safferstein, but I don't have a particle of proof. He has only to deny it, and then where am I?"

"Well," said the rabbi diffidently, "Miriam's breaking her strand of pearls gave me an idea. . . ."

As they drove to the Bernsteins, Miriam said, "I wonder how Safferstein felt when he found out that Aptaker didn't have a lease, that Mr. Goralsky had never got around to signing it."

280

"Probably not good," her husband replied. "I suppose Kaplan told him Sunday after the board had voted to sell him the property. But even if he had told him that Wednesday night, it was already too late. The train had been set in motion."

"Do you think he planned it from the beginning and that's why he offered to deliver the pills to Kestler?"

The rabbi shook his head. "I doubt it. How could he have known what Kestler's medicine would be? It could have been a liquid. No, he made the offer in good faith. He's reputed to be a kind and generous man."

"Kind? Generous? And yet he was willing to gamble with a man's life—"

"That's just the point," the rabbi said. "The man was a gambler, who believed in his luck. When your luck is running, you play it for all it's worth. If you start getting cautious, you're apt to lose it. That's the way gamblers think. And if it's running and you have a setback, you double your bets. That way you force your luck back into the groove. His luck was running along nicely. He had been able to buy up all the surrounding property and now he was practically certain of getting the Goralsky Block. The only hitch was the drugstore, and he had reason to believe that he'd have no difficulty in acquiring that. Aptaker was holding out only on the chance that Arnold might come back. But Safferstein had been dealing with Aptaker for some time, and as a shrewd businessman, he sensed that the likelihood was mighty small. And then he comes into the drugstore to fill a prescription, and there is Arnold working in the prescription room and Aptaker tells him proudly that it is his son. So there's the setback. But his luck holds. He finds he has two bottles of pills, the same size, the same number of pills, even the same shape. All he has to do is switch them and then get it known that the drugstore had made a mistake.

I don't suppose it even occurred to him that someone might get hurt."

"Well, I can understand how a man can get caught up in some great project and lose all sense of proportion. You read about artists and scientists who sacrifice everything for their work. And I suppose Safferstein may have felt that way about the mall he was planning. But having caused the death of one man, needlessly as it turned out, I don't understand why he called Dr. Muntz about the second bottle of pills. He knew they were the wrong pills. What's more, he now knew that Aptaker didn't have a lease."

"But he didn't know for sure, because I was trying to get the temple to give Aptaker his lease," said her husband, "and there was a chance I might be successful. And remember, there hadn't been the slightest hint that the police were investigating Kestler's death, so it looked as though the mistake in the pills would never become known. You might say it was Lanigan's fault for playing his cards so close to his chest, and my fault for—"

"By the same logic you might say it was Jonathan's fault," she said tartly.

"Jonathan's?"

"Sure, David. If he hadn't got sick in the middle of the night a few years back, Arnold Aptaker wouldn't have had to get up to deliver the medicine and he wouldn't have overslept the next morning. And he wouldn't have quarreled with his father and—Stop!"

He jammed on the brakes. "Now what is it?"

"You've passed Harris Lane again."

"Well, I'll just back up, and—"

"Against oncoming traffic? You certainly will not, David Small. You'll ride on and take the next turn."

"Oh, all right," he said meekly.

282

52

"I don't like it," said Lieutenant Jennings flatly.

"I don't care a hellova lot for it myself," said his chief. "And in addition I stand to lose a sizable hunk of change."

"You can charge it to the town."

"Sure," said Lanigan sarcastically.

"It's a departmental expense. It was incurred while doing police work," Jennings insisted, but without much conviction.

"If it works. If it doesn't, I pay for it myself."

"It's your funeral, Hugh. If it was me, I'd talk to the selectmen first. Then you could be sure that the town would pick up the tab."

"They'd never agree to it, Eban. You ought to know that."

"Guess you're right," said Jennings gloomily. "Okay, what do you want me to do? Would you like me to make the run? My car is older than yours. Another dent wouldn't make any difference."

"No, I'll do it myself," said the chief. "But I'd like you to go down to the garage and alert McNulty. And then hang around until we get there. The more witnesses, the better."

"Will do. When are you starting out?"

Lanigan glanced at the wall clock and said, "Right now. It's quarter past twelve."

As Chief Lanigan drove along Minerva Road, he noted with satisfaction that there was almost no traffic. Fortunately, when he spotted Safferstein's car at the curb there was no other car on the road. He slowed down and very deliberately swerved into the parked car, denting the front door with his fender.

At the sound of the crash, Safferstein came running out of the house. "Hey, what the hell, you drunk or something? Can't you see— Oh, it's you," as he recognized Lanigan. "What happened?"

"Swerved to avoid a dog," said Lanigan sheepishly. "I guess I swerved a little too much. Gee, I'm sorry, Mr. Safferstein."

"You sure didn't do that door any good," said Safferstein.

"I didn't improve it," Lanigan admitted, "and there could be some damage to the frame, too. I feel terrible. Tell you what, why don't you follow me to the town garage. I'll get McNulty to take a look at it. He does all the body work on the town vehicles. He can give you an estimate on the damage for the insurance company."

Lanigan got back in his car and drove slowly, occasionally glancing in his rear-view mirror to make sure Safferstein was behind him. As they neared the garage, he speeded up a little so that he was out of his car and waiting as Safferstein pulled in.

The mechanic circled the damaged car and said, "It looks as though it's just the door, but we better check it out."

As Safferstein watched, interested, McNulty pulled out the front seat.

"Hey, there's my silver pencil," cried Safferstein, "and my wife's earring, and a dime, and—"

From the other side, Lanigan pointed. "What's that?

It looks like a pill." He reached over and picked it up. He wiped it clean of the dust and grime and held it up. "So it is," he said. "A little oval orange pill, just like those delivered to old Kestler. There was one missing from the bottle, and I guess this is it."

"Oh my God!" And Safferstein buried his face in his hands.

The *gabbe* studied Reb Mendel appraisingly and said, "You look better this morning, Rebbe. Your cold—"

"It's all gone," said the rebbe, smiling broadly. "Look." With lips compressed, he breathed deeply. "Nasal passages clear. No coughing. No sneezing. I feel a hundred percent better."

"Yesterday, you looked—"

"Ah, yesterday, I was terrible. I ached all over. I'm sure I had a fever. And to add to my misery, you know how it is Sundays, there are always relatives. Yesterday it was my Uncle Elimelech and his oldest boy. He's a physicist at Cornell and he insisted on telling me about some research he was doing. I doubt if I could have understood it even if my head were clear. Finally, I excused myself and went up to my room. It was early, around six o'clock, but I couldn't keep my head up. I got undressed, took a couple of aspirins, and then some hot tea with lemon and honey and whiskey. Then I got into bed and fell asleep immediately."

"And slept through the night?"

"No, I awoke after an hour," said Reb Mendel. "I had this vivid dream, and it awakened me."

"A nightmare?"

"No-o. You remember that young man I used to call our young Viking?"

"Akiva, Akiva Rokeach."

"That's the one. He seemed to be in some sort of trouble. I saw him as clearly as I see you now."

285

"What kind of trouble?"

The rebbe shrugged. "You know how it is with dreams. So I read for a while and then finally fell asleep again. When I awoke this morning, I felt fine. It was the sweating from the aspirins and the hot tea, I suppose."

"Not to mention the whiskey."

"The whiskey, of course." The rebbe's face relaxed in a sunny smile. "I wonder how he's getting along, our young Viking."

"Why don't you lead the prayers sometime, Rabbi?" demanded Joshua Tizzik. "Then we'd get through at a decent hour."

Rabbi Small grinned at the sour face of his questioner. "I do. More than half the time. The trouble is you don't come often enough."

They were walking across the parking lot after the evening service. Although it was almost eight o'clock, the approach of evening offered little relief from the heat of the August day.

"I admit I don't get down often, mostly when I come to say Kaddish, for my mother this time, may she rest in peace. But when I do come, it's usually Chester Kaplan who leads."

"Well, this time it wasn't."

"So it's his son-in-law. Mind you, I've got nothing against young Aptaker, but it's like Kaplan wants to keep it in the family, like a monopoly."

"Mr. Kaplan had nothing to do with it," said the rabbi. "I called Arnold myself last night and suggested it. You see, it's a special occasion."

"I know, I know—the new baby."

"And he was most reluctant, I might add," said the rabbi. "I had to persuade him."

Tizzik's features twisted into a sour smile. "I can understand why, too. I'm no expert, but it seemed to me he stumbled a couple of times. And he read so slow like it was the first time. Maybe that's why Kaplan stayed away. Didn't want to embarrass him."

"Mr. Kaplan is out of town on business, as I understand it," said the rabbi.

"He is? But today is Wednesday."

"What's that got to do with it?" the rabbi asked.

"Wednesdays, Chet Kaplan has his At Homes."

"He still keeps that up? Then I suppose he'll get home in time for it. Do you still attend, Mr. Tizzik?"

"Now and then. The wife and I go to the movies more now that it's only a dollar for senior citizens. Besides, those At Homes, they're not like they used to be."

"Oh?"

"It's only what you'd expect," said Tizzik. "At the beginning, there's always a lot of enthusiasm, and then it tends to die down. And this Rabbi Mezzik who had a lot to do with it, he doesn't come down anymore. Got himself a pulpit in upstate New York, I understand. And maybe that last retreat that Chester organized didn't help matters."

"Is that so? What happened?" The rabbi was interested.

"Didn't you hear?" Tizzik was incredulous. "I wasn't

there, of course, but I got it from Bob Wiseman. A complete washout, Rabbi. It was the Fourth of July weekend and I guess it was the first time they'd been up there during the summer. According to Wiseman, who'd been to most of the others, what was nice about the place was that it was so quiet and peaceful. Of course, the other retreats had been held in the fall, after Labor Day. Well, it seems that in the summer the place is a madhouse, especially on weekends. There are houses all around this little lake and each and every one of them, according to Wiseman, must have a speedboat or an outboard. They were drumming up and down that lake all day long so you couldn't hear yourself think. And at night, it was worse with the radios and the phonographs going full blast with this rock-and-roll music. That's why the Catholic church gave it up as a kids' camp. Some of the guys came home the next day."

"That's very interesting," said the rabbi. They had arrived at Tizzik's car and the rabbi was about to turn away when he thought of something. "Oh, if you can manage it, Mr. Tizzik, you might try to come to the morning service this Sunday. Arnold Aptaker will lead the prayers again and you can see if he's improved. There will be a light collation afterward, tendered by the Kaplans and the Aptakers in honor of their new grandson."

"The usual cake and *kichel* and herring, I suppose."

"I suppose so."

"And whiskey in paper cups?"

The rabbi smiled. "Maybe in glasses."

"Well, maybe I'll try to make it. What else is there to do Sunday mornings? On TV it's all church services."